WHITE
BOY
FRIEND

WHITE BOY FRIEND

LEESHA McCOY

bookouture

Published by Bookouture in 2022

An imprint of Storyfire Ltd.
Carmelite House
50 Victoria Embankment
London EC4Y oDZ

www.bookouture.com

ISBN: 978-1-80019-972-9
eBook ISBN: 978-1-80019-971-2

To my children. You are the best four things that ever happened to me, and I love you so much, my little pumpkins.

Chapter One

"Because I'm not happy."

I blink at my boyfriend Bron through watery eyes. "Since when?"

He sighs as he shoves the contents of his sock drawer into the gym bag I bought for his trip with the boys last year. "For a while. We do the same things over and over, Nik. Every day is the same. You can't say you haven't noticed how boring our lives have become."

"So why are you waiting until *now* to say anything?" I long to step closer to him but I hold myself back. He recently showered and I love the way he smells afterward. "You could've told me you were feeling this way."

He looks up. "Like you did?"

"Don't do that." The tears run free when I blink, and I hate that I'm crying. I *never* cry. "I'm not the one breaking up with you over being a little bored."

He closes his eyes briefly, as if tormented. "You're right. I'm sorry. Look, I love you, Nik, you know I do, but I think we both need some time to get to know ourselves again. We're all we really know when it comes to relationships."

"What?" I croak out. "Are you saying you regret that?"

"No, not at all, but with our parents being friends... They've always been so heavy on us being together. Especially yours."

The memory of the day we met at a marketing event three years ago flashes before my eyes. He was the most beautiful man I'd ever seen. So tall, skin just a little darker than mine, a dazzling smile, but it was his almost-bronze almond eyes that hooked me.

I'd barely dated before he came along, and when I did it was in secret. My parents were against me so much as befriending boys growing up. Especially my dad. While my friends were living their best lives partying and having casual sex, I was taking extra classes or singing at church. I was terrified to tell them about Bron—even though I was twenty-three—but they adored him and his parents as soon as they met and even convinced them to join the same church as us a few months later.

"So... Are you saying our parents made you stay with me?"

"I don't know what I'm saying. To be honest, I don't know what I want."

Well, it's clearly not me. "Have you..." I pull my fingers as I mentally prepare myself to ask the question. "Have you met someone else?"

His reaction immediately tells me he hasn't. "Of course not. How could you think that, Nik? Have you not listened to a word I've said? I love you. I would never hurt you like that."

Thank God. I'm not sure if I could handle him cheating on me. "So that's it?"

He nods. "Yeah, and if you're honest with yourself, you know it's the right thing for both of us." He zips his bag before coming to kiss me on the forehead, like he always does.

"Bron," I whisper as I briefly close my eyes. *Will this really be the last time I experience this?*

The warmth of his arms around me is fleeting, and then I'm

cold and empty when he steps away. "We'll sort the lease out on this place later, all right?"

"Okay," I say. It's all I can do.

"I'll grab the rest of my stuff in the week while you're at work, but if you need me, call me. I'm still here for you."

He leaves when I don't reply, and after the front door closes, I fall onto the bed and attempt to process what the hell just happened.

How did I not see this coming?

I thought things were good. Yes, maybe a tad mundane, but it's not as if we fought or argued all the time. Our careers are steady, money is never an issue, and we always make time for each other. Date nights, weekends away, trips around the world.

That's not boring.

I could understand if I was needy or clingy—controlling even—but I was only ever supportive, encouraging him in everything he wanted to do. Even when he decided to start his own advertising firm last year.

Everything was perfect. Well, ok, maybe not everything... the only thing that maybe wasn't so perfect was the sex.

I cringe when I remember the conversation we had last month. Maybe that's what's triggered this? Perhaps me wanting to try new things in bed bruised his ego. He didn't take it well, which is why I never brought it up again, but if I had known it would lead to this, I would've kept my mouth shut.

It was only a suggest—

My cell vibrates on the stand beside me, but instead of reaching for it, I stare at myself in the dresser mirror. The curly lace front that's protecting my natural hair may be a little disheveled now, and I may not be a petite size six, but I know for a fact this isn't about how I look. It wasn't just Bron turning heads when we stepped out, and he never had any problems getting hard for me when we did get down to it. Hell, the bartender at our local is forever trying it on with me. He always says how much he loves a woman with curves in all the right places, and Bron would agree with him.

I don't get it.

My cell rings again, and I see Alicia's name before answering. "Hey."

"Uh, hello? Where are you? We've been here twenty minutes now. Since when do you rock up late?"

My stomach twists. "Shit, I'm sorry." I completely forgot I was having dinner with the girls tonight.

"Nik? What's wrong? Why do you sound like that?"

"Like what?" I hear Chay ask in the background.

I close my eyes in an attempt to swallow down the aching in my chest. "Bron just walked out. We broke up."

"You did *what?*"

"Yeah." I breathe out a laugh, shocked that those words have come from my mouth. "Wanna come here instead?"

"Of course. We're coming right now."

"We need drink. I don't have much here."

"We've got you, boo."

I dull my shock with the remains of a bottle of wine I found in the fridge, out in the back yard. It won't be light for much longer, but the sparkly lights Bron put up a few weeks ago in time for the warm summer nights seem brighter than ever.

We picked this house in Midtown because it was close to our parents' houses and where we work Downtown. Both of us were born and raised here in Memphis and that was something else we said was fate when we met in New York; that we'd traveled all that way and still found each other.

Our connection flowed from the get-go. Common interests, deep conversations about our upbringings between passionate rounds of sex, and he forever made sure I was okay emotionally and financially, even though I always had my own.

As passionate as the sex was, though, it wasn't very varied, and I often found it boring—even though I always came. Saying that as bluntly as I have sounds awful, but as perfect as he is in all other things, that was something I'd grown tired of ignoring.

Admittedly, talking about intimacy with Bron was tricky because of what he thought was and wasn't "acceptable". I secretly disliked some of his views—mostly on oral sex—but I never made him think they were a problem. I tamed my desires and accepted him for who he was unconditionally, because I never wanted to disrespect his beliefs or wound his ego.

Maybe that should've been a warning sign that things wouldn't last in the long-term.

I close my eyes as I take the last gulp of my rosé. It's strange to be out here on my own. Bron and I were always together. Maybe that was a problem too. Maybe we spent *too* much time together. *I can't remember the last time I missed him...* Now I wish I had pushed him to spend more time with his boys—not that I ever encouraged him not to.

Ugh. I hate these feelings, this crushing in my chest and the racing thoughts. I can't stop thinking about every single little thing that could've led to this. This is the first time I've been dumped and as much as he said it was about him, I'm undoubtedly finding it hard to not take it personally.

"Hello?" Alicia shouts from inside the house.

"I'm out the back!" I rest my empty wineglass down as my three best friends appear on the patio. Their expressions say it all. They can't believe it either. Everyone always says how perfect Bron and I are together. *A power couple.* How much they want what we have—or I guess now, had.

"Girl..." Rhian sighs, then they all rush to give me a hug before pulling chairs around me. "We're so sorry."

"So am I." I smile weakly but feel ten times better to have them here. "You all look beautiful." Unlike me. I'm still wearing my suit from work, and I know my makeup must be trashed.

"What happened?" Chay asks, teary-eyed herself.

I take a deep breath, hating how this tightness in my chest just won't quit. "He came back from the gym and said he wanted to talk. I thought we were gonna decide where we'd be going for our summer vacation... But the way he said my name immediately told me it wasn't that."

"Oh, sis..."

I smile at Rhian when she takes my hand. "He said he wasn't happy... That our lives were... boring."

Alicia's eyes widen in alarm. She's the mother of our group, and of her own two little girls. "He said *what?*"

I nod.

"Has he mentioned this before?"

"No. Nothing."

"So why not? I don't understand. To just up and leave after three years is a cop-out if you ask me."

There's no missing that the rest of the girls are thinking the same. "I know."

"He's not seeing someone else is he?" Rhian asks as she pours us all a glass of wine—mine until it almost overflows, and I have to lean forward to sip it.

"He said he isn't, and I believed him."

Alicia frowns, clearly deep in her thoughts now. "Boring? He's twenty-eight. What does he want you both to be doing? Going out raving every night? Bungee jumping? Making home videos? I mean, *God.*"

I choke on a sip of my full glass of wine, spilling a good mouthful down my blouse. "That never would've happened," I mutter. And the closest thing to a home video in Bron's mind would've been filming himself doing press-ups.

Rhian agrees with Alicia. "He should be thankful you're as mature as you are for your age. He's crazy to give you up."

More tears threaten to come. "I don't know what's going on inside his head, but if I'm honest, I can sort of see what he was getting at. Recently, it's seemed as if we were just existing—y'know? I mean, I can't remember the last time we did something spontaneous."

"But that's not all on you," Alicia retorts. "He's got a mouth. He should've used it."

"Yeah, I guess. Maybe I should've tried harder, because there were things that could've been improved..." I stop myself from saying too much, in case we manage to work this out in a few weeks and I have to backtrack. "Do you think I've been in denial? That I've missed the signs?"

"That depends. Were there any?"

"Not that I saw."

"Well then. Not to be the man-hater of the group, but sometimes, it's really not about us women. Sometimes, these men don't know what they want, or what they have."

"He did say he didn't know what he wanted."

"Maybe believe him then," Chay says. "Give him a chance to miss you."

Rhian scoffs. "Oh, hell no! We're not doing that. You better not sit around waiting for him, Nik. As amazing as Bron is, he made the choice. The last thing you're gonna do is put your life on hold while he figures out what *he* wants."

Her words strike a place within me that I wish they didn't. She's right. I've always believed that an ex is an ex for a reason. As much as I wish he'd walk through the door right now and tell me it was a mistake, deep down, I know we couldn't go back from what he's said. This has hurt me so much, I don't think I would trust him not to do it again.

"I know..." I burst into tears as the vision of my future with Bron slips away from me. "I'm dreading telling Mom and Dad too."

"Hey," Chay soothes, "don't worry about them right now. That's not important. *You* need to come to terms with this first. I mean, what a bloody arse. I never would've expected this from him."

I chuckle as I wipe my eyes. Chay's from England, and her accent cracks me up, especially when she drops phrases like that. "Me neither, but it says a lot about how he's been feeling, doesn't it?"

"Possibly." She shakes her head. "Wow, I just can't believe it."

She's not the only one. "I signed a massive contract at work today too. I didn't even get to tell him about it." I take a quick look up at the back of the house. "I don't know what I'm gonna do. I thought my life was set. I thought we'd get married, have babies, live happily ever after..." It kills me to think about him having that with someone else.

"Are you sure there isn't another woman?" Alicia asks. She always reads me well.

I frown as I have to slurp from my glass again. *When did she top this up?* "I really don't think so." I take a big breath. "But, if there is, that's not on me. I know I was loyal and gave my all, so I have no regrets."

"Exactly," Chay says, toasting me. "Whatever you do, don't make this about you. Don't take on his shit as your own."

"I won't." *Or at least I'll try not to.* "I know I'm still a queen."

"You better believe." She smiles softly and tucks my hair behind my ear. "We bloody love you, babe. Of course we know it hurts like hell now, but you'll get through this. We're all here for you too, all right? No matter what. You don't have to act strong around us. We know."

"I don't know what I'd do without you."

Chapter Two

This is the first time in my life that I've ever wished I suffered from hangovers. At least then I'd have a truth to use to get out of lunch with my parents.

I've only ever lied to them once, but trust me, once was more than enough. I was sixteen and desperate to go to my first ever house party with my friend Michelle. She lived with her dad who was always laid-back, unlike mine, so he agreed to let me sleep over so we could go.

It was the best, most freeing night I'd ever had until I ended up in the ER, wasted.

Little did I know, the "fruit juice" I was drinking was a lot stronger than I thought it was and went down a bit too easy. Hence I was found lying in my own vomit in the front yard after only an hour of being there, which prompted someone calling me an ambulance.

The look on my parents' faces said everything their mouths didn't when they arrived to pick me up, and I knew I was in with them deep. The tense drive home is still a bit blurry to me, but what happened the next morning when I woke up won't ever be.

Dad wanted to whoop my ass but Mom talked him out of it, not that what actually happened was any less painful. They spent the next few days reciting Bible verses about the repercussions of lying and being irresponsible. Telling me how I'd let Him down, that they couldn't trust me anymore, and that God would be "as disappointed in me as they were."

But what hurt most was how they compared me to my "mature," God-fearing brother who is two years my senior. They said they didn't know where they went wrong with me and that they were thankful they had at least one good child to be proud of, because I had embarrassed them.

Little did they know that my brother was ten times worse than I was back then. He was always sneaking out to a dance or coming home half lit, but I didn't snitch on him, even then. My brother James and I have always been close, even as kids, and we always had each other's backs.

Looking back, I think I would've preferred the asswhooping and had it over and done with, because the things they said to me really affected my life. They still do now. Not only was I banned from any future sleepovers or parties of any kind until I started college, but they also dropped me off and picked me up from anywhere I went for months after. I became almost obsessed with never disappointing them, ever again, which resulted in me going above and beyond in every way possible to live up to their expectations.

Don't get me wrong, I'm grateful to an extent because they're the reason I'm as successful as I am now. They always pushed and encouraged me, and although they were strict, I always felt loved, but there's no denying that I've missed out on things other girls got to do because of them.

Mostly fun.

Sighing, I stare into my bowl of lumpy oatmeal. I'm far from hungry. After all the tears I cried last night with the girls, the only thing I feel now is emptiness. I want to dwell in self-pity and misery, but I can't even do that. As much as I know my parents will be disappointed in me again, it would be even worse if they thought I was wallowing.

The laugh that escapes me is bitter, and it echoes around the room. I hate it. My hip-hop or Bron's reggae would usually be blaring out of Alexa by now. I'd be singing along while cleaning the house and sorting the laundry, and Bron would be getting the mower ready to cut the grass like he did every Saturday morning.

But today it's completely different. The house is eerily quiet, the coffee pot is still holding the dregs from yesterday morning, and the crumbs from Bron's post-gym bagel are still scattered over the marble side. I remember with a pang how that used to drive me crazy when we first moved into this place. I'd always tell him to clean up after himself, but then, as the months went on, I realized that he'd never change, so I stopped wasting my time asking.

I got the impression the girls think Bron dumping me is a good thing. I told them what he said about our parents pushing us together, and they agreed. My parents thought we worked well as a team. They thought we were a match. They wanted us to work.

They, they, they.

Alicia, especially, thinks this is a blessing in disguise, and I wonder if she might be right. If I'm truly honest with myself, it's not like I would have ever walked away. Boring sex and all. I would've carried on living life as I was. Work, home, dinner, missionary and an early night.

And repeat.

Not only would I never have dreamed of breaking his heart, but I also wouldn't have dared ask the heavens for someone better. Bron was almost perfect: driven, Godfearing, successful, loyal, and gorgeous. Who would I be to ask for an upgrade when I'd already received me a man that millions of women can only dream of? Sex isn't the be all and end all, is it? And definitely not worth breaking up with someone over.

I'm still stunned that being boring was.

I'm saved from my spiraling thoughts by my cell ringing. Alicia saves the day again.

"Hey, sis," I answer.

"How you feeling, boo?"

"Up and down. I'm trying to stay positive though, like you all told me to."

"Hey, it's okay to let it hurt, Nik. We just meant in general. Don't be up in your feelings too long. It won't change anything."

"Yeah, I know." I sigh. "I have lunch with my parents later."

"I remember. How are you fee—hold on a second—*No, I'm not buying you any more Robux. Does Roblox pay my bills? No... I don't care... No, I'm not taking it out of your trust fund... Then call your dad! The Bank of Mom is empty... If you don't move your ass*—Sorry about that. Damned kids and this damn Roblox. It's driving me insane."

"It's okay, honestly. How are they?"

"They're still breathing. Just. I took a few days off to spend with them next week while school's out. I'm regretting it already."

I chuckle. "It will be fine."

She says her girls drive her crazy, but everything she does is for them. I remember how long it took her to accept the promotion at the clothing store she works at because of the longer hours. The number of times she almost talked herself out of it drove all of us girls crazy, but after a million phone calls from us encouraging her, she finally accepted.

We celebrated hard after the contract was signed. Alicia more than deserved it after the shit she went through with the girls' father. He was part of the reason she almost said no. She'd been so used to putting herself last, especially while she was with him, it was as if she didn't know how to do anything to make herself happy.

Rhian, I think, is the reason why she eventually took it. She was relentless in making Alicia see that to put herself first was actually putting everyone she cared about first. "When you're happy, everyone around you is," she'd said. Rhian might not have kids, nor me or Chay, but we one hundred percent agreed with her.

"Yeah, let's hope we survive the week. So, are you nervous, Nik?"

"Beyond. I already know what they're gonna say."

"Well, I hope they surprise you by being sympathetic. I mean, it's not like *you* ended it."

I scoff. "I'm sure in their eyes they'll still see it as my fault."

She sighs now. "I know how much you love your parents, Nik, but you really do have to start standing up for yourself with them. It's your life, not theirs."

That's easier said than done. "I know."

"Things can't get better between you and them until you put your foot down. I've been there, remember? Look how long it took me to leave that bastard?"

"I know that too."

"It's hard, scary even, but you can't keep living your life for them. They give us life—they don't own it."

"Okay, okay, I get it, all right? Ugh. I'll put on my big girl panties."

"You're twenty-six, for goodness sake. Time to start doing your own thing, girl. What about taking up a class like Pilates or yoga? That would do wonders for your well-being and confidence, especially now."

I roll my eyes. She's suggested yoga before because she loves it, but I can't see myself really getting into it. Sticking my thick ass in the air and inhaling other people's gas is far from my idea of a good time. "Um... I don't think that's me."

"Do you even know who you really are though?"

I sigh. "I kinda hate how you call me out sometimes. Have I ever told you that?"

"Always. I'm serious though. There's a great yoga teacher in your area that I can put you on to. Think about it. Might be a good distraction."

"Okay."

She groans when Shyla, her youngest girl, mentions her dad. "All right, I've gotta go, but let me know how lunch goes, okay?"

"I will."

Chapter Three

I almost throw up on the drive to my parents' house. The only thing that prevents it is the fact my Benz is only three months old and the thought of having to scrape vomit off the seats makes me wanna cry.

This won't go well, so trying to convince myself otherwise would be pointless. Dad is gonna go off, and Mom, well, she'll probably take over once Dad's had his turn. She's gotten better over the past few years—not quite so judgmental—but when it comes to Dad and his tirades, she always backs him.

Maybe I should've asked my brother, James, and his wife, Vanessa to come, because as happy as they are, they always hoard the attention by arguing. They're the most stereotypical married couple I know, constantly bickering over the pettiest shit you can think of. Whose turn it is to make the coffee, whose turn it is to arrange date night; they're the worst but the sweetest at the same time. They sometimes made me wonder if Bron and I were even in a real relationship because we rarely argued. We just got things done.

I park perfectly on the drive and then brace myself as I make my way up to the door. The front of the house looks beautiful. Freshly planted flowers in all the tubs telling me Mom's been working her magic out here. She's a master in the garden, but all attempts to get me to pick up some gloves and buy a greenhouse have been futile. I've killed every plant she's ever bought me, so she doesn't bother anymore.

I don't blame her.

Dad answers the door, and after a hello and a brief hug, he looks behind me. "Where's Bron?"

My stomach does a flip-flop as I step inside the house, threatening to bring up my barely digested oatmeal again. I swallow hard to keep it down. "Um, he's not coming today. Where's Mom?"

"Out the back," he says, closing the door behind me.

"Great."

I make my way through the cramped hall decorated with Dad's collection of selfies with famous people. He was a promoter—an extremely successful one—and has worked with anyone who's anyone from DJ Khaled to Sara Blakely, the woman who invented Spanx. But my favorite picture on the wall is the one of him and Barney the Dinosaur.

They kinda look alike in that one.

He hardly leaves Mom now though. She had a cancer scare a few years ago so he stopped working so much to spend more time with her, pampering her and taking her to all the countries she's ever wanted to visit. They only got back from London a few weeks ago and are already planning their next trip.

I find Mom in the back yard tinkering with flowers in the middle of a table set with what looks like a lavish afternoon tea.

"Hello, Mom."

She looks up and smiles before coming to hug me. "Nicola, baby."

I hold her tight and kiss her cheek before she releases me. I have to bend because she's almost a foot shorter than me. My height comes from my dad. "How are you? This looks amazing. Thank you."

She turns to look at her masterpiece, then waves her hand dismissively. "Oh, it's nothing. Where's Bron? With your father?"

"He's not here." Dad answers before I can. "Did he have to work?"

My anxiety returns with a force. "No, I don't think so. Um, can we sit down?"

Mom holds my arm. "Of course."

After we're seated, I psyche myself up while internally shaking my head at how much effort Mom's put into this meal. We each have our own three-tiered stand with fruit cake, miniature pots of cream and jams, cucumber sandwiches, and tiny cupcakes.

"So...?" Dad prompts, pulling my attention away from my individual pot of tea.

"Bron and I aren't together anymore."

"What *on earth?*"

I blink at Mom's horrified gape, but then I recoil when Dad gives me a glare frosty enough to make me shudder.

"Not you and Bron. What will we say at church?" Mom says, clearly emotional, and it hurts my feelings because yet again, they're making this about them.

"It's okay, Annie," Dad soothes. He has one hand on her back, but his attention's still well and truly on me.

As much as these reactions were expected, they still catch me off guard.

"What happened?" Dad asks, his tone as icy as his look.

I debate sugar-coating it, but I decide to take Alicia's advice and just spit it out. "He broke up with me. Said he wasn't happy and that he didn't know what he wanted. That our life together was boring."

Mom's expression softens after that, but Dad's doesn't.

"And what did you say?"

"There wasn't much I could say. He'd already started packing his things." I shrug.

"Good God," he breathes. "When did this happen?"

"Yesterday."

He nods. "Good. It's not undoable yet. I'll call Toya and Calvin. I'm sure we can fix this."

Horror consumes me. "Call his parents? Fix it?"

"Of course. Bron clearly needs to talk this through with someone. When's the last time the two of you attended church?"

"Dad..." I take a breath to steady my emotions. What happened to, *How are you feeling, baby girl? We're so sorry?* Y'know, the normal shit parents say to their children when they go through a breakup? "Why does that matter? Bron made his choice, and as difficult as this is for me, I'm honoring it."

"Nonsense."

"Dad—"

"Don't 'Dad' me. You and Bron were made for each other."

"Clearly not," I mutter.

"Excuse me?"

I bite my tongue. "Bron doesn't want to be with me, Dad. Believe me, he's made that very clear."

"He does. He's just confused with how he feels, that's all. Men need to be needed, Nicola. Did you make him feel needed? I know how independent you are."

I give Mom a look, begging for her to save me, but she's busy repositioning a line of sandwiches on her stand.

"This wasn't about me. He said it was him." I barely cling on to my tears after those words come out. If they only knew how hard it was for me to even tell them this...

Dad shakes his head. "Women your age have no business being single. You can't afford to let a man like him go, Nicola. Find out what he wants and give it to him."

My hurt quickly switches to anger. "I'm not going to beg after a man who doesn't want me, no matter how successful or perfect they are. If he doesn't see my worth, that's on him, not me."

He pulls his hand from Mom's back before turning to fully face me. "Nicola..."

I open my mouth to continue, but I quickly shut up when Mom gives me a discreet shake of her head. I sigh instead.

"Byron, could you please get the scones from the oven? I think the timer's going off."

"Of course, baby," he replies, promptly getting to his feet and disappearing into the house. The tension only eases a little. I'm dreading what Mom's gonna say now we're alone.

"Are you okay?"

I try not to act stunned by her question. "Um..." I look up as Dad appears again with a tray of scones in his hand. "I'm fine."

She nods knowingly. "I'd *love* to go for lunch, thank you for asking. Just let me know what day."

Lunch? What? *I never invited her for lunch.*

"I'll check my diary," she adds, widening her eyes.

"Okay..."

"Great. Let's eat," she says to Dad. "I want to tell Nicola about our trip."

I slam my bag down on the kitchen counter when I get home. I knew Dad wouldn't take mine and Bron's breakup well, but I wasn't expecting it to be quite so bad. The things he said took me right back to being sixteen.

He's disappointed, again, and most likely embarrassed.

I can't bear it.

No way in a million years did I expect to be triggered this way. I broke up with my boyfriend, not my parents, so why are all the wounds from my childhood opening up? Why do I feel like a teenager again, letting my parents down by being anything less than perfect?

My mood worsens as I busy my shaking hands folding the laundry in the spare room and ten times worse when I finally get done putting all the clothes away.

Maybe I *should* try to make it right with Bron? Maybe he wants me to chase him, to show him how much he means to me? Maybe Dad was right by saying my independence pushed him away.

It's just... They raised me like this. They taught me to rely on myself, and I can't help that. I don't want to beg people for things I can do myself either. I like that I'm not needy; that's never been in me, and if I do things myself, I won't be let down.

Whenever I relied on anyone growing up, they'd always let me down, especially emotionally. Mom and Dad would tell me that dwelling wouldn't solve anything, that I can only rely on myself, so I learnt to be this way because I never wanted to appear weak to them.

Still, it's okay to care for others, isn't it?

I start typing a message to Bron when I get back down to the kitchen. Maybe I should check up on him. Maybe he's feeling the same way as me and doesn't know how to reach out? A quick text won't hurt surely?

Hey, just thought I'd text to see how you are?

He replies a few minutes later.

Bron: *I'm good. You? How was lunch?*

He remembered.

Me: *I'm good too. Lunch could've been better. Did you tell Toya and Calvin?*

Bron: *Yeah. I don't think they were happy, but they understood.*

Lucky him.

Me: *That's good. How are you feeling about it all?*

Bron: *The same. Don't take this personally, Nikki. I meant what I said—this is about me, not you.*

Tears threaten again, but I manage to hold them back.

Me: *I know...*

I want to tell him I miss him, that I could try to be what he needs, but as difficult as it is, I hold back. I don't want to look weak either.

Me: *...Should I email the landlady and ask for your name to be taken off the lease?*

Bron: *There's no rush. I've paid this month's rent already. I didn't want you to be short. I've found a place downtown for now.*

That message does make me cry. He always made sure I was good.

Me: *Thank you.*

Bron: *You're welcome. Take care, Nik. Here if you need me.*

Me: *Same.*

The tears really unleash when I put my phone back on the side, the sliver of hope I had for a reconciliation disappearing with each wave that comes. Finding out he already has somewhere else to live has really cemented the fact that we aren't getting back together.

It's really over, and my heart breaks a little more as that realization sinks in. No more Nikki and Bron. No more perfect couple. No more future engagement, kids, happily ever after.

I'm really single again.

The fear that comes with that thought makes me breathless.

I have to start all over.

I don't have a choice.

Chapter Four

I'm relieved when I manage to sneak into my office without being spoken to. I've already dished out all the fake smiles I could muster on the way in, and now, after one look at the eye-watering amount of paperwork waiting on my desk, I know that's all I can give today.

The telephone-based market research company I work for is one of the most successful in the country, with five locations, including one in Germany. I'm one of three project managers at this office, but when I first started, I was on the phones.

Initially, I wasn't great. Far from. There were days I had nothing but hang-ups or people dropping F-bombs on me, but following some after-hours training with my senior, Natasha, my success rate began climbing. I'd been going into the calls sounding like a desperate teenager trying to earn my next meal, but once I switched up my opening and relaxed my tone, I was smashing through my strike targets on every project.

My confidence grew and grew. I was more driven than ever, jumping on any new project that came in. Management soon asked me to be a trainer, and I quickly worked my way up from there. The hands-on experience was invaluable in allowing me to see all that this business entailed and undoubtedly made my major in Marketing Management a hell of a lot easier too.

I power up my MacBook and immediately feel my heart sink when I see the familiar desktop picture of Bron and me in the Bahamas on our first Christmas together. *I need to change that.* He surprised me on Christmas Eve with tickets, playfully saying he was sick of me moaning about the cold. He bought me four different bikinis at the airport, and I pretty much lived in them the entire time we were there.

That was one of the best Christmases of my life.

"Hey, Nikki," my assistant sings cheerily as she enters my office, pulling me back to the present. She's rocking another one of her handmade dresses; I can tell by the way it wraps around her slender figure so perfectly.

"Morning, Kelly." I take a deep breath to steady my emotions before finally switching my wallpaper to the first one on the drop-down list: a blue and purple swirly pattern that is as standard as they come. Maybe I should get a pet. Then I can have it as my screensaver.

It won't dump me either.

"Here's your coffee." She rests my "Boss" mug down on the matching coaster before sitting opposite me. "You have a conference call at eight thirty with MittCo. I've sent them the figures from yesterday. Numbers are good. They're hitting strike, no problem."

"Good." *At least work is still okay.*

"Marcus said he'll be down later to talk over who you want piloting the cosmetics account next week. He mentioned having the seniors work on it first to see how fruitful the sample is." She looks up from her iPad. "A word of warning. Apparently, when he looked through it, there were quite a few wrong numbers."

I groan. Marcus—my boss and owner of the company—and I both hate when the samples are talked up by the client but end up being trash. It not only lowers the strike rate, which costs us money, but it wastes IT's time. "Any chance of getting a replacement file?"

"Not sure yet. IT said they'll take a look to see if there's an error with the spreadsheet first. I'll let you know when they get back to me."

"All right. Hopefully it's an easy fix. I want that wrapped up ASAP."

The client said it would be straightforward, so I'm still holding out hope that it will be. Stress at work is the last thing I need. Marcus loses his shit when things don't go to plan, and we all dread when that happens.

"I hope so too." Kelly breathes a sigh of relief when she looks up again and tucks her auburn-streaked hair behind her ears. "Right, that's all for now. There is something else though."

"Yes?" I click open my emails but swallow uncomfortably when I see all the appointment cancellations from my joint calendar with Bron. Wow. He didn't waste any time scratching those.

It hurts.

"Well, when I checked your emails this morning..."

I sigh. "We broke up."

She recoils. "Excuse me?"

"Yeah." I know we only broke up a few days ago, but when is this feeling in my chest going to ease up? I hate how up and down my mood constantly is. One minute I'm good, next I'm like a recovering crack addict trying to resist reaching for the next hit.

"Nikki, I'm so sorry."

I shoot her a pathetic excuse for a smile, the absolute last I have left for the day. "Thanks, but could we not talk about it? Not yet." I don't want to bring my personal life into work if I can help it. There's no way I want the entire call center gossiping about my private life.

"There's nothing to be ashamed of, you know that, right? People get dumped all the time."

She's always telling me she's been ghosted by some new guy or another. "Doesn't it bother you?"

"No, why would it?"

"Because..."

"You think my feelings are hurt because someone doesn't want to be with me? Please. It just means they're not for me."

I frown. "Don't you have a heart?"

That makes her laugh. "Of course I do, but I know I'll get married one day. It will happen when it happens, and to be honest, I'm committed to myself these days. I don't have time for another full-time commitment. Being a strong independent woman with a diary full of dick dates is where it's at."

I'm taken aback by that. "And that's okay now?"

"Girl, yes! No one can make me feel a way about lickin' and dippin'. Besides, if a guy's letting me smash on the first date, they're easy too."

I snort. "Well, when you put it like that..."

"Trust me, no one cares. It's good to try before you buy too, y'know? Just make sure you get them to strap it up, no matter what bullshit they come out with. I could tell you some lines, believe me."

"Um, yeah, I will."

Her eyes narrow. "You don't sound sure. You're not going to do the whole 'feel sorry for yourself for months before you start dating again,' are you?"

"He only broke up with me last week, Kelly."

She shrugs. "So? Sooner you get back out there, the sooner that shitty feeling will eff off. You don't owe him anything if he broke it off with you."

"I know, but I'm not trying to make him jealous or hurt his feelings. We were together for three years. Revenge is the furthest thing from my mind."

"Who said anything about getting revenge on him? Dating is for you. Out with the old, as they say."

"I've never really dated," I admit. "I wouldn't know where to start."

She leans back as if I've slapped her. "Hold on, you've *never* dated?"

I roll my eyes. "Not really."

"Girl, then you *really* need to date. You'd have your pick of the pricks. You're beautiful."

"Yeah, well, Bron was pretty much perfect, so I'm not exactly sure what I'd be looking for."

"Rejection is redirection, remember? Trust me. I'll hook you up."

Panic grips me. I don't like other people taking control of my life, especially after so many years of not having any myself. "Uh, let me think about it."

She suddenly gasps. "Oh my God, you should *so* get Karl from accounts to read your cards. He got me perfectly last time."

I wonder if that's because she always tells everyone her business. "Karl does tarot?"

Her eyes light up when she nods. "I'll ask him for you."

Another wave of fear comes. "No, really, don't."

She gets up and practically skips to the door, completely ignoring me. "I'll get him to come up when you have your next break."

"I—"

She disappears back into her office, and I groan.

"Ready?"

I take a deep breath as I close my Mac. I don't know why I'm nervous. Tarot is just for fun anyway, isn't it? And it's not like he's actually going to tell me anything useful.

Karl came up here about ten minutes ago, but he spent five minutes lighting candles and burning sage. He said it was to "clear the energy" or something, and now my entire office stinks of it, even though I cracked the windows.

Let's hope it doesn't set the fire alarm off.

I lean back in my chair. "You really don't have to do this. I told Kelly that."

"I know, but I want to."

I trained Karl a few years back. He was going through his own breakup at the time but didn't go into details. He's engaged now, so I heard, to an accountant at a brokerage on the other side of the city. There's something about him that makes you feel at ease and he's funny, so there's no surprise he's been snatched up.

He's cute too. Kinda looks like Damon from *The Vampire Diaries*.

"You're not going to tell anyone what you find out, are you?"

He shakes his head. "Not a word. Promise. I like my job."

That makes me chuckle. I wouldn't be impressed with him for talking my business, but I wouldn't fire him for it. After all, it's not like me spending my work hours filling my office with naked flames and calling up spirits from beyond to get over my ex is exactly professional...

I hope Marcus doesn't come up here.

"How did you get into this?" I ask as he begins shuffling his cards.

"Through a friend. He's deep into the spiritual life." He shrugs.

"I see." I've heard about tarot, but I've never had a reading. My friend Stacey in college would always be reading someone's cards, but never mine. As a devout Christian I was always made to believe that tarot was the devil, and I should stay far away from it.

Better not tell Mom and Dad about this.

Karl speeds up his shuffling until a few cards fly out. "Ooh... Someone's going through a tower moment. I see a breakup—"

I eye him cautiously. "Did Kelly tell you?"

He frowns. "Tell me what?"

My stomach knots. "Nothing. What else do they say?"

"Wait a sec. I just need to clarify a few of these..."

More shuffling ensues, until he seems satisfied and rests the stack of remaining cards down next to the ones he's laid out. There are a few that catch my eye, specifically the one he called the tower card. A man's jumped out of a burning lighthouse and is clutching his charred ass as he runs away from it.

Another has a picture of a woman on the ground with what must be at least ten swords stuck in her back. *That's definitely me.* She's bleeding out all over the dirt with hardly any clothes on. Saying that, a few of the other cards are a little racy. The ace of wands looks a lot like a big glittery dick.

"So, I see a recent breakup that someone wasn't expecting. I assume that's you?"

I lift my head. "Possibly," I mutter.

"Seems the people close to you were shocked too. Parents not happy?"

I remain straight-faced, but there's no denying my unease.

He gives me a look but swiftly returns his attention back down. "Immediate future looks good. Spending time with friends... I see travel happening soon... You may need to let go of control issues though. The most important thing I see is the need to inject more fun into your life. Try new things. Emotional unfulfillment is screaming here."

My defenses are rising like a damn drawbridge. "Control issues?" I croak out.

"Yep. I recommend going with the flow for a while. We all like to be in control, but from what these cards are saying, you're doing way too much."

I swallow uncomfortably. "In what way?"

He looks up. "People pleasing. Not asking for what you really want. How old are you?"

"Um, twenty-six."

"Perfect time to find out who you really are. And just a word of advice, it's not who everyone else has told you to be. Be selfish and get to know what makes you happy."

I clear my throat, hating the whirlwind of thoughts and emotions consuming me. "All right, well, thanks for that. I better get back to work."

The faintest hint of a smirk hits his lips while he collects his cards, but I don't pull him up on it. I'm not clarifying his clarifications.

Even though I'm pretty sure he knows anyway.

"Stay positive, Nikki. Better is always around the corner," he says over his shoulder as he heads for the door. "Trust me."

I hum a reply as I dwell on what he said.

Perfect time to find out who you really are. And just a word of advice, it's not who everyone else has told you to be...

As uncomfortable as that last sentence made me, he might be right. I've done nothing but be who everyone else has told me to be my entire life. And people pleasing? That is *so* me.

"Ah, I love the smell of sage," Kelly says, arriving with a fresh coffee. "So, how did it go? He's good, isn't he?"

"Yeah." *Too damned good.*

"I remember when he first read me," she says wistfully, and then she shudders. "Think about what he said, all right? Some will hit, other stuff won't. They say 'take what resonates and leave what doesn't.'"

"Yeah, I will." The trouble is, pretty much all of it did.

"Alicia called while you were busy. Wanted to know if you're free for dinner at Railgarten with the girls after work on Thursday?"

"Tell her yes."

Definitely yes.

Chapter Five

I meet the girls inside Railgarten straight from work. We all love this place and come here often. It used to be Midtown's old rail station, but now it's home to food, fun, and games—indoor and outdoor—such as ping-pong and volleyball, and there's live music.

Right now, Third Coast are on the outdoor stage playing a soft rock set.

"I saw a tarotist."

Rhian shrieks, which draws the attention of the rest of the diners in our area of the courtyard. *"Let me see!"*

I roll my eyes. "Girl, I said a *tarot-ist*. Not a tattooist."

Chay and Alicia burst out laughing as Rhian frowns. "What's that?"

"It's someone who reads your future in cards."

"Oh... So what did they say?"

I pick at the tacos in front of me. Not even these are making me feel better and they're my favorite. "He basically said I people-please... That I'm too controlling... Reckons I need to have more fun and get to know who I really am."

Alicia snorts before clapping for the band. "Amen to that!"

"Hey," Chay says defensively. "Nik's good as she is, aren't you, babe?"

I'd usually give her a wink and agree but don't this time. "I think he had a point. All I've done since Bron left is overanalyze my life." *The overthinking is never-ending.* "Yes, he was stable, successful, fine as hell, and had a huge dick, but the more I think about our relationship... the clearer it is to see how suffocating it had been for him, for me, and, ultimately, us."

Alicia reaches over to rest her hand on mine. "I know that look. Spill."

I sigh. "I need to get out of my own way. I've been thinking a lot about my past and my habits. I need to go with the flow for a while and maybe stop working quite so much. It's all I do... I have a mountain of vacation time. I'm thinking of taking some."

We all wince when Rhian squeals again. "Please let me book us somewhere. *Please?*"

Rhian's always traveling. She runs a blog all about her trips and sells random but crazy-successful products on Amazon, like steering-wheel trays, spy cameras, anal bleaching kits, and pickle-flavored cotton candy—of all things. There's no denying she's free-spirited and lives life to the full, but am *I* ready to experience one of her adventures?

She eyes me. "You just said—"

"All right." I throw my hands up in defeat. Karl said have some fun. "Go ahead," I add, before I change my mind. "Let me know dates."

"Eeek. I will."

She's already scrolling through her phone, and I experience an unexpected twinge of excitement. It's been forever since I trusted anyone other than Bron or my parents to plan anything in my life.

Although I can't even remember the last time Bron did, come to think of it.

"Have you spoken to him?" Alicia asks softly.

"Yeah, about getting his name taken off the lease." I omit the part about me trying to see where his mind was at though, because it was far from on reuniting with me.

Chay eyes me over her fries-loaded fork. "How did that go?"

I sigh. "Better than expected. He doesn't think we should rush anything, so we agreed to leave it a while."

"I think he's right. I know he ended things with you, but surely he's not over what happened either. Do you think there's any chance you'll end up back together?"

I shrug. "I have no idea, but Rhian was right, I can't live my life like that, wondering and hoping he'll come back. If it's meant to be, it will be, and if it's not..."

Rhian smiles. "Imagine if you did? Chay could write a book about it. I love second-chance romances. They're hot."

"Right," Chay agrees as she tucks her long red curls behind her ears. "I still might, even if you don't end up back together. No harm in making some money off your heartbreak, huh?"

I roll my eyes. "Maybe I should start reading again. I've missed it."

"I'll send you some books you might like. There's one I'm reading at the moment where the woman gets together with three brothers." She smiles wistfully. "It's giving me sooo much inspiration."

I blink. "Actually together-together?"

"Yep. It's quite common these days, believe it or not. Imagine all those di—"

"Yeah, maybe let's not talk about that, considering I'm not even getting *one*."

She laughs, and so does the couple at the table beside us. My face grows hot.

"Sorry Nik, but you know you don't have to go without, right? Just build a toy collection."

The same couple smirks, and I wish the band was playing harder rock. "Can you not talk so loud?"

Rhian rolls her eyes as she reaches over to steal a handful of my barely eaten fries. "Oh, chill out. No one cares, Nik. Everyone masturbates."

I close my eyes. *God, you can kill me any time now...*

"You should try anal beads," Chay whispers. "Babe, those things will change your life."

As explicit as Chay can be, I still gape at her. "You use them?"

She leans back, as if I'm crazy for asking her that. "Damned right I do. Craig loves all that freaky shit. The first time he tried them on me..." She fans herself. "Let's just say that there was a minute I thought I was gonna die."

Alicia snorts.

"He asked me if I needed my inhaler after I came."

We all burst into laughter.

"Get some. You can thank me later."

Bron never so much as *mentioned* touching me there. Our sex life was basic: mostly missionary, doggy on special occasions, me on top when I had the energy. The orgasms were great, but the variety, not so much, and the one vibrator I do have hasn't seen the light of day for years.

I don't even know where it is.

Chay eyes me before catching the attention of a server. "Definitely get some. Life is way too short not to experiment. I've been with all sorts of men, and all have introduced me to different things. There's no shame in exploring what feels good to you, babe." She smiles sympathetically. "I know you had a pretty strict and sheltered upbringing, but maybe it *is* time to let that go. You're an adult now. You can do whatever you want."

"She's right," Alicia agrees. "Yes, your parents liked Bron for you, but maybe start thinking about what *you* think is good for you? I've told you this before."

"Hear, hear," Chay says. "The last thing you wanna do is

live with regrets of all the things you didn't do. Life is meant to be lived, not observed. Do whatever the hell you want."

"Yeah, maybe you're right."

"We are."

"Mom and Dad would lose their minds if they found out I had toys," I mutter thoughtfully, "or that I dabbled with tarot. They're barely speaking to me now as it is."

Alicia rests her fork down and eyes me cautiously. She's spent the most time with my parents and as fierce as she can be, even she's intimidated by them. "How did lunch on Saturday *really* go?"

"Not good. Mom wasn't too bad; I'm meant to be having lunch with her next Thursday, but Dad... He basically thought I should be begging Bron to take me back."

Rhian chokes on her drink. "You're not serious?"

"Unfortunately, I am. I think his exact words were, 'Women your age have no business being single. You can't afford to let a man like him go, Nicola. Find out what he wants and give it to him.'"

"Damn," Chay whispers. "My dad would *never*."

He really wouldn't. Her dad, Jonathan, does nothing but support her choices which, I'm not gonna lie, I'm envious of. I've only met him a few times because he lives in England, but the way Chay talks about him always gives me life.

"Yeah, well, I told him I wasn't going to beg after any man. That didn't go down well. I left as soon as I'd eaten, before he decided to whoop my ass."

Rhian laughs, but her eyes soon widen. "I still remember when he heard me cussing at your twenty-sixth. I swear I saw him reaching for his belt."

"Girl, my dad does not play." I sigh. "Let's hope my next man measures up to his expectations."

"I hate to break it to you," Alicia says, "but I don't think any man ever will."

I swallow a mouthful of taco. "Bron did. I don't think anyone will ever be good enough again."

"I'm more impressed that you stood up for yourself," Chay says. "It's about bloody time."

The others agree.

I smile. "Just a little bit."

"Well, keep it up," Alicia says, checking her phone and smirking. "You're a grown-up now, remember?"

I narrow my eyes at her. "Hmm-hmm. What's that secret smile about?"

She snaps her eyes at me. "Nothing yet. If it becomes important, I'll let you know."

"Gotta be dick," Rhian muses, waving her hand to order us another round of drinks. "Just not a stable one yet."

Chay snorts. "They never are with Alicia."

Alicia rolls her eyes. "I have kids, ladies. Dating isn't as easy as you'd think when you don't just have yourself to please. Count yourself lucky that you get a clean break with Bron, Nik."

"That's true."

"Just make sure the next one's rich so he can buy them Robux," Chay says to Alicia. "He'll have them eating out of the palm of his hand in no time."

"Ughhh, can we not mention that game? I heard the girls bargaining with my mom to buy them some as I was leaving out the door. Wait till you all have kids—then you won't think it's so funny."

I chuckle. "Let's hope it's lost its appeal by then."

"Doubt it." She eyes the drinks, and the server when he rests our drinks down. "He's cute," she says to me when he leaves.

I shake my head. "Stop."

"Y'know," she muses, "you really should think about trying

yoga, especially now. It will help with the sexual frustration too."

"I agree," Chay says enthusiastically. "It's something new."

I lift my glass. "I'm really not sure..."

"What have you got to lose?" Alicia asks. "Just try it, Nik. If you don't like it, don't go back."

I groan, frustrated by her going on about it. "Fine."

"See," Rhian says. "That wasn't so hard, was it?"

"I guess not."

"I'll give you the details. She's amazing."

My stomach churns with the mere thought of it, but I swallow it down with wine. "Thanks."

Chapter Six

After almost a week of going back and forth with the company of the cosmetics account, I arrive at work on Wednesday morning to an email from IT telling me we have a new sample and it will be good to go on Monday.

It means I can focus on LipLush. They want us to contact existing customers currently on their subscription plans to find out what made them sign up, so I've spent most of the morning rewording and reordering the questions to make sure we can get as much information from them as possible in each ten-minute interview.

My phone rings just as I'm reading through the questions one last time. "Kelly?"

"I have your brother on the phone. You okay to take it?"

"Yeah, sure. Put him through." I saw a missed call from him earlier and forgot to return it. "James?"

"Hey, sis. You good?"

I swivel around in my chair to face the window. I'll be distracted by work otherwise. "Yeah, you?" God, I love this view. Not only can you see a lot of the bustling city from here but the stunning arches of Hernando de Soto Bridge over the water.

"Uh-huh. I heard about you and Bron. How are you?"

I figured it was why he was calling, because we rarely talk on the phone. Maybe he bumped into one of the girls. "I'm okay. Who told you?"

"Mom let it slip last night when I checked in with them."

"Oh..." I'm literally stunned that they've told anyone, but hopefully that means Dad won't be talking to Bron's parents and trying to get us back together.

"So, how are you really? What happened?"

"Truthfully, I'm up and down..." I give him a brief rundown, sparing him some of the more intimate details, for his sake and mine.

"Well, shit. I didn't see that coming."

"Join the club."

"I bet. Y'know, sis, I understand this has come as a shock and it must hurt, but as a man, I can tell you, I'd believe what he said. Sometimes we really don't know what we want."

"Don't worry, I'm trying not to take it personally."

"Good. You're a catch, so don't let him make you feel any kinda way about yourself. He'll soon find out that the grass isn't greener, and when he does, make sure you don't take him back. As much as I liked Bron for you, make him stay where he is. He can't pick you up and drop you because he doesn't see your worth."

I smile. "Thanks, Jay-Jay. I appreciate that."

"Nessa said the same. She thinks he's crazy."

Bless her heart. I do love Vanessa. "Good to know. How did Mom sound when she told you? Was she disappointed?"

"I couldn't tell, but what does it matter? It's not them that broke up with him. Why...? What did they say to you?"

"Mom was okay, but Dad wasn't happy. He said he was gonna call Bron's parents."

"What the—"

"Yeah, I know. Said I should beg him back too."

He cusses down the phone, which makes me laugh. "Ignore him. Trust me, Dad doesn't see how he is sometimes. Remember that time we didn't speak for months? You gotta stand up to him, Nik. Don't let him keep railroading you with his idealist and outdated views."

"I don't want to disrespect him though."

"Whaaat? It's not disrespecting him to stand up for yourself. You can't let him keep living your life for you."

I groan. "I know. The girls keep saying the same."

"Good. I hope it will sink in then. I'm serious. He should be proud of you. I know I am. It's not like you've crumbled and let this ruin your life. You're at work, still being the boss you are. Whatever he feels is his problem, not yours."

Maybe he's right... "Thank you," I say quietly, suddenly emotional. *What the hell is wrong with me?*

"Come over for dinner soon, all right? I'll get Ness to arrange it with you. Gotta go, I have a client waiting, but we're here if you need us, okay?"

"I know. I will, and thanks."

I hang up and wipe my eyes. This has got to be the most I've cried for a long time. My emotions are all over the place.

"You okay, Nikki?"

I look up at Kelly at the door. "Yeah, all good."

She nods in knowing. "I'll get you a coffee."

"Thanks."

I sigh into the phone as I sit at the table to eat a chicken dinner I grabbed on my way home from work. "I have my first class Saturday morning, all right? Can you all get the hell off my case now?"

"Well done," Chay says on the three-way. "Practicing mindfulness will help you make better decisions for yourself."

I roll my eyes, wishing I never mentioned almost texting Bron again in the group chat a few days ago. "So you keep saying."

"It's true," Alicia says. "Yoga changed my life. Work and the girls used to have me stressed as hell before I started."

"Well let's hope it does the same for me because right now, I'm all over the place. I think this is the most stressed I've ever been."

"We know. Did you manage to get in with the instructor I told you about?"

I stab an undercooked potato. "Yes."

"Good. I miss Jenny. Giving up my morning classes with her broke my heart."

"I'll tell her you said that," I mutter, making a mental note not to buy this crap again. It's nasty.

"Do. Be warned though, she's a little blunt, but she'll change your life."

"Hmm, I hope she does something, because at this point I'm sick of being up in my head all the time."

"We get it," Rhian says sympathetically. "Try not to stress though, 'cause it won't make it better."

"That's easy for you to say. You should see the message I got from Dad earlier."

"What did he say now?" Alicia snaps.

I open the message. "He said, 'Have you made things right with Bron yet? You should come back to church like he has.'"

They all growl at that.

"He sent it an hour ago, so I should really reply before he calls."

"You should just ignore it," Chay says.

"Ha." If only. "I'll message you all later, all right? Rhian, do you have vacation dates yet?"

"Almost. I'll email you when everything is set."

"Okay." I say goodbye before I hang up, then I sigh heavily as I return to the message Dad sent.

No, I haven't spoken to Bron. I'll think about church. Hope you and Mom are well. Tell her I'm looking forward to seeing her tomorrow.

I already know that won't go down well, but maybe once I've spoken to Mom, she'll see my point of view and say something to him.

At least I hope she will.

I meet Mom at The Four Way Soul Food down on Mississippi Boulevard, dead on two o'clock. My parents love it here and visit at least once a week. Mom's favorite is fried catfish with green beans, buttered corn and rice, which she orders, while I go with the baked version and switch out the rice for fries.

The restaurant is busy, as usual, but we manage to find a table at the back that's a little quieter. It's not the ideal place to have the conversation I know we're going to have, but I didn't choose this place, Mom did. I offered to meet her at home and cook, but she refused.

She looks beautiful, as always, dressed in a summery maxi-dress and slides. Her toenail paint matches the yellow flowers on her dress, and I notice she's had her shoulder-length hair blown out, which reminds me that I should schedule in some pampering myself soon.

I've been thinking about dropping the lace fronts and rocking my natural hair for a while. Rhian recently went natural, and I've been having hair envy. I can't remember the last time I left my hair out longer than a few days, but I do know that it's past my shoulders now thanks to all the months of protective styles.

I ask Mom how she is and we pretty much make small talk while we wait for our food to arrive. She tells me more about her trip to England and that her and Dad have already booked their next one to Spain. I guess I'll be sampling paella next.

"Nicola..."

Ugh. Here we go...

"I'm sorry about you and Bron."

"Thanks," I reply warily, still unsure if this reaction's genuine or not.

Her eyes soften, like she's heard my thoughts. "Your dad is too, he just..." She sighs. "He liked you two together."

"So did I."

"And there's no chance...?"

I shake my head. "He completely blindsided me, Mom. I wouldn't trust him not to do it again."

"I understand, I do."

The food arrives, which saves me from having to talk more about it, or so I think until Mom drops her fork and the uneasy feeling returns.

"A few months before I got pregnant with your brother, I left your father."

I swallow my mouthful of catfish whole. "You never told me that."

"I didn't tell anyone, not even my parents. They disliked your dad from the moment we met, so they would've been relieved. My mother was always so hell-bent on me marrying a banker. Goodness knows why, but she was."

A banker? The hell? "Why did you break up?"

"Because your father lived in his ego and thought everyone should bow down to him. He also became more controlling the more successful he became, and I didn't like how he expected me to conform to his way of seeing things."

Well, that doesn't surprise me.

She sighs. "I don't always agree with him, baby."

"So why do you always back him up?"

"Because not only is he my husband, the man I promised in front of the Lord to support and love unconditionally, but I know that deep down, although it may not always seem like it, he does have yours and James's best interests at heart."

I'm not sure what it is about what she's just said, but something triggers me in a serious way. I think about doing what I usually do and keeping my mouth shut, but I can't. "Maybe so, but making your kids feel like constant disappointments isn't right, no matter how much it's for their own good."

Her eyes widen. "Is that how you feel?"

I laugh bitterly but quickly stop. "I don't think this is a good time to have this conversation, Mom."

She straightens in her chair. "No, it's the perfect time. Is that how you feel, Nicola?"

I nod. "It is. Since I was a child, I've felt as if nothing is ever good enough. I couldn't party with friends, I couldn't make mistakes, all because you'd make me feel so awful when I did. Like such a failure..." I bite my tongue, but it doesn't hold long. "I don't even think Bron leaving me was the worst part of what happened—it was telling you and Dad. I was dreading it because I already knew how you'd react."

She's clearly horrified by that. "Oh, Nicola. I'm so sorry."

"What I wanted more than anything was for you both to have my back. For you to be sympathetic to what had happened to me. I shouldn't leave my own parents' home feeling worse than I did when I got there. It's far from the first time I've felt like that either. I'm forever in fear of you and the way you react to things. Like Dad saying he was going to contact Toya and Calvin. Sometimes, I don't feel as if I'm in control of my own life—you are."

She remains silent, but I can't seem to stop now I've started.

"I'm twenty-six and still living by your rules and ideals. You have no idea how many things I've missed out on in my life because of the constant worry of whether you would approve of it or not." I stop myself then, because she has tears in her eyes, and it makes me feel terrible. "I'm sorry, I didn't—"

She shakes her head. "No, don't. I had no idea *you* felt this way. No idea at all."

"I don't want to upset you. You and Dad mean the world to me. It's why I've never said anything before."

She picks up a napkin to dab beneath her eyes. "So much of what you've said, your brother did a few years ago. It's why James and your father didn't speak for a few months, and then with the cancer scare, I convinced them to work it out. I should have realized you felt the same."

So that's what happened. I remember them not talking, but I didn't know what it was about. "I didn't know."

"A lot was going on at the time." She reaches for my hand and squeezes it tightly. "I have never been anything but proud of you, Nicola. I may not have always made that clear, but you are everything and more that I could ever have wished for in a daughter. I wish I was more like you."

"Really?"

"Of course. Your strength, determination, even how strong you're being over your breakup with Bron. I almost lost my job after I kicked your father out. I was a mess. But you... Your positive outlook on life is one of the things I've always loved so much about you. You never give up."

Well, this is news to me. I can't deny that hearing her say that makes me feel good. "I honestly never knew you felt that way."

"I know that now, and I'm sorry. Your father loves you just the same, and I know you might think otherwise for good reason, but I'll talk to him, all right? Give me some time."

If James has already confronted Dad and he's still the same,

I don't hold much hope in anything changing, but I don't tell her that.

"Okay."

She picks up her fork again, but as I watch her, it's not relief I'm feeling, it's guilt for making her almost cry.

More mental torture...

Chapter Seven

Just before one on Friday morning, Rhian sends me an email, CC'd to all of us.

Hey bitches!

The trip is all booked and paid for. My treat. Booking details are attached. If any problems with dates for you, Nik, you'll have to pull a sickie. Alicia's parents can only have the girls at the end of the month or not until the end of the year, and I'm not waiting that long.

Can't wait for this! Get your passports ready, and make sure you wax, Alicia. No one wants to see that shit. :D

Love, Rhi xx

End of the month? Pull a sickie?

I click open the attachment to scan the itinerary. We're going to Sedona, Arizona and she's booked us in for spa treatments, excursions, wine tasting, and wow, the accommodation looks stunning. I've always wanted to stay in a cabin. It even has a pool.

Nervous excitement wrings my insides as I read our schedule for the three nights' stay. Rhian is always the life of the party, so I know there's no way in hell she'll let me get out of any of the activities she has planned. I wouldn't be surprised if she chose some of these things on purpose to drag me out of my comfort zone.

I mean, karaoke night?

She knows how uncomfortable that shit makes me.

Cringe.

I email her back directly.

Hey bitch.

Thank you so much, but karaoke? Seriously? I agreed to go, and this is how you do me? Whyyyy?

No love, Nik.

She replies almost immediately.

Haha! You agreed, so suck it up. It will be fun, trust me. I hope to get you a dick tour too, but they didn't have that listed on the add-ons LOL.

Get out of your head and prepare yourself for fun.

Love you.

Rhi xx

I roll my eyes at her reply, but I can't help but smile because the excitement is still winning out. Even Karl said I needed more fun in my life, and this trip will definitely give me that. No work for five days either, liquor on tap, amazing food, lots of sun, clear waters, amazing company...

I call Marcus to ask for the time off, which he approves.

"Are you sure? I know it's short notice."

"Stop worrying, it's fine. You deserve a break."

"Thanks." I smile. I really do.

"I'll be down later to go over the cosmetics interview."

"No problem. I'm almost finished," I say before the line cuts out, and then I call Kelly to let her know I'm taking some time off.

"You know that's when the interview for LipLush is starting, right?"

"Oh shit, I forgot about that."

"Don't panic. We have two weeks and you'll be back for the finish. I'm sure we'll be fine. Besides, some time away would be amazing for you right now. There's nothing like a trip to clear your mind."

"I have to admit, I am excited."

"You should be. I'm gonna go grab some cupcakes for the team meeting later, but when I get back you can tell me all about where you're going. I love all that kind of stuff."

"All right. Can you make sure you get a mixture this time? I know everyone else likes chocolate, but I really don't."

"I know, I know. Casey got them last time, that's why."

"Okay, thanks."

Once she leaves, I reread the email Rhian sent, but it's not long before the conversation with Mom infiltrates my thoughts and trashes all my good vibes. What I don't get is how you can tell someone your feelings in a truthful and respectful way and still feel like the bad guy for it?

Everyone keeps telling me to stand up for myself and to say how I really feel to my parents, but no one said I'd feel like this once I did it. No one said I'd regret it or feel guilty. No one said that I'd wish I'd have kept my mouth shut so I wouldn't be all up in my head, replaying every moment.

I haven't spoken to Mom since yesterday, but I've thought about her non-stop. Even though she was nice about what I said, the look on her face when I told her and the tears in her eyes told a different story. The craziest thing though is what I did say wasn't even the half of it.

Dad still hasn't replied to my message either.

There are no words to describe the love I have for my parents. It's immeasurable, so the mere thought of intentionally hurting them in any way kills me. Ironic really, because they've done nothing but make me feel shitty, whether on purpose or not, but I just can't return the same energy.

I'm starting to think I care about people's feelings too much. Karl nailed it when he said I people-please. I always have, as if it's my job to make everyone around me happy so they can be happy with me.

No one seems to understand that either, as much as my girls try to. Maybe it's about time I found out what my brother said to my dad that time they spoke. I know he'll get this more than anyone. His relationship with Dad seems better than ever now too.

Me: *Hey Vanessa. Jay said to message about coming for dinner? Let me know when is good for you both.*

It's twenty minutes before she replies.

Vanessa: *Yass! We're free this weekend if you want to come over?*

Me: *I'd love to. What about Saturday night?*

Vanessa: *Good with us. Seven okay?*

Me: *Yep. See you then.*

I breathe a sigh of relief.

Hopefully talking to the both of them will help with this guilt.

My phone vibrates in my hand just before I rest it back down on my desk, but the dread that rises from the thought of it being Dad soon slips away.

Alicia: *Good luck for yoga tomorrow, sis. Remember to keep an open mind. Xx*

I forgot about that.

Me: *Do I have to go?*

Alicia: *Yes! Let me know what you think.*

I groan.

I burn rubber getting to the gym.

I'm late.

Why the hell am I always late these days?

I spilt my coffee, the yoga pants I wanted to wear had a hole in the crotch, and I was so nervous when I woke up that I had to use the bathroom three times before I left the house. Now I'm running, *running*, like a crazy woman through the gym toward the studios.

I'd usually take a deep breath and maybe say a little prayer before I did something like this, but all I manage is a hasty *please God, don't let me embarrass myself in this class* before I push the door.

To my absolute relief, when I get inside the large studio

with a wall of narrow mirrors ahead, everyone's still chatting and unrolling their mats across the shiny wood flooring.

I'm not too late.

I whisper a thank you before finding a space to inhabit for the next forty-five minutes, right between a young woman wearing the tiniest cropped top I've ever seen, and an older woman whose body is even more banging than the young one's.

Damn. "If yoga does that, then I've been missing out," I say to the older woman.

She smiles back, showing an immaculate set of teeth too. "It does, and thank you. First time?"

"Yeah."

"Ah, be warned, yoga is addictive. You'll love Jenny too. She's great."

"So I've heard."

She turns her attention to a man beside her, so I take a discreet look around to see who I'll be spending my time with. I thought there would be mostly women in here, but it's quite evenly split, which is cool.

"Welcome..." Jenny starts, quieting the room.

She's middle-aged but youthful, with olive skin, long dark hair, and a beauty spot just above her right top lip, giving me Monroe vibes.

She spots me and looks me up and down. "Hello, Miss Gray."

At least a dozen pairs of eyes latch onto me, and I'm positive I can feel their smirks too.

I daren't look away from Jenny though. "Uh, hello?"

Her attention falls on my body again, and I realize her disapproval must be related to my workout gear. My stomach drops as I notice that everyone else is wearing bright colors.

I'm the boring one in gray.

"Um... is there a dress code for yoga?"

The room erupts in laughter, and I suddenly wish I had the superpower of invisibility.

She smiles and I swallow uncomfortably. "Trust me, try bright colors next time. They'll lift not only your mood, but all of ours too."

"No problem," I mutter, making a mental note to prime some new workout gear. Alicia's also gonna get it from me.

Thanks for warning me, sis...

"Good." Jenny takes up her singing bowl, and I can finally breathe again. "Everyone, cross your legs—if you can—and close your eyes."

I slam mine shut and listen to Jenny's soothing voice, hoping it will help me forget not only the awful morning I've had but my current embarrassment.

"As always, we're going to start with some deep breaths, moving your shoulders up and around..."

We do a brief warm-up, breathing and stretching, and I can't say I don't feel a little paranoid when we finally move onto the first few moves. I wish I'd sat at the back so I couldn't be watched, because when I turn my head, I catch a few eyes on me.

It must be years since I sat cross-legged like this, and my poor hips are screaming. All sorts of joints inside me click as well. I sound like a little old lady with how loud they are.

"Now, back to center and we're going to dive onto all fours. Pointed toes, palms spread wide..."

Great.

I lean forward and my thoughts spiral again. Did I wear thick enough yoga pants? Will anyone see through these? What if the people behind me can see the crack of my ass? I'm only wearing a G-string and the man behind me feels pretty close...

"Tucking the tail, draw the navel up..."

My eyes widen when I arch my back and hear my stomach rumble.

Oh, no. Please don't...

Near-gas eruption aside, the past forty-five minutes have been exactly what I needed. I mostly kept up, I managed to shut my mind off, and I'm now the most relaxed I've ever felt, like I'm floating on clouds.

Why have I never done this before?

Some of the positions were a little tricky, and I know I'll hurt tomorrow, but it's already worth it. The breathing exercises were especially helpful. I'm not sure what kind of trickery she used, but for that full forty-five minutes I totally forgot that I had any worries at all.

I give Jenny a nod before making my way out to the hall, hoping she's seen the thank you in it. She was talking to one of the other women and there was a line behind her, so I didn't want to interrupt, but I wanted her to know I enjoyed her class.

Like, really enjoyed it.

"Don't mind her. She always embarrasses the newbies a little. Breaks down the ego so the good stuff can get in."

I turn my head. It's one of the guys from class. "Really?"

He smiles. "Yeah."

I smile back, but I'm not sure if it's because I'm still on a high or if there's just something about him that kinda forces it out of me. He seems friendly, is about a foot taller than me, undoubtedly fit—dark choppy hair with a few specks of visible grey in his short beard—and his glasses-framed eyes are, well, stunning actually.

A shimmery blue.

"Having a good look there, huh?"

I frown as he gets the door for me. *I wasn't checking him out, was I?* I decide not to answer.

"So, did you enjoy it?"

Ugh. Maybe he is going to make me answer him. "Enjoy, er, what?"

"The class?"

Thank God. "I really did. I'd heard great things about Jenny, and she didn't disappoint."

"She's the best, believe me, and I've been to hundreds of classes."

Hmmm. Hundreds? I wonder why, but I don't ask. "Good to know." I am intrigued to know what he wore for his first class with her though, so I ask.

He suddenly smirks and after getting another door for me, he breathes out a laugh. "I wore black, but that wasn't what killed my ego."

I slow my pace. "What was?"

"I'd been out drinking with a friend the night before..." He pauses, as if contemplating whether to say any more, and my interest is more than piqued.

"Did you have an accident?"

That question makes him grimace. "Unfortunately, yeah."

Oh my God. Did he shit himself?

"I threw up during the downward dog," he clarifies, seemingly reading my horrified expression to a T. "Needless to say, my ego was well and truly destroyed."

I bite my lip to stop from laughing, but it doesn't hold it back for long. "I'm sorry," I say, noticing the blush to his cheeks and feeling sorry for him. "And there was me praying that I wouldn't pass gas."

What the hell? Why did I tell him that?

"You wouldn't've been the first, believe me."

I smile at that, loving how he's making my moment of shame seem like it was nothing. "Do you tell all the newbies this?"

He frowns. "Actually, I don't."

Call me crazy but I believe him, and for some reason it makes me feel both good and a little nervous. "Well, I appreciate you telling me." I spot my car across the lot and quickly make a beeline for it.

Now I look weird. Why the hell did I run off?

I'm in my car with the engine purring before the butterflies settle and I find the courage to look for him, eventually spotting him in my rear-view, smiling to himself.

His smile is strangely cute, and those lips...

I look away. Why is my stomach doing cartwheels now?

And why am *I* smiling?

Chapter Eight

"So... How did it go?"

I prop my phone up on the side of the bath so Alicia can see from my shoulders up. "You were right. I loved it."

"Seriously?"

"Yeah. It was exactly what I needed. Thanks for warning me about the dress code though, bitch."

"Oh, shit. You didn't wear—"

"Gray? Yeah."

She smirks. "My bad—I honestly forgot."

I close my eyes and slip a little deeper into the water. "Sure you did. Luckily some guy informed me that the shame was a regular occurrence for newbies. Said something about an ego death or some crap."

The memory makes me smile.

I kinda wish I had his level of unbotheredness.

"It is. I wore black to my first class with her. I wanted to cry when she called my ass out. She's savage."

"Yeah, but what you said about her being amazing at what she does seems to be right. I'm kinda looking forward to next Saturday already. I even primed some new workout gear."

"Good for you. It's nice to have hobbies, Nik. It's also good to try new things."

"Yeah, yeah. So you all keep saying. Are you looking forward to our trip?"

Her entire face lights up when I mention that. "Hell yes. I'll miss my girls of course, but I could do with some *me* time. Mom and Dad are looking forward to having them too, so it's win-win."

"Good. I don't want you getting homesick or worrying yourself about not being with them."

"I won't, believe me. I fully intend to make the most of it, and I hope you do as well."

"Yeah, well, I'm not gonna lie and say I'm not nervous, but I'm excited."

"I think you'll be surprised. Rhian might come across as wild and free, but this is about you, and she knows us all better than we think she does. You can tell from the gifts she always gives us on special occasions."

"That's true." She gave me a personalized bracelet for my birthday in January. I love it so much.

Alicia kneels in her bathroom, rubber gloved up, and I frown when her body begins to jerk up and down.

"What are you doing?"

"One of the girls dropped a roll of tissue in the toilet and flushed it." She curses. "I'm trying to get it out with a coat hanger."

"Eww."

"Right." She sits back and sighs. "I'm gonna have to put my hand in."

My stomach turns.

"It's times like these I wish I had someone to share the shitty chores with. The trash bag split on me yesterday and I almost vomited clearing it up."

"I hate that too. Can't you hire people to do these things?"

"I have no idea, but if you find out then let me know." She slumps down against the wall and briefly closes her eyes. "I'm here if you need me though, all right?"

"I know, and same here. Not to put my hand down your toilet though."

She rolls her eyes. "Thanks. Oh, and now I know you like Jenny's class, I'll send you the link to her Facebook page. She posts lots of good stuff about wellness in there too."

"That would be good. Thank you."

"No problem." She smiles before she hangs up, and then I sink back down into the water fully, feeling the bubbles releasing from my hair.

That's it. I'm taking this lace front out after this and going natural. I wonder what my brother will think of that when I see him later...

I love spending time with my brother. We don't get together much these days with us both being busy with work. His company is making real moves now too, which takes up a lot of his time. Vanessa helps as much as she can with the book-keeping and acquiring new clients, but James carries the majority of the load.

James is a professional photographer, which, as you may have guessed, didn't go down well with Dad when he found out. He wanted his son to be a doctor or a lawyer, especially because he did so well in school, but James point-blank stood his ground and followed his passion, using Dad's lack of support as fuel to work harder, and it paid off.

Vanessa gets up from the table to clear the plates, but I tell her to sit back down.

"I'll do it. Dinner was amazing as usual. Thank you."

"You're welcome, Nikki. We'd love to have you over more often, but you know how it is."

"I do."

"I'll help," James says. "Why don't you go relax in the living room, Nessa? We'll deal with this."

She smiles up at him. "Thank you."

Once in the kitchen, I throw a towel at him. "You can dry. We both know how shitty your dishwashing skills are."

"Whatever." He pulls open the dishwasher. "Rinse those first and I'll put them in here."

I soak the pans before I begin to hand him the plates, smiling to myself because it's been a while since we did this. "Remember when Dad would stand over us to make sure we did it properly?"

"Didn't work though, did it?"

I smirk. "I guess not for you."

"Have you spoken to him since Saturday?"

"No." I tell him about the message Dad sent. "He hasn't replied though."

"He always used to give me the silent treatment too." He eyes the door before returning his attention to me. "We fell out that time because he didn't think I should be with Nessa."

I recoil. "Sorry, what?"

"Exactly. Said we argued too much and that it would never work, but what he failed to understand is how happy she makes me. The arguments are nothing. You know what we're like. We fuss, yeah, but give it a minute and it's like nothing ever happened. It's just how we are and, believe it or not, how we like it."

"Wow... I had no idea."

"Dad has his own views on everything, but he needs to understand that his views are exactly that. His, and they belong to him."

"How did he take it when you said that to him?"

"He cussed me. Tried to convince me that he knew best. It's why I cut him off. I said I'd be happier without him in my life, and I was. It was only because of Mom that I worked things out with him, but I told him straight that things couldn't go back to how they were before."

I sigh deeply.

"You need to put him in his place. Tell him how you feel. Make sure you're firm with him about Bron too. You don't beg that man back, no matter what Dad says. Yeah, you and Bron were good together, but he ended it, and that means if he wants a second chance, he needs to prove himself and fix whatever really happened between the two of you. It's not up to you to do that."

"I know." I turn to him when I rest the pot in the drainer. "Did you know Mom left Dad?"

He nods. "Yeah, she told me. I'm pretty sure she's why he apologized to me too. Mom might have his back on most things, but she's also the only one he listens to. When she stands her ground on something, he knows he's wrong."

"She said to give her time and that she'd speak to him."

"Let her lay the groundwork, but if it's anything like how it was with me and him, you'll need to say something. It won't be easy, but you have to do it."

"Yeah... That's what I'm afraid of."

"You can do it, sis. Look at all you've accomplished."

"True." I give him a hug before pinching his side, just like I used to do when we were kids. "Thank you, Jay. I really appreciate it."

"Any time. You know that. Your hair looks good by the way. You should keep it like that."

I pull on the ends of my bouncy fro, loving how free having my hair out makes me feel. "I intend to."

Fed up with analyzing the conversation with James yesterday and my own impending confrontation with Dad, I decide to ignore it by spending Sunday running around a million stores getting everything I need for the trip away with the girls. I'm still a little nervous about it because I know Rhian will encourage me to let go and "live my best life," but the excitement is winning.

This isn't my first girls' trip, but it is the first one I've been on single, so I won't have the excuse of not doing certain things because my man won't like it, which is both scary and thrilling. I can wear more revealing outfits if I want, talk to whoever I want, and even flirt with guys if I want.

Hell, men might even flirt with me.

The girls have been going on and on at me in the group chat about me getting back out there, and Kelly's been the same. I keep using the excuse that it's too soon, but they're not listening. To be honest though, regardless of how little time has passed, I wouldn't mind having a look, even if it is casual for now.

There's no harm in talking to someone, is there?

My happiness is almost at a ten as I head to the beauty salon for some pampering. I realized in the bath yesterday that I needed to take care of a few personal matters, and the gel on my toes is almost halfway grown out, so after I get those repainted and some infills, I prebook an appointment for the Saturday before we go away.

I've already treated myself to all new clothes, a few purses, shoes, slides, and cosmetics. It's rare that I ever splurge on myself, so screw it. I deserve to. I deserve to have fun. I deserve to treat myself. Besides, it's not as if I have a man to treat me anymore, so I guess I should settle into spoiling myself.

As much as I miss Bron, the more time that passes and I'm forced to see the relationship from the outside, I'm starting to think our breakup may have been needed, if only to make me take a deeper look at myself.

Although I wish it hadn't gotten to this...

Staying busy helps me to stop myself texting him too. I've

been googling "how to get over a breakup," and watching videos on YouTube, which have helped. They all say to focus on yourself and not to stalk your ex's social-media accounts, so after I changed my relationship statuses to single last week, I unfollowed him everywhere.

The last thing I need is to see him talking to or dating someone else.

I still feel a twinge of pain whenever I think of that, but I remember that *I* will have someone else one day too, so I need to really figure out who I am and what I actually want before that happens, because right now, apart from a more varied sex life, I have no idea what that entails.

The girls are right. I don't know who I am.

But I think I'm on the right track to discovering that. I now realize that I hate the color green, which was the tone of the décor in my bedroom until I ordered new lilac bedsheets and curtains to change the look. I love purple. I also bought a fancy coffee maker, new solar lights for the garden, and I've started a new skincare routine.

My determination to take care of myself better and consider my needs first is at an all-time high. I'm only wondering why it's taken me this long to do it.

After getting my brows threaded and a few intimate places waxed, I head home to pack everything. I know the trip isn't for another two weeks, but I always like to plan way in advance. Perhaps I should leave it and start trying to break my controlling cycle too, but I can't help myself.

There's a lot of stuff in my shopping bags but Rhian got us all hold luggage, so I decide to take almost everything I bought, leaving one floral jumpsuit and a pair of gold sandals out to wear to the airport on the morning of the flight.

Now there's only one last item on my bed, and that's my

package from Amazon with my new workout gear inside that was waiting on my front porch when I got home. I try it on before posing in front of the mirror for an absurd amount of time.

I *love* this.

It's lilac and fits like a dream. I have a bit of a belly in everything I wear, this included, but I couldn't care less about that. Not only does the color make me feel good like Jenny said it would, I look good as hell in it.

"Damn, sis. Look at you." I laugh. I barely recognize myself.

My go-to colors are usually dull, so to be wearing something like this and to feel comfortable in it is giving me life. These pants make my ass look amazing.

I wonder if that guy will like them.

Where the hell did that come from?

Chapter Nine

I'm smiling like a crazy person as I roll up my mat. After the week I've had at work, this was exactly what I needed.

Total peace of mind.

Even the fresh wave of body aches I'll have tomorrow isn't getting me down. They weren't too bad last time, but I went harder today and made sure to focus more on my form.

The guy that spoke to me last week is here, but I've kept my eyes strictly ahead, regardless of how hard my gaze has wanted to wander to the back left of me. Something about him has me intrigued. I just wish I knew what.

Jenny is alone when I get to my feet, so I take my chance to have a word and properly introduce myself.

"Hey, I'm Nikki. It's so nice to see you again."

"And you." She smiles. "Love the lilac. It suits you."

I smile as I take a look down at myself. "Yeah, well, you were right about the mood thing, and purple's my favorite color. If my friend Alicia had told me about not wearing black or gray, then I would've made sure to get these sooner."

"Alicia Johnson?"

"That's the one. She recommended you. Said she's still heartbroken over having to give up your morning class."

She chuckles. "Tell her I may be setting up a class over her side soon."

"I will. She'll love that. So, um, I really enjoy the meditation part of your class. I have a busy career and stuff, so it helps to take my mind off all of that. Do you have any book recommendations or anywhere online that I could get some more information on it? This is all new to me."

"Plenty. We have a Facebook group that I list all of that good stuff in."

"Alicia mentioned you did and sent me the link. I asked to join but I'm not sure if I've been accepted yet."

"My schedule's a little manic right now but I'll do my best to get you added soon."

"Great. Thank you so much."

"You're welcome. We're all going for our monthly get-together at Shelby Park if you'd like to join us?"

"Now?"

"Yep."

"Uh..." I suddenly hear the girls in my head, screaming at me to say yes. "Okay, sure. I'd love to."

"Great." She looks behind me. "Mike? Can she follow you?"

"Sure."

It's the guy...

"The area we meet is a little tricky to find, but Mike will make sure you don't get lost, won't you, Mike?"

I turn to see him nod. "No problem."

"Thanks."

Well, I didn't think I'd be spending my Saturday morning like this.

I silently follow him out into the corridor, trying to think of something to say.

"Nowhere to run off to this time?"

I get a flashback of me bolting to my car last week. "Uh, no."

"Cool. I'm Mike," he says, getting the door for me again.

"Nikki." I duck under his outstretched arm. "Do you always go to these meets?"

"Mostly. The people in Jenny's classes are nice and the conversations are always interesting. I overheard you ask her about books."

"Yeah, I'm finding these classes really help me…" I stop myself from divulging my recent breakup and self-discovery journey, but I can't say I'm not puzzled by why I would freely want to tell him that when I don't know him from Adam.

"Makes you think, right?"

"Yeah, it does."

His eyes soften before he points out his car, so I make my way to mine. The butterflies are back again, but are they because I'm nervous about meeting new people, or because I'm nervous about spending more time with him?

Once parked, I quietly follow Mike to an area beside the water under some trees, where several people are sitting on picnic blankets with drinks, snacks, and notebooks. There are a lot more people here than just those in the class I attend, so I assume the others are from Jenny's other sessions.

I've been to Shelby a few times before. It's beautiful, with lakes, forest, and bison roaming. It's busy today because the weather's nice. All blue clear skies with barely any clouds in sight. The warmth feels good on my skin and lifts my mood higher than it was already.

Jenny arrives shortly after me and Mike, and then all of us new members are introduced to the existing ones, which is about fifty people. Mike was right in saying that everyone is from different walks of life, but many have similar experiences to me when it comes to why they took up yoga.

The conversations go back and forth, with people suggesting vlogs, websites, and books of all types to add to their lists of mental-health resources, which is why many have brought notebooks with them. As I'm unprepared, I use my phone, but I notice that barely anyone else picks theirs up. Perhaps that's another rule of Jenny's. No phones during meets.

After several conversations and offers of water and healthy snacks, I find myself sandwiched between Jenny and Mike. Mike's sitting to the left of me and Jenny's to the right. I've just finished explaining what I do for a living and how my friend recommended yoga after my breakup.

Yeah, that last bit kinda slipped out, but I couldn't help it. These people make me feel insanely comfortable around them. It's almost as if I'm in some kind of group therapy session.

"Sorry to hear that," Jenny says. "Breakups aren't fun."

"You're not wrong, but to be honest, I'm starting to think it was for the best."

"Rejection is redirection," David, one of the new guys says, and quite a few of the others agree with him.

"My assistant said that."

"Gives you a chance to reinvent yourself," Jenny says. "How old are you?"

"Twenty-six."

"Perfect age for it too."

I laugh. "Heard that as well."

"There's a book that really helped me get through the biggest breakup I had a few years ago. I'll post it in the group. It sounds as if you're doing just fine though."

"I'm getting there."

She looks at her Fitbit before getting to her feet. "Well, as much as I'd love to sit here with you all afternoon, my son has a football game. See you all next week."

Everyone says goodbye to her, but no one else makes any moves to leave.

"Told you she's the best," Mike says, briefly leaning into my side.

"She seems it."

"It's because she cares about what she does," a woman named Olivia says. "She's been through a lot and likes to help others. You'll see that the more you get to know her."

"I can tell." There was no missing the way she listened intently while I was spilling the recent ups and downs in my life. "I still can't believe how much I'm enjoying her classes."

"Surprising, isn't it?"

I turn to Mike and nod. "It is. How long have you been doing yoga for? You said you've been to a million classes."

"About ten years. Yoga's been a part of my life since I was twenty-two."

"I see." He doesn't look thirty-two. I would've guessed my age. "So you live a life of peace and serenity?"

Stacey, another member of our class, snorts before she laughs. "Hardly. Mike might come across as cool, calm, and collected, but once he's had a few beers, he's low-key the life of the party, aren't you, Mike?"

He rolls his eyes dramatically, but I see the faintest hint of a smirk. "Can we not?"

"Oh, don't be shy," David chuckles. "That yoga class was the most eventful I've ever been to."

I realize they must be talking about the time he threw up, but instead of appearing uncomfortable, he suddenly laughs and shrugs it off.

"I learnt from my mistake," is all he says.

Olivia snorts. "Thank God."

He looks my way and shakes his head, and I get that fluttery feeling inside again. It makes no sense as to why he makes me feel this way. He's nothing like any man I'd so much as be slightly interested in like that.

The guys I go for are usually a lot taller and more built—

thick arms and even thicker thighs. Sure, Mike's clearly fit, but he's far from hench. I'm not a small girl and bigger men make me feel safe—they always have. He doesn't have a full beard either, and I love running my fingers through a man's facial hair.

I wonder if he's ever grown his.

"Don't judge a book by its cover," he says quietly, and I smile.

"Yeah?"

He nods and I watch his eyes wander over my face. "What do you do for fun?" he asks when the attention falls on someone else. "Have you been to Shelby before?"

"A few times, a while ago. And to be honest, I'm just jumping into finding out what's fun to me." I take a quick look around. "I like this though."

He nods. "Busy jobs do that. I used to have the same ailment."

Hmmm. Maybe he doesn't work anymore. "Ailment?"

"Yep."

"What do you do for fun then? Besides drinking."

He laughs. "I don't drink that often. Fun for me is doing whatever I want in the moment."

"Is that right?"

"Absolutely."

"Well, I don't have that luxury."

"Why not? Do you still live with your parents?"

"No, but sometimes it feels like it." I recoil, shocked by how that piece of information slipped out so freely. Why do I keep spilling my guts around this guy?

"Oh, I see." He leans closer. "The trick to having fun is not caring what they think."

"That's easier said than done."

His eyes narrow as he sits back. "Is it?"

I open my mouth to reply, but I can't think of a comeback to that.

He smiles as he watches me frown. Is it easier said than done? I don't know.

An unsettled feeling rises up in my gut, so I look away to strike up a conversation with one of the other guys here. Mike might not be anything close to my usual type, but there's no denying that there's some kind of attraction I'm feeling, and it makes me feel both unsettled and confused.

I wonder if he's always this nice to the newbies or it's because he feels the same intrigue I do. Either way, there's definitely something about him that has me wanting to get to know him better.

God knows why though. It doesn't even sound like he has a job.

A quick buzz from my phone Sunday morning pulls me from my latest round of overthinking, causing my eyes to hurt when I blink. I have no idea how long I've been staring at my bowl of oatmeal, but it must have been a while because the melted honey on top has now set again.

I didn't sleep the greatest last night, and that's because I got a message just before bed from my dad to say he'd give me a call today. A tiny part of me hopes that means Mom's been working on him and that he wants to talk it out, but I more think he's wanting to persuade me to go back to church on the Sunday before the trip with the girls. I told Mom about it, which might have been a mistake.

Probably wants me to consider my life choices before I go.

Grabbing my phone, I'm relieved when I don't see Dad's name. Instead, my stomach leaps when I see that I've been accepted to a Facebook group called *Yoga & Wellness with Jenny*, so I pass on breakfast and make myself a mocha instead and decide to be nosy.

I find a post from Jenny, made twenty minutes ago, about a

book titled, *How to Find Yourself After a Breakup*, but I also see a post made by Mike giving his reading list. It has at least a dozen books on it, starting with his number-one read for self-discovery.

Interesting...

What's more interesting though is the fact my finger seems to have slipped onto his profile and now I'm swiping through his pictures.

Most of them are of landscapes: him at the top of mountains or by water. He's always smiling too and seems like such a free spirit, which is admirable.

Completely different to how I live.

My life pretty much revolves around my career or spending time with my girls now. Mike never mentioned a job at Shelby last week, so I wonder what he even does.

Ugh. Why do I care?

I startle again at my cell, and my stomach immediately drops when Dad's name glares back at me. He must've only just got back from church with Mom.

"Hello, Dad," I answer, trying to sound upbeat.

"Good morning, Nicola. How are you?"

"I'm good, thank you. You and Mom?"

"Well. We were disappointed not to see you at church this morning. I thought you may be sick, but we haven't heard that you've canceled your trip away."

I close my eyes briefly. "I haven't decided if I'm going back to church yet."

"Bron has."

Good for him. "Well, if that's the case, I'd rather not go. It would be uncomfortable with us not long breaking up."

"But how do you expect to win him back if you don't see him?"

What? I thought Mom was going to speak to him? "Dad... Please. I'm not trying to win him back. I *have* said that."

"Nicola..." His words drift off when I hear Mom's voice in the background. "Your mother would like to talk to you. Have a safe trip." His tone tells me he's not happy, and I'm relieved when Mom says hello.

"Hey, Mom."

"I just wanted to say, have a lovely time away, baby. Sedona is beautiful and I'm certain you'll have an amazing time."

"Thank you. I hope so."

"I'm sorry," she whispers. "I'll talk to him again."

"Don't worry yourself," I say, defeated. "I appreciate you trying though."

She's quiet for a moment, and then I hear a heavy sigh. "Let me know when you get back. We can have dinner."

"Sure. Love you both."

"We love you too."

After making sure the phone has definitely cut out, I sigh. And groan.

I may as well bang my head against a brick wall.

Chapter Ten

I've been clock-watching for the past hour. Marcus has been on a rampage, and as the minutes tick down for the weekend, the less on edge I feel. Kelly is feeling it too and has barely said more than a few words to me when she's delivered my coffees.

Poor girl.

As expected, work has been a nightmare all week, and I don't think the stress has skipped a single soul in here. There's no doubt the business is growing to new levels and we need more staff. I just hope Marcus decides to hire at least another two project managers soon, or the entire place might end up going to shit.

Personally, to get through this week, I've spent my evenings reading to stop myself quitting the job I usually love. It's that bad. I had initially started with one of Chay's recommendations, but the romance was triggering, and I wasn't enjoying it, so I switched to one from Jenny's group instead.

The book she suggested on breakups is good—I'm about halfway through it now—but Mike's top book on self-discovery caught my attention and seems to have me hooked, especially the section on boundaries and how we should all stick up for ourselves, which I felt was speaking directly to me.

I've begun attempting meditation at home too, but yeah, that's not going so well. My mind stays busy, wandering to the relationship with my parents, whether I should move house, and finally settling on, of all things, the lack of intimacy in my life.

I'm really missing dick.

I try listening to my breathing like the book says, but that just makes me think about how sex would usually calm me down when I had weeks like this. I can't find my old vibrator either, which is making me want to start a collection like the girls told me to.

It's just that although I know a toy would do the job, I miss hands on my body. I miss the hugs after a long day, the kisses on the forehead, the deep conversations while I cook naked after a few rounds in the bedroom. I miss the morning texts, the naughty texts, the cooking for more than just myself. There are so many things I miss about being in a relationship.

Even so, despite all the stress, heartache, and lack of intimacy, there's no denying how much better I'm beginning to feel.

My phone buzzes a few times in quick succession, and I see a message from my brother pop up.

Jay: *How are you? You looking forward to your trip away with the girls next week?*

I smile. Him and Vanessa both keep messaging me. I get the feeling they're worrying, because they never text this much.

Me: *I'm good. More than looking forward to it. How are you and Nessa?*

Jay: *We're good. Just checking in*

Me: *All good here. Tell Vanessa I said hello*

Jay: *I will*

Swiping off my messages, I'm both surprised and slightly giddy when I see a friend request from Mike on the top of my notifications. He's changed his profile picture to one where he's laughing amongst a group of people. They all seem to be looking at him, men and women, and he has his arm around a mature woman and a man who looks a lot like him. Maybe his dad? Regardless of who it is, something piques my interest about this picture. It's completely different to any he's posted before.

I set my phone down, unsettled. *What is my obsession with this guy?* I even asked God about him last night because I keep thinking about him. The conversation we had at Shelby has played on my mind a lot too, and what he said about the key to having fun is not caring what other people think.

There's definitely truth in that, and it's had me thinking: why am I still holding on to this belief that I need to conform to society's standards—and, more importantly, my parents' opinions?

Glancing at my phone again, I watch Mike's picture fade to black. Why has he sent me a friend request? Does he think I like him? Does he like me? Is he friends with everyone else in the group?

Calm down, girl. Maybe I'm reading too much into this. Maybe he actually wants to be friends? That's okay, isn't it? I'm allowed male friends, aren't I? I'm single, and I would like to get to know him better. Perhaps I could find out what he does for fun.

Screw it. I pick my phone back up and accept his request.

I wonder if he'll message me.

I groan. *Stop.*

Chapter Eleven

I make my rounds to say hello or give a quick nod to everyone in the group when I arrive at the studio on Saturday morning. After the meet last weekend, it seemed rude not to, especially as everyone had such great stories and pieces of advice after I shared my baggage.

Mike still hasn't messaged me on Facebook, but he did like one of my recent posts last night. A quote I posted not long after I broke up with Bron that said, "When one door closes, another always opens."

I overthink that too, wondering if he checked out my page, until I eventually have strict words with myself about it. I need to stop living inside my head. It's actually starting to piss me off.

Thank God for this class.

The yoga session once again leaves my mind clear and refreshed. I managed the tree without losing balance for the first time, which has me buzzing. The added practice I've put in at home seems to be paying off.

Most of the other people in the class are clearly far more advanced than I am. Jenny gets them to do the harder poses while the newbies do the simpler ones, but that was something I loved about this class when I first saw the description, that all levels were accepted in one. It gives me something to aspire to.

Not only that, but there are all shapes and sizes: tall, short, heavy-set, curvy, slim, and everything in between, which just goes to show how inclusive yoga can be. I've never been into the gym or running, so I'm not going to pretend that I am. This though, this is me all over.

"Hey," I hear Mike say as I'm leaving the studio.

I try not to smile so hard but completely and utterly fail. "Hey."

He's quiet as he walks beside me toward the exit, so when he gets the door for me, I ask him if he's okay.

"I'm good thanks. You?"

"Uh-huh."

We walk toward the parking lot in silence, but I get the sense he wants to ask me something.

"Do you have any plans for the rest of the day?"

I knew it. "Nope. Why?"

"I'm hitting the Greenway and wondered if you wanted to come along. The track's not too tricky, and the views are incredible."

I stop beside my car, which he seems to have followed me to. He's asked me somewhere one-on-one, so does this mean... I stop my overthinking before it can carry me away. *Just say yes. It means you can get to know him better.* "I'd love to—oh, but I don't have a bike."

"You can hire one there."

"Oh, okay. Sure. Why not." I'll only be sitting at home otherwise, and it has been years since I went on a bike ride. I also wouldn't mind exploring some more of my local nature spots.

His smile is genuine, but I also detect a hint of relief. It's contagious too, like usual, and my excitement begins to take hold. "Great. Wanna follow me there?"

"Yep, but I'll need to stop at a store on the way." I wave my empty water bottle. "I don't have water or anything on me."

"Don't sweat it. I've got everything we'll need."

Was he betting on me saying yes?

Ugh, stop it. He's just asking you on a bike ride, Nikki, not for your hand in marriage.

"All right."

After hiring me a bike and refusing to let me pay, Mike lends me one of his spare helmets and we're on our way. I haven't ridden a bike since I was a teenager, and my ass is a little bigger than it was back then. Luckily though, the seat is comfortable and I'm able to keep up with him.

Or maybe not.

I pedal faster to catch him but get preoccupied by the sight of his incredible ass in the cycling shorts he changed into in his car. *It might even be perkier than mine.* He's got great legs too, and I wonder if he does anything else as much as he does yoga.

Shaking my head, I up my pace and finally level with him. We have to stay quite close because there are a lot of people here.

"Have you been here before?" he asks, giving me a quick glance.

"Um, I think once with my friends a few years back? We got drunk by the river. To be honest, I haven't done the outdoors much, but I enjoyed last weekend."

"You've been missing out."

"So I'm beginning to see." Sitting at Shelby last weekend made me realize that. It was so peaceful by the water. The sun was out, and it made me feel amazing. In all honesty, I'm really starting to see the beauty in the simple things these days.

He swerves around a fallen branch on the track but soon

levels back beside me. "You mentioned last week that you work in market research. What kind?"

"Telephone-based. I work for PVR." I glance his way. "Do you know of them?"

"Not really. I've seen the building though. How long have you been there?"

"About six years now. Where do you work?"

"Anywhere I choose to on the day. I'm self-employed."

"Oh." I look his way again but snap my attention back to my handlebars when I hit a little dip in the trail and the bike wobbles. My heart pounds.

Almost went ass over tits then.

"What does self-employed entail?" I ask, keeping my eyes ahead this time.

"Me and my laptop mostly. Online stuff. Stocks, shares, affiliate marketing. I'm kinda into a lot of things. I don't 'work' much anymore. I had a car accident a few years ago trying to rush to my corporate job. I didn't go back after."

"Oh, damn. Was it bad?"

"I died for a few minutes, but it could've been worse."

"Wow..."

"Yeah. That was *my* moment to find peace. Since then, I've made my money work for me and pretty much take each day as it comes."

"Don't you get bored?"

He laughs. "Bored?"

"Yeah, I mean, what do you do with so much time on your hands?"

"A lot, believe me."

"Do you not have a girlfriend?" I ask, immediately regretting it. What the hell inspired me to ask him that?

"Nope, not for a few years now."

"And you don't get lonely?"

"Not really. I have my friends and my family, and I do work. Apart from that, I enjoy my own company."

"Yeah, I get that. I'm kinda enjoying my own company too."

"People think you have to be with someone to not feel lonely, but that's not true. Spending time with yourself can be eye opening."

"Hmm..." He's not wrong there. "I wanted to say thanks for the reading list you posted in the group. I finished the book you recommended on self-discovery last night and found it very inspiring."

"I loved that book and reread it often. Not everyone is ready for that kind of read though. Most people I knew when I started meditating thought I was going insane, especially when I started yoga after." He laughs. "They thought I was going through a midlife crisis."

"In your twenties?"

"Believe it or not. Have you tried the meditations?"

"Yeah, but I'm finding it hard to stop the thoughts, regardless of how much focus I put into my breathing. Maybe I'm going crazy the other way."

He chuckles. "It doesn't come overnight, but the more you do it, the easier it becomes. For now, just observe the thoughts that come, then try to release them."

"Release them?"

"Yeah. A lot of things that pop up in our quiet moments are things that are hindering us in some way. We aren't our thoughts. Let them pass."

"I see..." *That makes so much sense.* "How long did it take for you to get used to it?"

"A while. I think I gave it up at least a handful of times before I stuck it out. It kept making me feel weird."

I chance another look his way. "Weird? In what way?"

"What do you think about when you meditate?"

"The relationship with my parents, my job, my breakup,

and..." I stop myself from confessing the last thought, just in time.

"I'm pretty sure that one you don't want to talk about was the same as mine."

"Oh..." I feel a blush creeping up my cheeks and almost wobble on my bike again. "You might be right."

He laughs. "I bet I am. How long has it been since you rode a bike?"

I was hoping he hadn't seen that. "Years. Can you tell?"

"A little. Wanna race?"

I turn to gape at him but really do almost fall off the bike this time. "You want me to race when I can barely stay upright?"

He laughs again. "You'll be fine. You're wearing a helmet."

I shake my head in disbelief. "I'm not a competitive person. Never have been."

"Oh, come on. You can do it. Just to the bend up there. It's not far. I'll even give you a head start so I don't distract you."

I take a quick look down at my legs, not liking the thought of falling off and scraping them to shreds. "What about my knees?"

"Three..."

"What? I didn't say yes!"

"You didn't say no either. Two... I'll give you five seconds."

"But..." My gut twists with anxiety. I've never raced anyone. "I can't."

"You can. One. Go!"

A random and very strange squeal escapes me as I switch the gears on my bike and begin to pedal like a maniac. *What the hell am I doing?* I'm twenty-six, racing a grown-ass man. I must be absolutely crazy.

Once I hit the five-second count in my head, the adrenaline really kicks in, causing me to pedal even faster. The thought of being chased makes my heart pound, but when I look up from my wheel and see the bend approaching and how close I am, the excitement of possibly winning takes over.

"Mike?" I shout, hoping to hear how far behind me he is with his voice, but when he doesn't reply, I kill my legs to make it the remaining few yards and scream when I get there first. "I win!"

Turning narrowly to stop, I expect to see Mike, but I frown when he's nowhere to be found.

Surely that's longer than five seconds.

I cycle back around the bend and to my horror, I see him sitting on the ground a way back, waving people away from him, so I cycle faster to see what happened.

"My God..." I rest my bike down beside his when I see his torn-up knee. "What happened?"

He glances down. "Rock on the trail. I'm good—I just need a second."

I kneel beside him, recoiling slightly when he looks up. "Um, are you sure you're okay? You look a bit pale..."

"I'm not good with..." He doesn't say it, but I know he's talking about blood.

"Uh, do you have anything in your bag you could use to cover it? A spare T-shirt or something?"

"Yeah, I think there's one in there." He takes off his rucksack, but I take it from him.

"I'll rinse it first, then wrap it. Wanna look somewhere else for a minute?"

He blinks, but then his eyes soften. "You don't have to."

"Honestly, I don't mind." I think of something to take his attention away from the blood while he looks away and I pour a bottle of water over the wound. "Least you haven't thrown up."

He laughs. "I still might."

"Thanks for letting me win too."

He snaps his head back to me. "Believe me, I didn't."

I smirk. "Hmm, sure. Isn't this one of the oldest tricks in the book?"

He shakes his head and laughs harder when he turns his head. "I promise you—I did not do this on purpose. I'm not into self-inflicted pain for any reason, not even to impress a girl."

"Sure." I find a grey T-shirt and wrap it around his knee. It's not the best, but I make it work. "All gone. I'm not sure what you're gonna do about it when you get home, but at least for now it's out of sight."

He looks down. "Thank you."

"No problem. Wanna head back? You should probably get that cleaned properly."

"Yeah." He helps me up once he's got to his feet, then we both push our bikes back toward the parking lot. "That win doesn't count, by the way."

I laugh. "Is that because of the head start or your accident?"

"Both. Want a rematch?"

That makes me smile on the inside. "Yeah, why not. I wouldn't mind beating you fair and square next time."

"No chance."

"I guess we'll have to wait and see."

He turns to face me and smiles. "We will."

I drift off into my own little world after that. Although this didn't go exactly as I thought it would, it's still been the most fun I've had in a while. That feeling of winning was everything too. It might not have been technically fair, but the fact I did something so completely out of my comfort zone and actually enjoyed it has me on a high.

No wonder everyone in the yoga group seems to like Mike. He makes me feel comfortable, and even though he's nothing like anyone I've spent time with before, I really enjoy his company.

"Thanks so much for inviting me out here," I say as we arrive at my car. "I had a really good time."

He uses his T-shirt to wipe the sweat off his face, and the brief glimpse of his lower torso gets me heated. I was right about him being fit. He's not shredded, but there's no doubt in my mind that he takes care of himself in all ways. However, when he lifts it a little further up, I notice the beginning of a scar, quickly reminding me of his accident, so I search for my keys in my tights pocket before he sees me looking.

I can't believe he actually died.

"So did I, accident and all. Next weekend?"

The excitement of that thought is instant. "I'd love to."

"All right, well, enjoy the rest of your weekend."

"You too."

I smile all the way home.

Chapter Twelve

I spend Sunday cleaning house and making sure everything is nice for when I get back from my girls' trip. We don't leave until Tuesday, but going by last week at work, this one's gonna be just as hellish and I'll more than likely end up finishing late again tomorrow.

Today has been productive, and amongst all the cleaning, I managed to drop a few bags of donations to the thrift store too. Just knowing the house is lighter has somehow made me feel it, and I plan on getting an early night while I'm not so stressed.

There's just one more thing on my list to do before I forget...

My stomach twists in knots as I look for the incognito area on my Google search—not that this is necessary because no one other than me uses my phone, but still. Once I find it, I Google "sex toys."

Walmart?

Walmart sells sex toys?

I shudder. That's just weird—shopping for groceries and dildos at the same time. It's two-day shipping anyway, and I'd kinda like something to take away with me.

I eye my suitcase. *Thank God for that hold luggage.*

Scrolling on, I find Lovehoney. I've heard of them before, but I keep looking. Amazon... The Coy Store... Olivia Ocean... I try LELO.

My eyes immediately light up when the page loads and something called an Enigma pops up. *What the hell does that do? Two hundred dollars?* I almost have a heart attack at that price. Will it clean itself and tuck me into bed afterwards?

As I scroll through, I'm continuously surprised by not only the cost of these things but the selection. So many choices for so many different things. Even 24-carat gold ones. *Where the hell have I been?*

There's even an electronic range for men.

Wow... Okay... Mind definitely blown there.

I find the menu and go directly to vibrators. *Maybe start slowly, Nik.* I'm not trying to damage any internal body parts by trying to do too much too soon.

There's a lot here again, so I filter it down to sex toys for women. *Definitely want a good one... Hmm...* I decide on something called a Smart Wand and a Rose. The reviews on the Rose are not only the highest I've seen, but they have me screaming.

***** *Babaaaay. Buy it. Just buy it.*
***** *After buying this, I wasn't even sad about breaking up with my girlfriend.*
***** *I wasn't ready. Lawd...*
***** *Ruined my mattress. Use several towels.*
***** *What kind of demonic invention is this?*
***** *It snatched my soul.*

Damn. I'm excited for that one. I also grab a standard vibrator before heading to the checkout, and once selecting express shipping, I'm good to go.

Almost three hundred dollars though. Whew. These toys better be good. Let's just hope I'm not too shy to use them on myself. I've always stuck to my trusty hand to get me off when I'm single, or the BOB—Battery Operated Boyfriend—that I still can't seem to find, but looking at all those sites and reviews makes me realize how much I've been missing out on.

The first person I met that used toys was Tanisha, my dorm mate at college. She would wash her dildo in the bathroom sink and leave it on the side of the bath with no shame whatsoever. It had a suction cup on the end, so it would be standing to attention every time I'd go in there.

It was green, *of all colors.*

Not only that, but a guy I was seeing at the time found it and came into the bedroom waving it in the air, asking if I wanted him to use it on me. I was horrified in the moment but screamed telling Tanisha about it later.

I wonder what she's been up to?

After twenty minutes of searching, I find her on Instagram. She's in Maryland now, married, pregnant with her first child... Wow. I'm so happy for her. She was with some real assholes back in the day, so she deserves to have found her king. She struggled a lot with body dysmorphia too, which I never understood because her figure was everything.

I smile wistfully as I scroll through her feed, but I also feel a little sad. I thought that would be me soon: buying my first house, changing my last name, having kids. Even though I'm a little envious, I push it down, because no matter what my love life currently looks like, I refuse to hate on someone else's happy.

Besides, *I* love me, and I have so much to be grateful for.

I need to remember that.

"Is that all?" I lift my head from my crossed arms. "Can I go now?"

Kelly ticks off the last thing on her to-do list—extravagantly, may I add. "Yep. All done."

I don't know how she can be so cheery all the time. "Thanks. I've gotta be up in six hours and I'm hanging already." Anyone would think I'm going away for a month with all the shit I've had to do today.

"Hey, least you won't have to worry about work for the rest of the week."

I rest my head back down. "Doesn't help me now." All I can say is that thank God I packed everything I needed ages ago so I can go straight home and pass out.

She chuckles. "Tiredness aside, are you looking forward to your trip away?"

"Very."

"You gonna try get laid?"

"Kelly..."

"My bad." I feel a hand on the back of my head. "Go on, go home. I'll handle anything else that comes up. You sent the email with the passcode, right?"

I nod as I look up. "I did."

"All right." She smiles and then I see her send a look to my hair. "Y'know, I've been meaning to say this for a while... I love your hair out, Nikki. It really suits you.

That makes me smile from the inside out. I even sit up straight. "Right? I think I'm gonna keep it like this. It gives me Viola Davis vibes."

"I agree. You should. Now go home!" she shouts on the way out the door. "And have an amazing time."

Trust me, I'm going. "Thank you."

Once home, I manage to drag myself into the shower before eventually falling onto my bed, still in my towel. I'm not as sleepy as I was, and the excitement has finally started to kick in.

I check the group chat with one eye open and see over a hundred messages I've missed. My phone started vibrating like crazy just after four this afternoon and I had to put it on silent.

God knows what they've been talking about.

After scanning through a load of messages about outfits, Chay's plans to wear out Craig tonight, and Alicia crying after she tucked her kids in to bed, I roll over onto my back so I can write out a reply.

Me: *Hey, girls, not long home from work. Chay, I like the green bikini best, and hugs, Alicia. Think of how much fun the girls will have and how excited your parents are to spend time with them. You deserve this trip too. It's not selfish to take some time for yourself at all xxx*

Rhian: *Bless you, boo. Are you gonna get some sleep now?*

Me: *I plan to. I'm exhausted.*

Rhian: *Don't worry. You'll have plenty of time to relax when we get there.*

Me: *I know. You okay?*

Rhian: *All good here. Get some sleep, boo. We'll see you in a few hours xx*

Me: *All right. Night sis xx*

Chapter Thirteen

The girls make an entire scene when I meet them outside Departures in the morning. As early as it is, there's no doubting how hyped they are for this, and although I barely had enough time to wipe the sleep out of my eyes after snoozing through two alarms, their excitement is contagious.

It's just after five so we have a little while to eat and grab a drink before our flight at six thirty. It will only take us around three hours to get to Arizona, but the shuttle to Sedona will take a while too. I offered to hire a car when we got there, but Rhian wouldn't let me.

Alicia and Rhian walk ahead toward check-in, but I hold Chay back a little before we follow them.

"I bought a few toys over the weekend," I whisper as I lean into her side.

I'm nervous to talk to her about this, because as much as I used to hype up the sex with Bron, I never went into details. I couldn't about certain things anyway, because I knew they'd be judgmental if I gave them full exposure, especially over what Bron *didn't* do.

He had Jamaican roots, so oral sex wasn't an option. I tried to go down on him a few times when we first got together, but he wouldn't allow it. He didn't agree with it and said that he wouldn't kiss me afterwards if I did. I didn't understand it until I learnt more about his culture, but even when I did get it, I didn't really, and it sucked.

Or not.

"Oh, shit," Chay hisses. "Which ones did you get?"

"A standard BOB, a wand thing, and something called a Rose."

She widens her eyes at me before smirking. "Those Roses ain't no joke, girl."

"So I heard."

"You not used it yet?"

I shake my head. "I brought it with me though."

"Thank God I brought EarPods," she mutters. "It takes a minute to adjust but when you find the sweet spot, Lawd have mercy."

"The reviews pretty much said the same. I ain't gonna lie, I'm excited."

It has a tongue, so I'm intrigued to see how it's gonna work. I used to love the feel of a man's head between my thighs, just as much as I used to love kneeling between theirs. There was always something about having that control with a guy... I've missed it.

"You should be. Didn't you get the beads?"

"No, that section was intimidating."

That makes her laugh. "It's cool. You have a few to get you started. Toys are like Pringles—once you pop..." She leans a little closer. "I have an entire chest full. You name it, I've probably got it."

"Don't you enjoy sex without them?"

She frowns. "Of course I do, but sex is supposed to be fun. No harm in playing, is there? It's not like I bring other people in."

My eyes almost escape my face. "Have you ever?"

"A few times, but not with Craig. It's not as great as it's made out to be anyway, especially if you don't like sharing."

I shake my head. "I can't believe I've known you for all these years and not even really known you."

"Well, let's hope now you're discovering who you really are, we'll all get to see the real you too."

"Yeah..." *Whoever that is.*

I wonder how much Craig has played a part in Chay being so open and free. They met three years after Chay moved here to gain her diploma, and she always talks highly of him.

"How's Craig feeling about you being away from him now?"

Her smile tells me all I need to know about how last night must have gone. "Let's just say he could barely open his eyes to kiss me goodbye."

I snort.

"Besides, I promised to make the trip fun for him too. You aren't the only one who packed extras."

Oh God. "Maybe *I* should've brought headphones."

She laughs. "Don't worry, you won't hear a peep. I'm an expert at not getting caught."

I shake my head as we catch up with the others.

"What's that look for?" Alicia asks.

"Usual Chay," I reply, getting my passport ready. "I think I need a drink."

"Don't worry, sis," Rhian says. "Once we're done here, we're going straight for the lounge."

"You booked us into a lounge too?" Chay practically squeals. "How did you manage that?"

Rhian pretends to rest an imaginary crown on her head. "Perks of being me. Now hurry up, their breakfasts are a-mazing."

· · ·

We land a few minutes after schedule, and after collecting our bags, we make our way through Phoenix Arrivals.

"Our shuttle should be waiting," Rhian says after checking the time on her cell. "Hurry up so we don't miss it."

"Yes, sir." Chay salutes as we pick up the pace.

We all drank a little too much on the flight and Chay especially is in full-blown "happy" mode. So is Rhian.

I think I'm the most sober one of us all.

A few stumbles aside and we make it outside to find our shuttle, and after handing our bags over to have them loaded, we make our way to the door of the bus.

"Hold on," Rhian says as she rummages around in her purse, following behind with Alicia. I need to find the—"

"Rhi!" I shriek, rushing toward her as she falls in what seems like slow motion—but I don't reach her in time. She's already on her ass, laughing while clutching her elbow.

"Fucking hell," Alicia says, kneeling beside her. "Are you okay?"

Rhian nods. "I'm fine. Help me up."

Chay picks up her bag while I run to grab the lip gloss rolling away down the sidewalk before it ends up under the bus.

"Got it."

"Oh shit, I'm sorry, babe," I hear Rhian say.

I turn to see the girls looking at Alicia's dress where Rhian's bled on it, and I'm immediately reminded of Mike.

The memory of our bike race makes me feel all warm inside.

"Screw my dress. As long as you're all right." She looks in her purse and pulls out a Band-Aid. "Give me your elbow."

"Aww," Chay gushes. "It's Minnie Mouse."

"Love it," Rhian says, twisting her arm for Alicia. "The driver's staring at us though, so best hurry it up."

Once Rhian's bandaged up, we finally make our way onto the coach to a mass of people staring at us. I feel like the naughty kid with all the disapproving glances aimed our way, and I barely resist the urge to flip them the bird.

"Nothing to see here," Chay says, leading us to our seats near the back. "Nosy assholes," she mutters.

The rest of us giggle as we take our seats.

"We made them late," Rhian hisses. "Bad girls."

Alicia shrugs. "Tough."

An hour later, I'm beginning to doze off while resting my head on Chay's shoulder. Rhian's doing the same to Alicia behind us.

"I think I'm getting old. I'm not handling my drink very well," Chay says.

Alicia agrees. "Do you remember when we partied all night and still went to lectures in the morning?"

I shake my head. "I can't believe you did that." I hardly ever stayed up with them, but I remember the state of her and Chay, walking into lectures wearing the same clothes as the night before.

"Those were the good old days," Rhian says. "Take me back."

Chay gives me whiplash as she spins around. "Are you crazy? Girl, no."

"Do you smell that?" Alicia suddenly asks.

I turn around now. "Smell what?"

Her nose crinkles. "Vomit."

"No..."

"I'm so sorry," a young woman with choppy blue hair says, turning in her seat. "It's my little boy. He doesn't travel well."

"Oh, hell no," Chay mutters beside me, mirroring my thoughts. "I don't do well with sick."

The consensus from the passengers around us say they don't either, and there are several groans of disapproval.

The woman's face falls before she spins around and begins yanking baby wipes out of the pack. "It's okay, sweetie..."

I feel awful, so I make Chay apologize. Me, however, I pull out a bottle of Chanel and start sniffing it.

Alicia slaps me from behind. "Don't do that. You'll get high."

I turn around, already feeling green. "Do you want to clean up after me? 'Cause if I don't do this, you will be, and don't forget everything we've eaten on the way here."

Her cheeks puff before she shudders. "Sniff away."

"Thank you."

"I'm glad that's over," Chay says as we finally arrive at our cabin.

"Me too." My thoughts of the shitty ride here are soon overtaken by the wonder of the red rock and pointy hills around me though.

This place is incredible.

I've never been to Sedona before, but I've heard all about it. Alicia and Rhian have both been and I can see why. It's so peaceful, and so vastly different to the hustle of Memphis. I'm excited to get inside the cabin, but I take a minute to soak in the sights around me first, and so do the others.

After dropping her bags on the dusty path leading to the cabin, Alicia makes a beeline for a hammock attached to the trees out front, while I walk around the rocky area that has a picnic bench and parasol to the right. The mountain views and the sound of a creek in the distance are what really excite me. So beautiful. I can't wait to spend the next three days here. I already know this is gonna be the best thing I could do right now.

"This place is amazing, Rhian. Thank you."

She turns as she opens the front door. "You're welcome,

babe. I just know you'll find your peace here. I might be wild a lot of the time, but I know what is needed and when."

"Yeah, well," Chay says, "I think we could all do with some peace after that crazy journey." She shudders. "I feel dirty, and not in a good way."

Same.

"There might be kids around here too," Rhian says, dragging her suitcase inside. "Just so you know."

Alicia shrugs. "They're not mine, so I don't care."

I snort as I follow them all inside. "Right." I couldn't care less about kids being around. I just want a shower so I can get to the pool and soak up this amazing sun while I take in these picturesque views.

Inside the cabin is just as nice. It has two open staircases, high ceilings, and a cozy atmosphere. Warm colors, the scent of the outdoors, and there is plenty of space too—which I knew there would be because of the pictures Rhian sent, but it looks even bigger in real life.

"You did good, babe," Chay says. "We appreciate you."

Rhian does a twirl but stumbles a little before Alicia catches her by the arm. "I know. So, should we pick our rooms...?"

"Yes..." My attention's diverted by my phone vibrating in my jacket pocket. *Work?* Why the hell are they calling? "Hello?"

"Hey, Nikki, it's Kelly. Sorry to bother you, but we can't seem to open the file that LipLush sent you."

"Hold on." I roll my eyes. "Girls, I need five minutes."

They all reassure me it's fine, but I know they aren't impressed.

"We're gonna pick rooms and then we'll meet by the pool," Chay says. "Hurry your ass up."

"I will."

Please don't tell me I didn't send the passcode...

· · ·

The girls are relaxing by the pool by the time I get outside. Chay's pulled her lounger into the shade and is covered in factor-fifty sunscreen because her red hair and freckles make her prone to burning, while Alicia is directly in the sun, as usual, trying to fry herself.

Alicia always tells me and Rhian how lucky we are to have dark skin. Her brother is also black and white, but has a much darker skin tone, and she is forever complaining that he's selfish for stealing all her dad's melanin. Alicia may act the most mature of us, but the things she comes out with sometimes make me scream.

"Hey, loves."

I slip my glasses down from my head as the reflection of the pool almost blinds me. I already love it here. It's ten times nicer than I expected, not that I thought Rhian had bad taste, but I honestly didn't think she would've picked somewhere quite so stunning or quiet.

"Did you sort it?" Alicia asks when I settle in the lounger beside her to screen myself up.

"I did. The file was encrypted, that's all. They're all dialing on it now." I thought I had emailed the passcode to Kelly but for some reason it had gone to my drafts instead. Holiday excitement had clearly kicked in early.

"That's good. Least now you can chill out."

"Yeah. Sorry. I just don't want my job going to shit along with my relationship, y'know?"

Chay nods at me as she sips her drink. "We understand. It's something you can control."

"Exactly."

"You thought any more about dating yet?" Rhian asks before sipping her own cocktail. She and Chay ran into one of the stores on the way here and bought enough drink to keep us well and truly lit all day.

"Actually, I have."

They all gape at me, and I roll my eyes.

"And?" Alicia presses.

"Why not?" I shrug. "You're right. I should live a little."

Kelly hasn't stopped going on about it either. I told her point-blank that I wasn't swiping left or right for anyone, but she reassured me that if she hooked me up it would be with a reputable website.

We don't screw bums, she said. *But their superpower is usually slinging dick.*

"Thank the Lord," Rhian gushes. "I mean, you're fun, successful, beautiful... You have so much to offer, Nik. You'll be snatched up in no time. If you were gay, I'd be straight in your DMs."

That makes me laugh. "You still are."

"Are you gonna date outside of your race?" Alicia asks, catching me completely off guard.

My stomach tightens. "Um, I dunno about that, sis."

"Why not?"

I shrug. "I dunno. I've just never considered it. Melanin has always been my weak spot." Although... Mike's white and he's cute—smaller build and all. We're very different though, so I'm not sure we'd work romantically. I like a career-driven man, one with a five-year plan, but Mike's a very free spirit...

"Same," Rhian agrees. "The darker the better for me."

She's not wrong. I, personally, have always been drawn to my black kings. There's so much about them that I love. From how spiritual and caring they are, to the glow of their skin, right down to the way they carry themselves.

"But how do you know if you've never dated anyone else?" Chay asks. "Craig's the first white guy I've been with, and trust me, it's not true what they say about black men being bigger. My boo is hung."

I snort, and the others laugh.

"So that's why you're always walking funny," Rhian mutters.

Chay scorns us. "Hey, don't hate. It's not a good look, loves."

I laugh. "I'm not hating, and I never said anything about it being because of the size of their dicks."

"Well good, because I've had all types of meat—from pink to dark, and all the shades in between—and believe me, it still all comes down to how well they can use it."

Alicia groans. "Girl, really? Too much."

Chay rolls her eyes. "Trust me. They say the darker the berry, the sweeter the juice, but lychees are just as sweet, and they're white."

Rhian frowns. "Aren't they pink?"

"White, pink, same shit."

I shake my head in disbelief. "How the hell did we go from talking about dicks to lychees?"

"It's your fault."

I blink. "Mine?"

"Yeah," Chay retorts. "When we told you to date, we meant give *every* type of man a chance. This is meant to be the time to broaden your horizons. Try new stuff. That includes men, Nicola. This isn't the era to be holding on to those old beliefs. Love is love."

I glare at her. "Don't use my name like that. You sound like my dad."

"Maybe you'll listen then."

Ugh. "It's not that I have anything against white men or interracial dating, I just know what I like."

"So you're saying you've never found a white guy attractive?"

"Of course I have..."

"Well then. You've gotta be open to receive what's good for you. Don't write any type of man off. Love and happiness are feelings, not shades."

"Hear, hear," Alicia agrees with her. "This new guy I'm talking to is half Chinese and half black, and he is *fine.*"

I eye her. "Oh yeah? I thought he wasn't relevant. Does he have a name?"

"Not yet, and don't try to change the subject, Nik. You gonna give everyone a chance or not?"

Could I date a white guy? Or anyone outside of my race? I mean, I was with Bron and our cultures were different—him with his Jamaican customs and me with my American ones—so I suppose I could... I sigh. "Fine, I'll be less picky. He has to wash his meat though, because I've heard white people don't— and I'm not talking about his dick," I add, before one of them says something.

Chay gives me a look to kill. "Hey, I wash my bloody meat and I'm white."

"You're black at heart though, babe," Rhian says, saving me.

"Whatever the hell that means. I'm just me. It's the best way to be."

"And that's why we love you."

"You better. Seriously though, don't judge, Nik. The older generation did enough of that shit for all of us."

Rhian agrees with her. "Now that *is* facts. I'm sure my great-granny is still trying to beat my lesbianism out of me from beyond the grave."

That makes me laugh. I can't even with her sometimes. "I'm sure she sees things differently now."

"Hmm, maybe. Anyway, how's the yoga going? Still enjoying it?"

I nod. "Very. It's been exactly what I've needed. They had a monthly meet at Shelby and I got to meet the other members of Jenny's groups. It was nice."

"I remember those meets," Alicia says. "Everyone was so chill."

"They are. It seems a lot of people take up yoga for similar reasons. I've even started switching up my food because of the benefits they've talked about."

"Good for you," Rhian says. "Do whatever you need to feel good, especially now. You aren't dieting though, are you?"

"No, not at all, I love my body." I always have. "It's more that I'm pushing myself to try new things. I've also started reading books about self-discovery, and they're changing my mindset too."

"Well, damn," Chay gushes. "Seems as though that group has been amazing for you."

"It has. With being so busy with work all the time, the problems with my parents, and now the breakup with Bron, it's really helping to clear my mind and help me breathe."

"You have always been go, go, go, babe. It's about time you slowed down a little."

"I haven't had a choice. Now I don't have a relationship to pour into, all I can do is focus on myself." I sigh. "Sometimes it doesn't seem real that Bron and I aren't together anymore."

"Hey, it's normal to feel that way," Alicia says sympathetically. "Even with us suggesting that you try dating, it's meant to be fun. We're not telling you to start looking for a husband."

"Right," Rhian agrees. "This time is about you finding out what you want in your life. It's about you getting to know yourself."

"Yeah…"

Alicia leans over Rhian to squeeze my arm. "We know, boo, and we understand."

"I know you do. Anyway, less of the sad shit," I say, before I knock back my drink. "Who's ready for a refill?

"Me!" Chay says, jumping up. "Give me your glasses."

Chapter Fourteen

Yesterday was a complete write-off. We all overdid the liquor and, as a result, ended up passing out before it got dark. I had hoped to sample that new toy I brought with me, but yeah, that wasn't happening. If those reviews are anything to go by, I might really have died.

Today has been much better so far.

We started the day with the first excursion that Rhian had prebooked: a jeep tour of Old Bear Wallow. We were going to do the Canyon, but it was ten hours long and none of us were feeling it, so we did a wine tour instead, which is why we're all now tipsy again.

"Look at my toes!" Chay gushes as she slumps down on the leather couch beside me. She lifts her bare feet in the air. "How pretty?"

"I love them." I opted for good old-fashioned French manicured, but Chay's dusky pink is giving me toe envy.

We've been in the spa for a couple of hours already, having had facials and pedicures, and now Alicia and Rhian are having hot stone massages on tables ahead of us. This place is quite busy so they couldn't fit us all in at the same time, but they let us all hang in the same room while we waited.

"What should we do after this?" Rhian asks during a swift rise of her head. "The weather looks nice. How about we check out the water?"

"Sounds good to me."

"Same," Chay says. "We'll have to run back to the cabin to change though."

"That doesn't—"

A sudden sound resembling an old creaky door hitting a hollow wall renders me speechless. I know what I think it was, but I notice the masseuses don't bat an eyelid.

Chay suddenly giggles. "Alicia, did you just fart?"

"I'm so sorry," she says, keeping her head firmly buried in her towel, and even though I can't see her face, I know she's feeling a way.

"It happens all the time," one of the masseuses says, "really."

Alicia keeps apologizing though, no matter how many times we try to reassure her, until Rhian lets one out.

"Can we get over it now?" Rhian says, sounding not one bit bothered.

I see the two masseuses smile knowingly at each other, and so do Chay and I.

I swear, I love that girl.

"This is so nice," Alicia says as she dangles her feet in the stream. "If I didn't have my girls to go home to, I'd never leave."

We agree with her. This is *so* nice.

There is nothing but towering jagged mountains around us, and the weather is the perfect temperature. The shallow water is crystal clear, not too fast-flowing, and most importantly, it's quiet. No kids here, only a few small groups of friends playing music and chilling like us.

I decide to take some pictures to post on my Facebook and Insta, but I end up taking some selfies too, of my feet in the water, the classic "thighs that look like hotdogs," and a few provocative ones of me lying back on the grass from the waist up.

I look hot in my metallic purple bikini top. I had to adjust my breasts a little because they kept slipping out the sides like fried eggs, but I managed to get a few good pics.

Once posted, the likes begin to flood in. I haven't posted for a while, not since I blocked Bron on everything. My thoughts drift far from him though. I'm more wondering if Mike will see them, and if he does, what he'll think.

"I'm getting in," Rhian says, getting up from beside us.

"Please be careful," Alicia tells her. "You've been drinking."

"I'm good." She starts stripping off down to her hot-pink bikini beneath her booty shorts and tank top. Her body is banging, I ain't gonna lie.

"That's not leaving anything to the imagination," I say to her, trying not to stare.

Rhian shrugs. "Oh well."

I swear she's said that a million times today.

She runs from behind us and then jumps into the water, hands and legs flailing before she disappears, but to Alicia's relief, she emerges just as quickly.

Without her bikini top though.

My eyes escape my face. "Sis... Your titties!"

She looks down but doesn't cover them. "Nice, aren't they?"

Alicia gasps and immediately looks around for something to throw her, but I'm too stunned to.

"How the hell do you have such perfectly perky boobs that size?"

"Right," Chay agrees. "They're a cracking pair. I can't take my eyes off them."

"Neither can anyone else," Alicia hisses. "Cover them up." She throws her tank top at her, but Rhian doesn't use it. She lies in the water and floats.

"You'll get us arrested!" Alicia admonishes her.

She leisurely strokes her arms through the water. "Oh well."

I shake my head. *This woman...*

After our eventful afternoon, we go home to freshen up before hitting Olde Sedona Bar & Grill for dinner.

I feel amazing in my glittery dress and matching heels, and my girls look equally as gorgeous. It's one of the things I love about us: we never leave the house until we're all happy with how we look, and if one of us isn't, the rest of us will do whatever it takes to make sure they are.

"They do karaoke here," Rhian says with a twinkle in her eyes. "Get those lungs ready."

I ignore her and scan the menu instead.

"A-hem?"

I look up at her. "You must not be talking to me."

"I'm talking to *you* especially. No one knows you here except us, and I'd bet money you'll never see any of these people again in your life."

"It's karaoke though." I take a quick glance over at the stage. "It's cringey."

"No it's not—it's fun, Nik." She waves the server over to order a round of tequila shots. "I hate to use alcohol this way, but something needs to break you out of that damned shell."

"I can't believe that shit hasn't worked yet."

"What hasn't worked?" I ask Chay. *What are they up to now?*

She sighs. "Nothing. What you having?"

"I dunno. Everything looks good. How about we share?"

They agree, so we get seafood, tacos, ribs, and a grilled mixed platter to share between us. The food is delicious and goes down well, but after we finish dessert, the topic of karaoke resurfaces.

"Can't I just watch you?"

"Oh, come on," Chay says. "Alicia's ass is even up for it."

Alicia shoots her a glare. "What's that supposed to mean?"

"Exactly what I said. Look, no one cares, Nikki. Rhian had her tits out earlier for the entire world to see—do you think she cares about what anyone thought? No. So I don't know why you give a flying bollocks about singing a few songs out of key. No one's asking you to audition for bloody *X Factor*. Most of these people in here are smashed anyway and will forget about you before you've even left the building."

"She's right," Rhian says, backing her up. "You really need to lighten up."

I grind my teeth. "Fine."

The girls look between themselves as if they can't believe I've conceded, and then the next thing I know, we're all up on stage with mics in our hands ready to sing "Three Little Birds" by Bob Marley and the Wailers.

The eyes boring into me are unsettling, and so are the laughs that come when we start singing—Chay the loudest—but then something makes me remember Rhian today and how she saved Alicia from her embarrassment and showed everyone her tits like it was nothing, so I decide to take a leaf out of her book.

Screw it.

I close my eyes and start belting out the lyrics like I would if I were at home, pretending no one can see me. I don't even open them when people start cheering and Alicia whispers, "What the hell, sis?" in my ear.

God, why have I never done this before?

It feels so good to let go.

"That's right, sis!" Rhian cheers. "Let it all out."

And I do.

As many times as I've listened to this song before, I never really paid too much attention to the lyrics, but while I sing them now, I find them soothing to all my current problems.

"'Don't worry about a thing, 'cause every little thing gonna be all right...'"

God knows what's gotten into me. Karaoke is something I've hated since I was in college. My friends all loved it, but I'd stay at the back, hiding so they couldn't drag me on stage. Drunk people screaming out of key and getting in their feelings over sad songs would make me wanna throw up.

Being up here now has given me a completely different view on it though. I feel so liberated, and although my heart is pounding and my hands are shaking, being able to let go and not care what anyone thinks is kinda exciting.

The crowd seems to love it anyway, giving me a standing ovation when the chorus comes around again. Every so often I open my eyes to see the smiles and cheers, but most of the time I keep my eyes closed so I can live in my own world.

"Let's go again," I say when the song ends and I soak up the fresh round of applause. "That was so much fun."

The girls stare back at me with expressions of shock and awe.

I shrug. "I was wrong. It's not cringe."

"Let's do 'Born This Way,'" Alicia suggests with a glimmer in her eyes.

"Whatever is good with me."

She smiles like a proud mother, and I feel something inside me shift.

I'm proud of me for doing this.

I never do things like this.

Perhaps it's the alcohol or the rush I'm feeling, but not even the dozens of eyes staring at us from around the bar gives me second thoughts.

I don't know what it is, but I have so much fun, they have to drag me off stage in the end for hogging the mic.

"Cheers!" Rhian says before we knock back a round of shots at the bar, bought by a group of cute local guys.

They knock back theirs too, before getting us all refills.

"I've never seen someone light this place up like that before," Dante says, and his friend, Ben, agrees with him. "I guess you really can be beautiful as well as talented."

That makes me laugh. "Thank you."

"How long you here for?" Dante steps a little closer, to I think, the annoyance of Ben.

"Unfortunately, only one more night."

"That's a shame. I'd love to get to know you better." He steps back so Chay can hand me my shot. "You single?"

"She is," Chay answers, wiggling in beside me and Ben. "She's a catch too."

His eyes travel the length of me. "I bet she is."

There's no doubt his attention is doing wonders for my confidence, even with the high I'm already feeling. I'm not trying to start a holiday romance though, and after everything I've thought about while I've been here so far, I think my focus should really be on me, not a man.

"Wanna dance?"

One won't hurt. "Why not?" I say, shocking Chay.

Seeing that look on my girls' faces is getting quite thrilling.

I knock back my shot before Dante leads me over to the dance floor, and then we dance along to a soft rock song that I don't know. I'd be lying if I said I wasn't enjoying feeling a man's touch on my body, but by the time a few songs have passed, I make my way back to the girls.

"Have fun?" Alicia asks, handing me a water.

"Actually, I did." I don't say anything else when they give me the "why have you left that guy out there look", though. I may have just smashed through my fear of karaoke, but I'm not about to have a one-night stand.

Besides, I feel as if I've just stepped into a new version of myself, and I want to spend it with the ones who helped me get here.

"I can't believe you've been hiding a karaoke-championship-winning voice inside you all these years," Rhian gushes when we get back to the cabin. "You smashed those songs."

"I think that was the most thrilling thing I've ever done." I still feel high off the moment. We must have been up there at least half an hour in the end. We sang Michael Jackson to Queen, and I loved every minute of it.

I was fearless.

"I don't think I'll ever forget it," Alicia says wistfully, and the others agree with her. "If that's the highlight of the trip, I'm so glad we did this."

"Me too," Rhian says. "Worth getting my tits out and all."

Huh? "What?"

Alicia elbows Chay. "Let's leave these two. See you in the morning, girls."

"Night," Chay says as she disappears upstairs with her.

I turn my attention to Rhian. "You got your tits out for me?"

"Maybe." She grabs two bottles of water from the fridge and tells me to come outside with her.

We sit at the picnic bench in near darkness. I can hear the water and the birds but not much else.

"So?" I say, wanting an answer.

"Kinda. I wanted you to let loose and gathered if I did some 'embarrassing' stuff, you would feel comfortable to as well."

I shake my head. "Sis..." There have been so many moments today when she's acted a fool. "You were right, you did inspire me to."

She smiles. "Then it's mission accomplished. How did it feel up there, not giving a shit?"

"I can't even put it into words." I'm smiling now, thinking about it.

She holds my hand across the table. "That's what life should be like, sis. Exciting. We all love you so much, Nik. We don't say it just to say it—we say it because we mean it. We want you to be happy. Not fake happy, truly happy."

"You'll make me cry," I warn. "I love you all too, so much. You've always supported me, cheered me on, not just tonight but since I met you. You might not realize this, but you've already changed my life in ways you couldn't imagine."

"Well, this is just the beginning. I know it's hard going through a breakup, especially when someone ends it with you, but I'm so proud of how you haven't taken this personally, because a lot of women would."

"I just know it's not about me."

"It's really not. Those guys tonight were telling the truth when they said how beautiful you were. Why didn't you take that hot guy's number?"

"I don't want to rebound," I tell her honestly. "I think it's why I've been so hesitant to start dating. It's only been a month, and I want to heal first."

"Are you broken?"

I blink. "I don't feel broken."

"Well then. Don't take everyone's breakup advice to heart, Nik. Love comes when it's time, just like the changes in our lives. Some people meet their forever person as soon as they leave the one that wasn't, some don't meet them for years. And some people are only meant for a season, as a lesson. Just trust that whatever happens for you happens because it's meant to.

As long as you stay true to who you are, and I mean who you *really* are, you have nothing to be scared of."

"Hear, bloody hear," Chay shouts, drawing our attention to the bedroom window she and Alicia are hanging out of.

"Facts," Alicia agrees. "Everything she said."

I smile up at them. "I really do love you girls."

"We know," Alicia says for them all. "Now, bed."

"Yes, Mom," I say as I get up with Rhian, but she hugs me before we go inside.

"Say yes to life, boo. So many amazing things can happen when you do."

Chapter Fifteen

I'm awake before the others, so I decide to take a walk by myself to clear my head. There have been so many conversations here that I haven't had time to process, so what better way to do that than to spend some time by myself, without any alcohol in my system?

I don't intend to go far, but I end up halfway up the small mountain closest to the cabin, where I sit on a rock to take in the views.

Rhian really did good, picking this place.

Suddenly, I'm emotional, and as hard as I try to contain the tears, I can't.

"I've really just been watching my life pass me by," I say to no one. "I'm twenty-six and I can honestly say last night was the best night ever... How sad is that...? And this place... How have I never known how much I love the outdoors?"

I couldn't've picked a better destination for a getaway with my girls if I'd tried.

"I need to start living life..." I close my eyes and remember how I felt up on that stage, how free I felt, how little I cared that anyone was watching. I've always cared so much about the opinions of others, but the way I felt last night makes me wish I let go more.

"I need to take more chances, more risks... I need to stand up for myself too..."

My life has literally turned upside down over this past month, but even with the disappointments and hurt, I'm starting to believe that the upheaval is the best thing that could've happened to me.

"I just need to figure out who I am. Who is Nikki?"

I sigh. I have no idea, but if she's anything like the woman I'm beginning to see emerge, I can't wait to get to know her better. I need to leave the old Nikki here.

My phone vibrates on the way back to the cabin. It's a Facebook message from Mike.

Mike: *Still up for a rematch this weekend?*

He actually messaged me. I almost trip down the mountain.

Me: *Good with me. Hope your knee's okay? Maybe you should get some knee pads.*

I overthink my reply as soon as I send the text, but I needn't have worried.

Mike: *Wow, savage. After I win on Saturday, we'll see who the butt of the jokes is. And the knee is good thanks. Got my stepmom to handle it.*

I'm equally amused and intrigued by his reply.

Me: *We will, and good to hear that. See you at yoga.*

Mike: *You will.*

I'm excited already, but I try not to get ahead of myself. I don't know Mike, as nice as he seems, so I need to not start imagining all sorts until I do know him better. Still, there's no denying there's something there, even if it's just a friendship.
Ugh.
I'm doing it again, and I was supposed to leave the old Nikki back up the mountain.

"Where have you been?" Alicia asks as I walk into the kitchen to a breakfast of eggs, bacon, and toast.

"I woke up early so I went for a walk." I don't explain further because I know they'll get it, and their expressions confirm it.

"This looks great," I say as I sit beside Chay. "Thank you, whoever cheffed it up."

"We all did," Chay says, but then she side-eyes me. "Why don't you ever get hungover?"

Alicia hands me a plate. "Because she's a lightweight and never drinks enough to cause one."

"Shut up, bitch. I can drink my fair share actually."

Chay heaps a mountain of bacon onto her plate. "That shit ain't fair."

"I ain't sorry."

"Pass me your phone," Rhian says, holding her hand out.

I frown. "Why?"

"Just give it to me."

I hand it over once I unlock it, thanking God I used Incognito when I was looking for those toys. And talking of toys, I still haven't used my Rose yet.

Maybe tonight...

Rhian keeps my phone the entire time we eat, doing whatever she's doing, until finally she hands it back.

"Tinder? Are you serious?"

"Calm down. I thought you could practice your game before tonight."

That unsettled feeling rises in my stomach again. "What's happening tonight?"

"I booked us in for speed dating."

"Oh God..." I groan.

"We're coming too," Chay says, referring to her and Alicia. "Just for fun though."

"And what does Craig think of that?"

She smirks. "You don't want to know."

I shudder. *Those two are seriously freaky.* "All right, fine."

"We should use fake names and hometowns," Chay suggests. "I'll be Emily from London. Craig loves that one."

"Okay... I'll be Chinita, from Texas."

"Bea," Alicia says. "From New York."

Rhian smirks. "And I'll be Becky from Florida. We'll have a few drinks before we go, and you can swipe on that app, Nik. We need groceries too."

"I don't mind going to the store," Alicia offers. "Wanna come with, Nik?"

"Sure."

I can't psyche myself up anymore, so I finally bite the bullet and take a seat in front of my first guy when the next round of dating starts. The rest of the girls are already two rounds in, and they seem to be having fun.

There are a few cute guys here, but they're far down the line. The first one I get leaves a lot to be desired. His shirt is so dirty it's as though he's been through a round of competitive eating.

"Good evening," he says when I sit down. "Your dress looks good on you."

"Thanks. Your... hair is nice."

Alicia sends me eyes before rolling them, and I send her back a "what?" with mine.

I'm rusty, okay?

Tinder did nothing to help my chat game. Most of the guys that jumped in my DMs today have either made us all crack up laughing or asked me to send them nudes.

Or offered to send me theirs.

"Are you local?"

I turn my attention back to the guy in front of me. "No, unfortunately not. I'm from Texas. I'm here on a girls' trip."

"I see." He tells me he lives in the next town over, but that's as far as he gets before it's time to switch seats.

The next guy stares at my tits the entire time and only manages to ask what I do for a living. The next two do pretty much the same, until I finally get in front of one of the cute ones in here.

He's mixed as far as I can tell and has beautiful eyes.

"I've been waiting for you to sit in my chair."

"Yeah?"

He nods—at my tits though. "What's your name, gorgeous?"

"Chinita. Yours?"

"Keith. Nice to meet you, Chinita. Are you from here?"

"No. Texas."

He nods. "How long are you here for?"

"A few days."

"And how are you finding it so far? Have you visited before?"

"Nope, never. It's beautiful."

He leans back in his chair, adjusting his tie as he smiles. "Like you."

I smile back but I'm not really feeling him, and I'm relieved when I move to the next table.

"I saw you at the water today," I overhear Rhian's new guy say.

Oh God.

"Did you like the view of my tits?"

I snort out a laugh, offending the guy in front of me. "Sorry. I wasn't laughing at you." I tilt my head toward Rhian. "That's my friend."

"I'm gay," I hear Rhian say, yanking my attention back to her. "I've never tried dick before. Do you know what it tastes like?"

I almost choke on my drink as I hear Chay screaming with laughter beside Alicia.

"Is she really gay?" my guy asks.

I nod before the giggles take hold. "She is."

"Then why's she sitting in front of men?"

"No idea."

Switching again, I end up in front of a guy who looks a lot like Mike.

"Hey," I say as I sit down. The smile comes without me forcing it, and I almost frown.

"Joke?" he asks.

"Uh, sure." *Please be a funny one.*

"What type of ship has two mates but no captain?"

"Um... I don't know."

"A relationship."

"Oh God..." I chuckle. "That was terrible."

He smiles. "I never said it would be good. You have a beautiful smile."

"Thank you."

He asks me my name and I find out his is Lewis. He makes me laugh by telling me more corny jokes and seems unbothered when I tell him how bad they are. Still, as strange as our conversation is, I'm genuinely disappointed when I have to switch seats, and when I sit down in the next chair, I wonder what Mike's doing.

We all fall out of the door laughing harder than ever.

"Sis, why did you have to go do that guy like that?"

Rhian shrugs as she links arms with Alicia. "What? I was just being honest."

"You're lucky they didn't kick you out."

"If they did, they did."

Shaking my head, I smile, not only because of my crazy-ass girl, but because as much as I'm loving being here, I'm looking forward to going home so I can see Mike on Saturday morning.

"I need a wee—badly," Chay hisses as we head toward home.

"Why didn't you go before we left?" Alicia snaps, and it reminds me of how she talks to her kids.

"I forgot."

I get the giggles again and feel the need to pee myself. We did some shots at the end, paid for by the men who took a liking to us. Including Lewis.

"Maybe there'll be a bush on the way that you can squat in," Rhian says.

"We need to hurry up. I don't think I can hold it much longer."

We take off our shoes and begin to jog haphazardly along the trail, until we find somewhere suitable to hide.

"You go first," I say to Chay. "We'll keep a lookout."

She pulls up her little black dress and crouches just out of sight, but then she shrieks. "Aw shiiiit, I pissed on my dress."

I laugh so hard I almost piss myself, so I quickly climb through the bushes to squat next to her, making sure I don't do the same.

"I'm gonna smell all the way home," she says sadly, and I feel sorry for her.

"We can find some water on the way if you want?" I say, pulling my panties up.

She stumbles out from the trees, and I follow. "It's okay. Craig might like it. We've never done watersports."

My stomach turns.

"Is there anything you and Craig *don't* do?" Rhian asks, shaking her head.

"Not much."

"I feel like a virgin next to you," I mutter. "You're forever shocking me with your confessions."

"Hey, I'm a writer. The experience helps."

Maybe I should get back into her books?

I can't believe it's our last night here already. Our time here has flown and we're all sad that it's almost over. We've laughed, cried, preached, and, dare I say, this trip has changed us all.

"Come over one day next week after work," Alicia says as I sit in the lounger beside her. "I'll tell you all about the new guy then."

"You better. I want details."

"We all do," Chay complains. "Anyone would think she's dating a celebrity and signed an NDA."

Alicia rolls her eyes. "Shut up."

I look around at all my besties as silence falls over the group. I really am so blessed to have such an amazing group of queens in my life. "Thank you all for such an amazing time."

"You're welcome," they all reply.

I look over at Rhian in the water. "Especially you. I'll never ever forget this."

"Neither will we. We should do this every year. Make it like an annual thing. We should brand it or something and have T-shirts."

"I'd so be up for that. You can do the branding though, Rhi. You're the expert on that."

"Hmmm. Leave it with me. Y'know, we're all going to have the blues when we get home. We should book something soon. Maybe Vegas next time."

"Let me sell an organ first," Alicia says. "Those slots are addictive."

She's not wrong. I remember the one time Bron and I went for a last-minute weekend away when we first started dating. He left me for half an hour and I'd blown one hundred dollars by the time he returned. He wasn't impressed at all and wouldn't leave any money with me the rest of the time we were there.

Thinking about that now, I feel like he was kinda acting like my dad.

Maybe that's why they got on so well.

My eyelids droop, but I'm trying to stay awake so I can use my toy. It's quiet, so I'm not worried about the girls hearing it; I'm more concerned about those reviews and if I'll be able to keep quiet if it's as good as they say it is.

I hope it is.

Once I'm sure everyone's fast asleep and I haven't heard any noises for a while, I slip it under the sheets and turn it on. I'm sure every little thing sounds louder at night; even the covers ruffling have me paranoid that someone can hear me.

Get a grip, girl.

I gasp a little when I make contact, but what those reviews said about having to adjust it end up being right. It does feel better after I move it around a little bit, but it's not as mind-blowing as I expected it to be.

Undeterred, I twist it this way and that, open my legs, close them a little, lift and tilt my hips, then just as I'm about to give up, I find the sweet spot.

The first moan out of my mouth shocks me, but I manage to muffle the next one.

And the million more that try to come after.

"Oh my God," I hiss at the ceiling. "Oh my... *God.*"

I almost squeal like a seal at one point, so I bite the sheets, then before I know what's happening, my soul has left my body.

Snatched all out.

My toes might even have curled.

After my senses return, I pull it out from the sheets and look at it like it's attacked me. It all happened so fast. One minute I was celebrating finding the right angle, the next... I don't even know.

I hope none of the girls heard that cry for help at the end.

Chapter Sixteen

It's late Friday evening by the time I get home. Sedona was amazing, no doubt, but I'm definitely looking forward to sleeping in my own bed tonight. It will also be nice to use my toy without the fear of being overheard.

I'm also glad to be alone. As much as I loved spending time with my girls, I have a lot to think about. The conversations we had have inspired me, and I'm excited to start implementing some changes in my life.

Although I'm not exactly sure where I'm going to start.

First though, I'm thinking of making some more food switches. I'm feeling shitty after all the crap I've eaten this week, and I'm pretty sure half my bloodstream is alcohol. I have yoga class tomorrow morning too, and I don't want to embarrass myself by passing gas practicing any of the positions. I know Mike said it was a regular occurrence and Rhian didn't care in Sedona, but I'm not quite at their level of not giving a shit yet.

Probably best to stick to water and unprocessed stuff for the rest of the day.

My phone pings as I'm loading the washer. It's Mom, asking if I got home okay.

Yes, I got home about an hour ago. Had an amazing time but glad to be home. How are you and Dad?

Not speaking to Dad directly is making me feel uncomfortable because I don't know where his mind is at. There's a part of me that keeps thinking he's still planning to talk to Bron's parents too.

I really hope he doesn't. God knows if I'd be able to hold my mouth if he did. I'm preparing myself to stand up to him if it comes to it, because the girls are right, it's long past time I did. I just don't want to fall out with him because it would hurt deep if I did.

Mom: *So glad to hear that, baby. Dad said so too. Let us know when you're free for dinner please. We want to hear all about your trip.*

They probably wanna know if I got up to anything I shouldn't have, but I push those thoughts from my mind. I'm trying not to take things personally, like Rhian told me, so I'm careful with how I reply.

Thanks. I will. Love you both.

Instead of putting my phone down, I decide to start the changes in my life right away by sending an email to my landlady about removing Bron from the lease. I know he said there wasn't any rush, but if I take him off, I can fully accept that we're over and hopefully put an end to these lingering thoughts of us reuniting.

The lease ends completely next month so I'm secretly hoping she'll cancel it early. I wouldn't mind moving into a new place and having a fresh start. I'd move to Germantown, closer to the girls and away from my parents. I'm not leaving Memphis.

I still miss Bron a little, and it's strange not having him to come home to, but I'm growing to enjoy my own company and learning what I truly like. Like the girls have said, life is supposed to be fun and thrilling, not stagnant and boring, and the more that time goes on, I see how right Bron was about us just existing. All that being said, he was my world for three years, and being in this house with all the memories isn't helping either.

It's time like these when I wonder what he's doing, and if he's okay. I would have loved to have stayed friends with him, but I don't think I could handle it, especially if he moved on with someone else.

I guess I'm not as over him as I thought.

After yoga, I follow Mike to the Greenway, smiling most of the drive there. There's always something about being in his presence that's exciting to me. I'm not sure if it's because of the different stuff we do or if it's all him. Either way, I already know this is gonna be fun.

"Ready for this?" he asks once we've collected my bike.

I chuckle at his game face. *So serious.* He looks different all round, because he's had his short beard trimmed and he's had a cut. *Cute...* Kinda like John Krasinski with a more defined nose.

Really cute.

"I'm more ready than the first time."

"Good. You're still going down though."

I smile as we push our bikes toward a quieter part of the track this time. Mike's wearing shorts again but a tank top instead of a tee. I'm guessing it will help against wind resistance or something.

I snigger.

"What's so funny?"

My attention lands on his arms before settling on his face. Nice biceps too. "Are you wearing a tank top so the wind doesn't slow you down?"

He smiles, but a little glimmer in his eyes tells me there may be some truth behind my accusation. "Hardly."

I don't believe him.

"So, how was Sedona?"

"Amazing, and just what I needed. Let me guess, you've been?"

"I have, many times. I saw the pics on your feed."

"Oh yeah? Does Mike like a good scroll of social media?"

He blushes a little, and I find it sweet. "You got me there."

"Uh-huh." I wonder if he checked out the selfie I posted in my bikini. I'm not saying he was the reason I posted it, but I'm not entirely saying he's not.

"It looks like you had fun."

"I did. No bike races, but I did try karaoke for the first time."

He raises his fist, and I roll my eyes as I dap him. "Well done, you. Did anyone care?"

"Not in the slightest. I actually got a standing ovation."

His eyes narrow when he looks my way. "Is that so?"

I nod. "I'm pretty good."

"You must be. You didn't sing Whitney Houston, did you? Everyone sings her."

I laugh. "No, but they did have to pull me off stage in the end. I might have enjoyed it a little too much."

"There's no such thing as too much fun," he says as he comes to a stop. "Here to the bend up there. That good with you?"

"Sure," I say as I fix my helmet. "You're still gonna lose."

He shakes his head, but he soon grins. We're both grinning when we position ourselves to start.

Thick thighs, don't fail me now...

"No head start this time."

"Fine by me," I say, sensing his competitiveness rise. *I can't let him win now.*

"On your marks... Get set... Go!"

I push my starting pedal as hard as I can and then cycle like my life depends on it. After all the shit I've been talking, I need to win this.

He huffs before he chuckles, and then I see his front tire in my peripheral.

"Careful of the bumps," I tell him. This part of the track has quite a few.

"Worry about yourself, Nikki."

The tone of his voice when he says my name makes my heart skip a few beats, so I decide to block him out and focus on winning this, so I can tease him after.

Please...

My lungs begin to burn when I'm halfway there, but I keep pushing, determined to win. *Almost there...*

The bend approaches quickly, and the thrill makes me laugh, causing people walking our way to smile and cheer when they realize we're racing.

So close...

After chancing a swift look to the side of me as I reach the bend, I shriek when I don't see him. "I won—again!"

I hear him groan as I brake, and then I laugh. Who knew how competitive I could be?

"You must have cheated," he says breathlessly, pulling up beside me. "You said you haven't ridden a bike in years."

"You know what they say about riding a bike. Maybe your knee is still sore and hindered your performance."

He gasps. "That's a low blow."

I bite my lip to stop from smiling, but it still appears. "It was, wasn't it?"

"Nikki..." He shakes his head before offering me his hand. "Congratulations."

"Thank you," I say as I shake it. "Well done to you too."

"For what?"

"Not being a sore loser."

That makes him laugh. "Who said I'm not?" He uses the hem of his tank top to wipe his forehead like last time, and again I can't seem to stop myself from checking out his abs.

Maybe he could lift me up...

My entire insides shudder with that thought, and it throws me.

He is not my type...

"Having a good look?"

I lift my head to see a beaming smile plastered over his face and feel mine heat up in seconds. "I'm just trying to figure out how you lost with muscles like that."

He laughs. "I guess looks can be deceiving."

"I guess so."

"Thanks for a fun afternoon," I say as we walk to our cars. "I had a great time."

"So did I, loss and all. What are your plans for the rest of the weekend?"

"Laundry, mentally preparing to return to work on Monday. You?"

He reaches into his bag to retrieve our keys before handing me mine. "I have dinner with my dad later; tomorrow I have a few calls to make."

"Thanks. Well, I hope you enjoy dinner. I'll see you at yoga next weekend?"

"You will."

My face hurts from smiling by the time I get home.

. . .

I spend Sunday looking at houses in Germantown. Mrs. Lucas emailed me last night to say I could end the lease early if I wanted, as long as I'm open to allowing viewings. I said yes and jumped straight online to look for a new place.

After looking at a handful, I run into a gem, so I decide to be spontaneous and let them know I'm interested. I'm hoping I get to go have a look one day this week, because if it's as nice as it seems in the pictures, I'm going for it.

Now I'm lying in bed looking at new places to walk nearby. I went to my local park earlier by myself and felt amazing when I got home. God knows what's gotten into me these days with the whole nature obsession, but it's doing wonders for my head and heart.

But then, so is spending time with Mike.

I was on a high for the rest of yesterday when I got home, and I have been for the last ten minutes since he texted me about doing something next weekend. It's why I'm googling open spaces at the moment.

Mike: *No races this time. We can use our legs. Have you found one yet?*

Me: *Haha. Are you still licking your wounds? No, not yet. I'm still looking.*

Mike: *No. *Cough* Maybe an invisible one. I still can't understand how someone who hasn't ridden a bike in years beats a pro.*

Me: *Is that your ego talking? And I'll have you know, I won because thick thighs don't just save lives, they win bike rides.*

Mike: *LOL. I see that. I clearly still have work to do on that. Look up Overton Park. That's another good one.*

I google it and agree.

Me: *Looks beautiful.*

Mike: *It is. Let me know if you're free after yoga on Saturday and we can go.*

Me: *Will do.*

Smiling, I put my phone on charge. There's no doubt I like Mike, but I also need to not overthink the situation between us. We're friends, and we have fun. My head has ruined so many things in my life, I don't want to let it ruin this.

I'm gonna go with the flow.

Now, where's my Rose...

Chapter Seventeen

"Hey, hey, hey. Welcome back."

I smile at Kelly as I arrive at the office. "Thank you."

She follows behind me. "Coffee's already there."

"You're the best." I take a sip once I've sat at my desk, then I open my Mac to check my emails.

"I know." She sits opposite me, cross-legged with her iPad on her lap. "I'm so glad you're back. I missed you. Marcus had me earning every cent of my paycheck while you were away."

"I bet." Marcus is no joke.

"He'll be down soon to discuss LipLush."

"Okay..." That doesn't sound good.

"Right, let me fill you in quickly so we can get to the good stuff."

She tells me about the new projects starting in a few weeks, then gives me updates on the LipLush project, which concerns me a little because we still have a lot of interviews to get before it's completed. A lot more than I was expecting with only five days left to go.

I'll need to keep an eye on that.

"All right. So how many new interviews need scripting this week?"

"Three. I'll get you the files after we're done."

"Thanks." Straight back to being busy, and I'm not sure I'm looking forward to it quite as much as I usually am.

She rests her iPad on my desk. "So, how was your trip? I've been dying to hear all about it."

I ignore the staff email in my inbox about the low conversion rates on LipLush and turn my attention to Kelly's beaming face. "It was amazing. Exactly what I needed, just like you said."

"And? Did you get D?"

I chuckle. "No, I didn't. We did speed dating though, which was fun. I tried karaoke too."

She frowns. "What, like your first time?"

"I know. I've been missing out."

"Damn right you have. Karaoke is amazing. I've won competitions with my Aretha Franklin."

"Really? I never knew you could sing."

"Yep. I spent a year in drama school as a child." She shudders. "Wouldn't recommend it. What else did you do?"

"Drink, eat, see the sights. Usual stuff."

"Sounds amazing. I'm so glad you had a good time. Glad you're back more though."

"As busy as it's gonna be, I'm glad to be back too." I look at my emails again. "I should really get to work on those files."

She jumps up, happier than ever. "Let me grab them."

"Thanks."

I wonder if I could quit my job...

That thought is so unlike me, but after only two days of being back, I'm seriously considering it. My mind keeps wandering back to Sedona and how peaceful I felt, and every time I look at my emails, I wanna cry.

Marcus needs to hire more staff, and the fact he's not is starting to piss me off. He should be happy the company's growing like this. I never had him down for being a tight-ass, but he's acting like it.

"Sorry, Nikki, but I have another file for you."

My response is a nod—it has to be, otherwise I might scream.

What would I do if I didn't work here though?

I love market research, that isn't the problem, but this work-life off-balance is getting out of hand. It was past eight when I got home last night, and I'm always in the office by eight every morning.

"Rumor has it," Kelly says, sitting at my desk, "that the other project managers have been complaining about the workload. Apparently, Marcus caught Frank crying in the breakroom yesterday."

"Are you serious?"

She nods. "His wife's been on his case about never seeing him, and you know their baby's due soon. He's even mentioned leaving."

"Damn..." Frank's been here forever. He's in his forties and started here in his early twenties. He always says how much he loves it here and won't ever leave, so if he's feeling like this, it has to be bad. "I hope he doesn't."

"Me too. Frank's so sweet, and so is his wife."

"She is."

"I'll keep you posted, but in the meantime, try not to stress too much. I know it's difficult at the moment, but better to be busy than to have no business."

I glance at my emails again. "True."

"Y'know what keeps me happy?"

That gets all of my attention. "Tell me, I'd love to know."

"Date nights and lots of sex."

I groan. "I don't do that either."

She rolls her eyes. "Well, whose fault is that? I told you to get on that site. You could be being wined and dined three days a week and getting D all the others."

"I don't really want uncommitted D though."

"But what about dates? Surely you wouldn't mind being taken out every once and a while? Trying new things, meeting people?"

"I wouldn't mind that at all..."

"So sign up to that site. I know you said your girls put you on Tinder while you were away, but that's not gonna get you anywhere. Just have a look—it's not gonna hurt."

"Yeah, maybe."

"I'll send you the link, all right? Let me know what you think. Make sure you up the age range if you don't want the lames in your DMs though. The older ones are more mature."

I nod, but I'm not really paying attention. I've just seen a message pop up on my cell, and my stomach's just jumped into my throat.

Bron?

"I'll leave you to it. I'm going out later—do you need anything?"

"Cupcakes," I mutter as I pick up my cell. "Please."

"Got it."

I unlock my phone when she leaves to read the message.

Bron: *Hey, hope you're well. Mrs. Lucas just called to confirm I wanted my name off the lease. You didn't mention that you'd spoken to her about it.*

Shit, I forgot about that.

Me: *Hey. Sorry, I was supposed to let you know. I'm good, hope you are too.*

Bron: *I've been better. Your dad said you'd been away with the girls when I saw him at Sunday service. Did you have a good time?*

Anger rises inside me. How dare Dad tell him that!

Me: *I did. Thanks.*

I pause before I send the message. Do I ask him what's wrong? I mean, I want to, but would that be leading him on? I do care, and he's clearly said that for a reason, but I quickly remember that he broke up with me and that his happiness isn't my problem anymore, so I send the text how it is.

Bron: *All right. I'll confirm it with her then. Take care, Nik.*

My chest tightens. I should have asked what was wrong. *Ugh.*

As I reread his messages in an attempt to read between the lines, my concern for Bron is quickly replaced by anger. How dare my dad tell him about my personal life? We aren't together anymore.

I take a deep breath, remembering the advice from the breakup book Jenny recommended. *Don't let him get to you...*

It's really hard not to though.

After dinner, and another session with my Rose to ease my stress, I take the leap and sign up to the elite dating site that Kelly sent me the link to. I then spend the entire time in the bath thinking about what I'm actually looking for.

I'd like to meet a man on his grind, who I can grow with. I want him to be fun too and open to trying new things. But above all, I'd like to meet someone wanting something serious, because I've never been into long-term casual dating and I'm not about to change that now.

I fill out the questions about myself pretty easily. What I spend ages on is the one-line bio for under my profile picture. I write, delete, and rewrite it a million and one times before deciding on one.

Successful Queen seeks fun adventures.

It's not the most exciting, but it fits in with what everyone else on this site is saying on theirs.

I groan.

Hopefully my pictures will save me.

I choose four in total. One of me at my desk that Kelly took a few months ago for the company website, one full-length of me in a fitted green sequin dress that Bron took of me when we last went out for dinner, and two selfies—one being my favorite by the water in Sedona.

After I set the desk snap as my profile pic, I spend roughly an hour accepting and declining endless profiles until I'm bored. I tick anyone who I feel an attraction to, regardless of color, trying to step out of my comfort zone.

I am a little nervous if I'm honest though, not because of judgment from my loved ones—there are countless mixed couples in my family—it's more that I worry about being able to connect to someone who isn't black. It's all well and good being attracted to someone physically, but I want to have things in common with them. I want to be able to understand them and vice versa, and I worry I'll miss out on those things if we aren't the same.

Maybe it's sad to think that way, but when you've grown up

black and had people around you that have dated interracially, you see and hear things that leave impressions on you. My cousin Erikka had the worst time from her now-husband's family when they first met, and there's no way I want to deal with that.

Regardless of how happy they are now.

But then I think of Mike and how I seem to be being pulled to him. He's fun, completely different to anyone I've known, and although he seems like a free spirit—which is the complete opposite to me—there's definitely something there that I feel needs to be explored.

Saying that, I was supposed to have messaged him about Overton.

Me: *Hey, Saturday after yoga is good with me.*

He replies almost immediately.

Mike: *Great. See you then.*

Maybe I should focus on this thing with him instead of messing around on another dating app. *But we're just friends...* Exactly. But Overton is huge, so there's no doubt I'll have time to get to know him better on Saturday.

Maybe I might get a better idea of his intentions then too.

My thoughts divert when I'm alerted to a flurry of notifications of matches and a few messages.

Mack: *Hey beautiful...*

Jonny: *Hey beautiful...*

Roy: *Hey beautiful...*

I groan. It's the same weak-ass shit that I got on Tinder. Is that all men say as an opening these days? What happened to, "nice to meet you, how are you?" or someone introducing themselves? Or do I have a completely skewed idea of dating? I hope not.

Maybe they'll say something a little more interesting after I reply.

On my break, I reply to the girls about drinks after work on Friday, then I check my DMs.

Wanna meet up?

Wyd?

Do you have any more pictures?

What's your favorite color?

I groan. Kelly said this site would be good.
"What's wrong?" she asks, making me jump.
"Nothing."
Her eyes narrow as she hands me another file. "Just one today."
I take it from her to give it a scan. This isn't too bad. A quickie. I could probably get it done by lunch and then help dial for the rest of the day. "Thanks."
"You looking at dick pics?"
I look up. "What? No."
"Have you not gotten any yet?"
"No, and that site you said was good isn't."
She frowns. "That doesn't sound right. Let me have a look."
I hand it over and watch as she begins tapping around,

bewildering me with how she manages to do anything with her hands with nails that long.

She shakes her head. "No wonder you're not getting any good matches. You're looking at men too young. I *told* you, you want the thirty-five to forty age range."

"I know you said that, but I'm twenty-six."

"So? All the guys our age are still in their emotional immaturity stage. The older ones are more stable, and they're always up for trying new stuff in the bedroom."

"Um..." I'm not sure.

She rolls her eyes. "Just trust me. I'm a pro when it comes to this."

Still not sure. "All right."

Chapter Eighteen

Shoving my phone back into my jacket pocket, I wait for Alicia to answer the door. I left work at five after seeing the team only had fifty interviews left to get. I'm usually a team player, but after all the extra hours I've put in this week, as soon as I knew I wasn't needed, I was out of there.

My phone pings multiple times again, and I roll my eyes. I'm not even going to bother checking it because it will just be the same old shit.

Wyd? Wdyd? Wruu2?

You'll be snapped up, they said. *You're a catch*, they said. *It will be fun*, they said.

Fun?

This dating life is *far* from fun, and I haven't even made it to an actual date night yet.

"Hey, boo," Alicia says, finally appearing at the door.

"Hey." I try to sound cheery, but my enthusiasm's buried deep in my pocket, beneath my phone.

"Oh dear. Come in and tell me all about it." She closes the

door but instead of heading to the kitchen where we usually get into it, I pop my head into the front room to find the girls.

They're sitting cross-legged on the couch in front of the TV that's blaring out *Nickelodeon*, but they're not paying the tiniest bit of attention to it. They're on their tablets playing a game that looks a lot like Lego characters with unicorn hair, running around.

"Hey, girls."

Shyla looks up first. She's almost six and wears the cutest pink Peppa Pig glasses. "Hey, Aunt Nik."

"Hey, Aunt Nik," Aliyah follows. She's seven. "Wanna play?"

I eye their screens again. I was never good at video games as a kid, but my brother was. I was too busy playing with Barbies and did way after my friends were done with them, and even as I got older, whenever any of my boyfriends would ask me to play video games with them, I'd never be interested.

"Um, not right now. I need to talk to your Mommy. Maybe later?"

"Okay."

They barely look at me during the entire exchange and most likely don't realize when I've left the room. I'm sure they weren't as bad as that the last time I saw them. I thought Alicia was overreacting...

What the hell do they put in that game?

"You'll regret that."

I frown at Alicia as I sit at the island with her. "Regret what?"

"Saying you'll play with them. They're like elephants. They don't forget a thing. You might as well download it now."

"They seemed pretty engrossed to me." I shrug. "If they do, they do." I love Alicia's girls, so for them I'd make an exception.

"Don't say I didn't warn you. Drink?"

"Yeah, water please." As much as I could kill for a glass of wine right now, I force myself to be good. I might not stop after one either.

She recoils before getting to her feet. "You okay?"

"I'm good, I'm just trying to take better care of myself and I'm doing really well with it."

There's no doubting how much better I'm feeling after switching up my food and drink. The extra energy in the mornings hasn't gone unnoticed, and I even had time to do a quick yoga and meditation session this morning. My mind still refuses to shut off completely, but I'm determined to keep trying.

"Good for you. We did go wild. I'm surprised we didn't do something crazy and try to become blood sisters or something."

I snort. "I'm surprised we all came back in one piece after how hard we went in."

The memory of Rhian's tits still makes me randomly smile, and Chay pissing over her dress in the bushes on the way home from the karaoke night. We really did drink our body weights' worth of liquor. Still, I'm glad we went in.

Alicia returns from the fridge with a bottle of water, and then I ask her about the guy she's seeing.

"It's still early days yet, but so far..." She's smiling her face off. "It's promising."

I almost fall off my chair. "Well, damn. I never thought I'd see the day you'd describe any man as 'promising.'"

Alicia went through the worst with her ex-husband. He didn't support her career or her when she was suffering with depression, and was in general a lying, cheating, manipulative piece of shit. He still sees the girls every other weekend, but he barely says two words to Alicia. He hates the fact she bossed up and made it without him, and I reckon he's intimidated by her.

"I told you, I've got kids—"

"Yeah, so you've said a million—"

"But so has he, so he understands."

"Really?"

She nods. "He's a single dad to a girl and a boy. Widowed."

"Oh..." That's awful.

"Yeah, I know. He's so amazing, Nik, and the way he treats me is everything. He knows what he wants, has all his shit together, and you'll never guess what he does for a living."

"Go on..."

"He builds apps for kids."

"Are you kidding?"

She shakes her head. "He has a world on the game the girls play."

"Well shit, girl, you kept that real quiet. Where did you find him?"

She laughs. "In Walmart two months ago. I was telling the girls I wasn't spending any more money on that game, and I heard him laughing behind me. I was ready to cuss him out, but when I turned around and saw him, I could barely speak, I swear."

"That sounds like Chay wrote him into existence."

"It does, doesn't it?"

"And no catches?"

"Not so far. Like I said, we're taking it slow right now, but so far, so good."

"Well, I'm happy for you. After everything you've been through, you deserve the world and more."

"Thanks, boo. I do, right? But anyway, how are things with you?"

"How am I?" I pull my phone out to open my dating DMs. "'What does the Sistine Chapel, you, and a pineapple have in common?' 'Could you tie me up?' 'What color are your nipples?' 'Do you eat ass?' 'I love black girls. Can you twerk?' 'You got Snap...?'"

Alicia's laughing now, but I'm rubbing my temples from an impending migraine.

"Wait, it gets worse: 'My wife thinks you're hot—fancy a

three-way?' 'You look like a plus-sized Beyonce—I love that.' 'What's your body count?'"

She snorts at the last one and then is full-blown hollering again.

"Not funny." I put my phone down. "Y'know, I had to Google 'body count' to find out what that was. I thought he meant actual dead bodies, sis."

Who the hell knew it meant how many people you've had sex with?

She screams but tones it down when I glare at her. "I'm sorry, honestly, but it is kinda funny. I should send you some of the ones I got. One guy straight out asked me if I'd sell him my worn panties."

"Eww." I shudder. "Where are the normal men? The men that don't wanna have sex before dinner? The ones that know how to hold a decent conversation? I don't see any leading going on anywhere."

"I thought your assistant sent you a good site?"

"Most of those *were* from the good one."

Her face falls. "Oh."

"There have been two, maybe three guys that have kept my interest, but even they're getting boring now. There's only so many times you can be asked what you're up to today."

"It's hard, I get it. You know how long I've been single for."

"Yeah, but I *don't* have kids."

She rolls her eyes. "Look, at least you're finding out what you don't want. This is a good thing really. It means you're fine-tuning what you do want. Besides, there's no harm being single for a while. That's where the growth is. And you don't want to settle again, do you?"

"No..." I press my fingers into my temples. "I dunno if I'm losing my mind or not, but I've kinda been feeling a way about a guy from my yoga class."

That comment catches her attention. "Yeah? What does he look like?"

"He's hot but a bit nerdy, kinda. Looks a bit like John Krasinski, but it's not even really about his appearance. He's interesting and, not to sound weird, but it feels good to be around him."

She smiles. "Good vibes, yeah?"

"Yeah, but a little unsettling. Y'know that monthly meet I went to before we went away? Well, I ended up kinda spilling my guts about shit I had no business talking about." I shake my head and smile. "See. It makes no sense."

"Hey, it's okay to smile. You're single, so you don't need to be restricting yourself. Don't take that dating shit too seriously either. We told you not to. You're grown, so just have fun."

"Yeah, I'm trying."

"How are things with your mom and dad? Did you see them over the weekend?"

My mood instantly drops. "No. They invited me over, but I was tired, so I told them I'd see them this weekend instead."

"You need to get that talk with your dad over and done with. Longing it out is only going to make it worse. Look how stressed you are about it."

"I'm stressed because my life is all over the place."

"No it's not. Stop saying that."

I sigh. "I think I just need a good hard D that's not attached to a weirdo."

"Aunt Nik?"

I look down at Shyla, praying she didn't hear what I just said. "Yes, sweetie?"

"Are you ready to play now?"

"Um, yeah. Sure."

"Told ya," Alicia says as she leaves the room with her phone. "Hey—"

"Do I need to download the Roadblocks app?" I ask Aliyah.

The girls laugh. "Ro-blox."

I hand them my phone so they can do it, and after naming me "AuntNik22," I'm all set up and ready to go.

"If you buy Robux, you can get nicer things," Shyla says.

That makes me laugh. They didn't waste any time there.

"You can buy us some too, if you want," Aliyah adds.

"She is not buying you Robux!" Alicia shouts from upstairs.

Damn, her hearing's good.

The girls look disappointed, but they soon smile when they see me reach for my purse.

"Don't tell Mommy," I whisper.

Finally, the LipLush project is complete, and I couldn't be happier. Me going to Sedona before it started probably wasn't the greatest idea, but we got it done and kept our unbroken record of success, so that's the most important thing.

The call center's mostly empty now, but Kelly's stayed behind with me to get the figures organized and ready to send to the client. She's amazing and always committed when it comes to her job, and I'm so thankful she decided to stay when her old project manager quit. Marcus always comments on how well we work as a team too, and we do, but I also know how valuable Kelly is and have gotten her pay rises more than once. I think she's paid more than any other assistant in here.

As I'm attaching the zip file to the email, my phone buzzes. *Bron... again?*

Bron: *Just signed to come off the lease. She said she'd email you a copy. Hope you're good?*

I take a minute to think about my reply this time. He didn't need to let me know he'd signed the papers, and my gut tells me he's used it as an in to talk to me. It's been six weeks since we broke up, so why is he messaging now?

Me: *Thanks for letting me know. All good here. Hope you are?*

Bron: *Getting there. I went back to church. Mom kinda suggested it and it's been helping. Your dad said you might be coming back too?*

I grind my teeth when my dad is mentioned again. I need to call him.

Me: *Good to hear you're finding your peace. Dad asked me but I haven't decided yet. What else has he said to you?*

Bron: *Not much. Don't let him bully you into going back, Nik. Just tell him no.*

A flurry of mixed emotions rush through me after reading that text. My heart aches a little too. It would be so easy to continue this conversation, but I decide to put an end to it before I get in my feelings too much.

Me: *Thank you.*

He doesn't reply afterwards, and even though I'm relieved, I'm also a little hurt. This is how I felt a few weeks ago when I was up one minute and down the next. Constantly thinking of the past and what could have been.

I need to not go there again...

Besides, I have more important things to deal with right now. I need to call my dad.

. . .

"Nicola? Are you all right?" Dad seems surprised to hear from me, but I rarely call him without arranging it first.

"I'm good, thank you," I reply, barely keeping my frustration in check. "I wanted to ask you something."

"Go on."

"Well, Bron messaged me about the lease on the house and mentioned that you'd seen him."

"I did, at service, which is where you should have been. Will you be joining us this weekend?"

"I don't know yet," I almost snap. *I've told him this.*

"It would be good for you, Nicola."

"Dad... I understand how much you'd like for me to go, but I honestly haven't decided yet. I'm calling because Bron said you told him about me going away, amongst other things."

"I did."

"But why? What I do is none of his business anymore, and I feel uncomfortable knowing that you're telling him things about my life."

"Don't be ridiculous. He asked how you were, and I told him you were well."

"That's fine that you've said I'm doing well, but he doesn't need to know details."

Dad mutters something that I don't quite make out, and when I ask him to repeat it, he refuses.

I sigh. "Please don't tell him things about me," I plead, hoping that he accepts that and doesn't berate me instead.

"Fine."

"Thank you. How's Mom?"

"Good. She's out at the moment, but I'll tell her you called."

"All right."

After telling him I'm still at work and making my excuses to go, he hangs up before I do.

I stare blankly at the phone. *Well, that didn't go as badly as I expected.*

"That sounded tense."

I look up to see Kelly standing in the doorway. "It was."

"I wasn't being nosy; I overhea—"

"It's fine," I reassure her. I should've shut the door before I called him.

"Overbearing parents are the worst."

I remember what she told me about hers. "You aren't wrong."

She smiles sympathetically before glancing at my Mac. "Are you done?"

"Pretty much."

"Then can we go now? I have a dick appointment."

That makes me laugh, and it's direly needed. "Go on. Go. I only have to send the email now."

"All right. See ya."

Once she's gone, I send the email, then I get ready to leave myself. My phone buzzes again though, and I see Bron's name.

Bron: *Always here for you. Take care, Nik.*

I sigh. Deep down, I know he is, and that's what makes it worse, but I also need to set my boundaries and not feel guilty. He lost the right to my love and support when he ended it, and I can't let myself feel bad about not being there for him, so I text back a simple: *You too.*

And strangely, although the guilt lingers, it feels good.

I stuck up to my dad too.

"Progress," I say proudly to myself as I leave the office.

Chapter Nineteen

I join the girls on the couches inside Alicia's local bar, happier than I've been all week. It seems like forever since I saw them. I've missed them so much, and after the news I got at the end of the day, girl time is well and truly needed.

LipLush has been spreading word of our recent project with them and how much detail we got from the interviews, so it looks as if the mania at work will be sticking around for a little while yet as we get flooded with approaches from other businesses.

I'm not sure how that's gonna work with me packing. I finally signed the lease on the property I liked in Germantown on my lunch today and move in at the end of the month. There have been viewings after viewings at my place while I've been at work, and Mrs. Lucas has finally found a young family to move in.

My new house is completely different to my current one. It's two-bedroomed, has a slightly smaller kitchen, but the back-yard sold it to me. It's full of beautiful plants and trees that remind me of a secret garden. It is so peaceful and made me feel good as soon as I saw it. And to top it off, the landlord said it might even be available to buy in a few years' time, so for me it's a win, because I would love to own my own house one day.

"That one's yours," Chay says, eyeing the sparkling water on the table. "I dunno how you drink that nastiness."

I chuckle. "It's good once you get used to it. How are you all?"

The consensus is that everyone's good, and then Rhian asks how I'm doing.

"I'm good." *Really good.* "Work has been manic, as you know, but yoga has been amazing, and I've been doing a few new things…"

Chay eyes me. "New things like what?"

This girl's mind. "Not what *you* think. I've been going on bike rides and—"

Her eyes widen. "Bike rides? Who the hell with?"

"A guy from yoga. His name's Mike."

The girls all give me a look, but I ignore it.

"The hot nerdy one you told me about?" Alicia asks inquisitively.

I give her a nod, but more of my attention goes on the twinge in my gut when she called him nerdy. "He's a really nice guy. Funny, different. Adventurous too."

"And… where's he from?" Chay asks.

I roll my eyes. "I don't know originally, but he's white if that's what you're asking."

They're shocked again, and I shake my head. "Calm down. He's just a friend."

"Sure," Chay retorts. "Is he tall?"

I frown. "Yeah, a little taller than me. Why?"

"And what's his build?"

"Athletic, muscly. Whyyy?"

"I bet he's got a big dick."

Oh God… This woman. Thankfully there's no one close to us this time. "And how do you know that, Chay?"

"Because those tall, fit guys are usually the ones hiding all the meat, and if he's a little nerdy too... Whew."

"Sis... Thanks for the insight, but like I said, we're just friends. He's fun to be around and I can be myself with him."

"Better to be friends with someone first," Rhian says, "so you're doing it the right way."

Ugh. I don't even argue with her because I already know it will be futile. Yes, there is definitely something between me and Mike and I'd be an idiot to think there wasn't, but he hasn't so much as mentioned these outings being dates, nor has he tried anything on with me, so as far as I'm concerned, we're just friends.

Even if my mind's been trying to convince me otherwise.

I ask how things are going with Alicia and her new boo instead, so I can take the heat off me.

"Good. We're having dinner tonight." She turns to Rhian. "What about you, boo? How are things going with you and Joi?"

I recoil. "Hold on. You and who? Are you dating someone, Rhi?"

She tries to tame her smile, but she fails epically. "Kinda."

"No, not kinda. How did I not know this? Spill, bitch."

She laughs. "You were busy with work when I called, remember? You never called me back."

"Oh shit. I'm so sorry. I completely—"

"Hey, don't worry, all right? Alicia filled me in and said how hectic things were. It's cool."

"It's not, but thanks. Now spill!"

"Well, it's crazy really because we knew each other in high school and I haven't seen her since we graduated. We bumped into each other in Costco of all places and just started talking..." She smiles again, as if remembering it. "She was always beautiful but... Anyway, she asked me out for lunch, which I thought was just to catch up, but she ended up telling me how much she liked me back in the day."

"Wow, that is crazy."

"Right. We've talked every day since and I see her most days. She's a food critic now and has a blog too, so we have lots in common."

I shake my head. "That's another story for Chay."

"I already said I'm writing a story about it. I'm loving all this inspiration. First Alicia with her boo, now Rhian..." She looks at me. "I'm just waiting to see how yours is gonna go."

"You might have to wait a while for that, although I started talking to a guy from Ohio on the app today. He's a little older, is in the same line as work as me, and he hasn't mentioned sex yet."

"What about Mike?" Alicia asks.

"I said we're just friends."

"I smell a love triangle," Rhian mutters. "It's definitely gonna be a book."

"It's really not. To be honest, I'm doing what you said and taking each day as it comes. I'm focusing on myself, saying yes more, and all around having more fun. From now on, if it feels good, I'm going with it."

Chay toasts me. "About bloody time."

"How are things with your parents?" Alicia asks. "Have you seen them yet?"

"Mom canceled and rearranged for this Sunday, so no. I spoke to Dad though, and he did try to convince me to go back to church again, but I said I still hadn't decided."

"Progress," Rhian says. "Like you said, one day at a time."

"Right. Oh, and before I forget, I've found a place in Germantown."

They're all ecstatic about that.

"I can't wait for you to be closer," Rhian gushes.

"Me either. I hope you're all gonna help me pack."

"Of course we will."

. . .

I meet Mike at Overton straight from yoga on Saturday. He's changed into jeans and a sweatshirt, same as me. I forgot to change before I left the gym though, so I had to pull over on the way here and may have flashed a few people my tits and ass as I scrambled around in my Benz changing.

It's cooler today and might rain, but not even that was enough to put me off coming. I tied my natural hair up into a bun and skipped the makeup too. That's something else I like about spending time with Mike. No pressure, and I never feel as though I have to be anything else but myself.

I didn't even feel comfortable wearing my robe around the house with Bron because he'd make little comments about it. It's funny, the things you notice about someone when you're not so close to them anymore.

Mike, as usual, stays quiet for the first few minutes of the walk. I've noticed whenever we go somewhere, he allows me some time to take in the sights around us. He leads me to a bench that looks over a green and a small stone bridge, and when we sit down beside each other, I smile because I always feel so relaxed in his presence.

"This is so peaceful," I say quietly.

He gives me a look as he leans back, but then I notice his gaze drift to the loose curls around my face. It's not the first time he's given my hair that look either. "It *was* peaceful."

I smirk. "You could've come alone."

"Where's the fun in that?"

He smiles and then more silence falls between us. I wonder if he feels the same as I do when we're together. Our quiet moments are never uncomfortable, and as strange as it sounds, it's as if we both know when something needs to be said and when it doesn't.

"Have you ever been here before?"

I shake my head. "Nope. This is a new place for me. You?"

"I come here often, to work too. Just me and my Mac."

"Is all of your work done online?"

"Ninety percent. I have a small team that I sometimes meet up with to coach in stocks, but that's a rare occurrence."

"I see. So you don't have an end goal toward anything?"

"My only goal is to enjoy every day as it comes. After my accident I realized that life was pretty much out of my control, so now I try to go with the flow."

"I don't know how you do it. My job keeps me grounded and, dare I say, is part of who I am."

"Have you always worked as hard as you do now?"

"Since I was eighteen."

He nods, as if he understands. "That's why. It's all you know."

"You might be right about that. I'm starting to see things differently though. I've wanted more fun in my life, so I've been saying yes to new things. That trip I went on to Sedona was so much fun and I never would've done that before, well..."

"Let me guess... Your breakup?"

"Yeah. Don't get me wrong, Bron didn't hold me back or anything, and he's not a bad person, it's just, well, he kinda ended our relationship because he felt it was boring, and he was right."

There's a definite hint of something in Mike's eyes when I tell him that. "Sometimes, it takes something drastic to make us see things for what they are, to open our eyes. When you're in the picture, it's difficult to see it."

"That's so true."

His lips straighten as he studies the water, but when he looks back at me, his eyes soften in understanding. "I've been there, so I know. Comfortable is nice, safe even, but it's not living life to the extent it can be lived."

I don't know why I smile, but I do. "You're very wise."

He chuckles. "I read a ton, so I have a good range of knowledge."

"I would ask if you're older than thirty-two, but you don't even look as old as that. You should be a life coach."

"And I'd say you're old beyond your years." He swats a fly away from me. "If you hadn't told me, I'd never have known you were twenty-six."

That makes me smile. "Why thank you."

He shifts down a little so he can rest his arms over the back of the bench. "I did consider coaching at one point, but people aren't my strong suit. Most are too judgmental for my liking."

I scoff. "You'd hate my parents then."

"Why?"

"They're the most judgmental people I know."

"That sounds tough."

"Yeah..." I debate telling him any more, but I finally decide to open up, hoping he'll give me some outside insight. "My upbringing was pretty strict, and I wasn't allowed to do a lot of things I really wanted to. My mom isn't too bad anymore, but my dad... I don't think he means it, but yeah... I've pretty much lived my life under their constant judgment."

"Caring about what our parents think is natural, but it's not always healthy. Have you ever stood up to him?"

"I'm trying. Do you get along with your parents?"

The smile hints that he does, but there's no mistaking the sadness I see in his eyes. "My dad and I are close; my mom passed when I was a teenager."

I reach for his hand to squeeze it, surprising myself, but it doesn't seem to faze him. If anything, he welcomes it, and it feels good. "I'm sorry to hear that."

"Don't be," he says, running his thumb over the back of my hand. "She had a very fulfilled life. She was the complete opposite to how you've just described your dad. If anything, my mom encouraged us to make mistakes. Said it was the only way we'd learn."

"Wow... I can't imagine what that would be like."

He releases my hand when he sits up, then he leans forward to rest his elbows on his knees. "There was one time I really liked this girl. I must've only been ten, but I remember coming home one day and telling Mom about her. I'd been trying to talk to her for weeks but no matter what I tried, she ignored me." He shakes his head and smiles. "So I asked Mom if I could do more chores to earn some extra money, thinking a gift would get her attention..."

I smirk, already having my suspicions of where this is going.

"Mom was dead set against it and point-blank told me that a gift wouldn't change anything, but of course me knowing better, I insisted, so she agreed. Long story short, she was right. I spent the best part of a month saving to buy this girl a locket, just for her to accept the gift and still not give me the time of day."

"Your mom sounds like a smart woman."

"She was the best."

He stands and helps me up, and then he leads me back to the path before he releases my hand. "Did you have any childhood crushes?"

"Barely," I say, as I try not to show how disappointed I am that he let my hand go again. "Like I said, I wasn't allowed to do a lot. I grew up in church and spent most of my free time either there or in extra classes. The one time I did decide to run wild, well, it didn't end too well." Again, I spill my secrets to him, telling him about the time I drank too much with Michelle. "That well and truly put me off."

"But you're grown now. Why don't you tell him how you feel?"

"I've tried, believe me, and you're not the first person to tell me I should. I just..."

"Fear his reaction?"

"A little." I pull a leaf off a tree we pass and begin to tear little pieces off it. "My brother eventually had to stand up for himself, and deep down I know I'll have to too, at some point. I just don't want to disrespect him."

"Saying how you feel isn't disrespect though."

I scoff. "Maybe not to you, but when you haven't done something before, I guess you fear it."

"You said you weren't competitive but you still raced me. Twice, to be exact."

"True, but that's different."

He glances my way. "Why is it? You were scared of something but did it, and look how happy you were after. It's the same thing."

True. I did feel proud of myself after we raced. I did when I sang karaoke too.

"I think you're stronger than you know, and perhaps maybe you're finally starting to see it."

"Perhaps."

"How about racing me now?"

I laugh. "Oh hell no. No chance. I detest running."

He bumps my shoulder with his. "Spoilsport."

"I wouldn't want to hurt my knees if I fell over, and I probably would. I'm sure you don't want to throw up at the sight of my blood either."

He grimaces. "Maybe you're right."

"Have you always had a fear of it?"

"Since I was a kid. Dad almost sawed his hand off. I was helping him in the garage at the time."

"Oh God. Was he okay?"

"He was fine, no lasting damage, but as a kid I thought it was the end of the world." He shudders and I laugh. "Do you have any phobias?"

"Not that I know of. I have a thing about the color gray now though."

He smirks. "Not surprised. Your comment about the dress code was funny. I'd never heard that one before."

My first instinct is to be embarrassed by the memory, but I take a leaf out of his book and shrug it off. "Well I was right, wasn't I? Jenny does have a dress code."

He chuckles. "I suppose."

Silence falls between us again, but then I remember what he asked. "I don't like slimy food. Does that count as a phobia?"

"Slimy food?"

"Yeah. Okra makes me heave."

He widens his eyes. "You don't like okra? Who doesn't like okra?"

"Me."

"Not even fried?"

"Is it slimy?"

His smile after I ask that makes my heart race. "Not the way I make it."

"Then maybe I'll have to try yours."

He sends a look to my lips when I say that. "Whenever you're ready."

Chapter Twenty

I'm quietly disappointed when I see the parking lot ahead. There's no denying how much I've enjoyed spending time with Mike again.

"What are your plans for the rest of the day?" he asks as he retrieves his car keys from his pocket.

It's just after one now. "Nothing much. Probably find something to cook and then maybe do some reading. I could do with some chill time though. Work is gonna be a little manic for the next few weeks. What about you?"

He stops as we reach my car, and then sends another heated look not to my lips this time, but a sweeping one from my feet to my face. "Wanna eat with me?"

That completely catches me off guard. I was no way in hell expecting that, and I'm immediately nervous. "Um, I'm kinda on a health kick right now. Where were you thinking?"

He appears deep in thought for a moment. "There's a place on Concourse Avenue that's good. You'll like it."

"Aren't you sick of my company yet?" I tease, but it's more for my benefit. I want to, but a part of me is starting to wonder if this is an offer of a date.

"Would I be asking you if I was?"

"I don't know."

He regards me carefully, until I get the impression he's read my mind. "It's just food, Nikki. I don't have any sneaky intentions, if that's what you're worried about."

"I never said you did."

"Well then. You're hungry and so am I. If the answer's no, just say so. I'm not going to pressure you or be offended. You should know that about me by now."

I do know that. "Okay, sure. Let's eat."

In the car, I try really hard not to get all up in my head about Mike while I follow him to this restaurant. But I fail epically. Yes, I'm all for going with the flow, but what is actually going on here?

We're spending more and more time together, and now we're having lunch... I've never believed in fate before, but something tells me that for whatever unknown reason, I was supposed to meet this guy.

"What sort of things do you eat on your 'healthy eating kick' then?"

I stoop under his arm as he opens the door to a restaurant called Vegan Sistas Meal Preps and More. "I'm trying to stay away from anything processed for a while."

"Well, you're gonna love this place."

He's right.

As soon as I look at the menu, I experience another dose of fate. Everything they serve is something I would eat, and the best thing about it is that they do meal preps. I end up setting up a weekly service that will be delivered to my house every week, starting for when I move into my new place. Salads, casseroles, tacos, wraps, and it's all organic and vegan.

Mike and I both order the spaghetti special and an apple strawberry smoothie, and I swear, I don't miss the meat at all.

"So you're moving, huh?"

I find him watching me when I look up from my plate. God knows why I picked this dish. I haven't looked down at my top because I'm sure it's spattered with sauce, and I'm having to lick my lips so often they feel chapped. "Yeah, at the end of the month. I'm moving to Germantown."

"Nice. If you need boxes, I have plenty."

"I do actually. Thank you."

"Don't mention it." He twists his pasta. "I helped my dad move a few months back and he never threw them out. I guess you're the reason why."

That makes me smile. "And I guess I really was meant to meet you."

"Hmm, you might be right."

I laugh. "Oh no, I think we're spending too much time together. You're picking up my mannerisms."

He gives me a look that causes the fluttering inside me to rise again. "Never." Then his expression switches to a serious one. "I enjoy spending time with you."

His confession hits me somewhere I never would've expected it to. "Me too," I reply, but then I look down at my food when I begin to wonder again what's actually going on between us.

Are we just friends?

"Where did you grow up?" he asks, pulling my attention back to him. The expression on his face is still the same, and it takes a second for my heart to settle.

"Mostly Midtown, but as a kid, Raleigh. You?"

"Blackhaven until I was fifteen, Collierville ever since."

I blink, surprised by his answer. Whitehaven, known more commonly as Blackhaven, is a predominately black area. "I wasn't expecting that."

"I told you not to judge a book by its cover."

He did, and I still did. "I'm sorry, I never—"

He chuckles. "It's cool. People are always surprised when I tell them where I grew up. I still think of it as home because that's where we lived with Mom. We didn't move until after."

I nod. "I bet it was hard for you to leave."

"It was. I begged Dad not to move us, but of course I didn't have a choice. It worked out for the best in the end because we all needed the fresh start, y'know?"

"I get it." My mind begins to wander, mostly to if he's ever dated a black woman before. I probably shouldn't ask, considering I seem to have already stereotyped him, but as I finish up my meal, I can't help myself. "Have you dated a black woman before?"

He immediately smirks. "What do you think?"

Doubt sets in. "I think... Yes?"

"Mostly. What I'd really like to know though is if *you've* ever dated outside of your race before?"

I shake my head. "Never."

He seems disappointed by that, but I'm far from. I wonder if that's a sign that this is something more and that he thinks he doesn't have a chance now?

I hope it is.

"Why not?"

Damn, he really asked me that. Although I shouldn't be surprised that he did. "A few reasons..."

"Which are?"

"Black men have always been my type, and I suppose I've stuck to what I've known. I always worried about not being able to connect with someone who doesn't understand my roots."

He nods thoughtfully. "I respect your honesty, and I get it, but if a person cared enough about you, they'd make the effort to understand everything that's important to you, and the reasons why."

"That's true... My friends have been changing my view on that as well. They've opened my mind to a lot."

"They sound like good friends."

That comment makes me smile, and for the first time, I wonder if they'd like him. "They really are. Do you have any close friends?"

"A few. My friend Kevin is the person who knows me best. We've been friends since elementary."

"Is he chilled like you?"

He shakes his head with vigor. "Not at all."

I narrow my eyes at him. "I think you should elaborate."

That makes him laugh. "Do I have to?"

"Absolutely."

"Well, after Mom died, I wasn't always the most well-behaved kid."

I mock gasp. "Was Mike naughty?"

He laughs. "A little. He was worse than me though. I may or may not have hotwired a few cars and done a few other things I'm not proud of now. It was an outlet."

"For your pain?"

"Exactly that."

"I always wished I had friends to lead me astray. Not to the extent of breaking the law, but my parents forever had a way of knowing who was good for me or not, so I had very few friends, and fewer and fewer as I got older."

"So you're having your naughty stage now?"

That makes me laugh. "I wouldn't say that. It's more that I'm taking chances. Although, my parents might say different. They've been on my case recently about going back to church."

"I see."

"I'm assuming since Bron and I aren't together anymore, they feel as if I should be focusing on my relationship with God."

"But you don't have to attend church to do that, do you?"

"Right. I talk to God all the time. My parents are old-school though, like most of the older generation. Do you believe in God?"

He falls silent, and I wait with bated breath for his reply. "Sort of. I believe in God, but not in the way the Bible says."

I'm not surprised by his answer. "Like my friend Alicia."

"Don't get me wrong, I respect everyone's religion, but what I don't understand is, if God created everyone in his image, how can anyone be condemned?"

That gets me in my feels because I agree with him. "That's something I've always wondered."

I wonder what my parents would think to that.

After we leave the restaurant, we take a slow walk back to the car, and I decide to bite the bullet and ask Mike about his dating life.

His quick glance my way tells me he was expecting my question too. "I haven't dated for a long time. I've been single for almost four years now."

"Any particular reason?"

He sighs. "Initially I had some things to work through due to the timing of the ending of my last relationship. Now, I'm just seeing what happens."

I sense he's suffered some heartbreak too, by the way that sounded. "I think that's the best way to be."

"What about you? Do you think you'd get back with your ex?" he asks, giving me the impression he's invested in the answer. "You said at the yoga meet you were together three years."

"I don't think so. We haven't really spoken since we broke up, except for a few messages about the house and his things, and we'd both have to be wanting to get back together, which we're not."

I look for a reaction from him, but when his expression remains even, I continue. "Besides, I think he was right about the boring thing. Yeah, we traveled and went to social events together, but we didn't do anything spontaneous or new. We were more friends really. I'm starting to think my parents loved him for me more than I did. Dad especially."

"Sounds like it."

"I don't think I could trust him now anyway. It was so sudden, y'know? He didn't even talk to me about it. He just left one day."

"That must have been difficult."

"It was, but as time goes on, I'm thinking it was for the best." *And I wouldn't be here now if it hadn't happened...*

"Do you think you'll stay single for a while?"

Another question I wasn't expecting. "I don't know. I'm on a few dating sites, and there's one guy that I talk to here and there..." I give him a look after I tell him that, but he doesn't seem bothered. "We're in the same career and have similar interests, but right now, I'm trying to focus on me and find out what I actually want in life. I've spent so long being someone I'm not. Striving for perfection, people-pleasing..." I laugh uncomfortably. "This conversation's just gotten really deep, hasn't it?"

His eyes soften, and once again he gives me a sense of safety to share. "Most of our conversations end up that way."

He's not wrong. I love that though, how he makes me laugh one minute then has me thinking about my life the next. "You're very easy to talk to. It's nice having someone other than my girls in my life that I can open up to."

"Same. I'm very private, but with you... I sometimes wonder why certain things come out around you when I have no intention for them to."

My heart warms with that comment. "So I'm not the only one who's noticed that."

"Not at all." He remains silent as we walk the last few steps to the car, so I pull my keys from my sweatshirt to distract myself from a flurry of mixed emotions.

Was this a date?

"Thanks for the company, Nikki. As always. I had a really good time."

I feel a blush creeping up my neck as we reach my car. He always walks me to it after our outings, same as how he always opens doors for me. I love that. "So did I."

His glance lingers as I unlock my car, but although I think he's going to say something else, he doesn't. He simply closes my door when I get inside and then disappears in my rear-view to his own car.

As long as we've spent together today, I'm kinda wishing we had more time, and when I see the expression on his face when he turns, it tells me he might feel the same.

I love that we can seem to talk about anything, and although our backgrounds are very different, I feel as if we click.

It's hard not to think about how different my life is to how it used to be, but there's no doubt the change was needed. There isn't much I don't say yes to anymore for one, and I can actually say my life is fun, which makes me realize exactly how much I'd been letting life pass me by.

Chapter Twenty-One

Once home from work, I heat up some leftover meatloaf before getting started on some more packing. I've barely gotten more than five hours' sleep all week, but at least it's Friday and I have the girls coming over to keep me company tonight.

Mike said he'd give me the boxes he has after yoga tomorrow, so I don't have that many here apart from the few I managed to find stashed in the attic. I've made decent progress in the living and dining rooms, but I still have most of upstairs left to go.

I finish another drawer in the kitchen and quickly move on to the next, but my heart leaps when I find the stack of anniversary cards from Bron and me to each other.

I forgot those were in here.

Pulling them out, I smile when I remember the last one I gave him. It's a little worse for wear because I gave it to him in the bath, and he dropped it when he pulled me in with him. The twinge of sadness that comes with that memory is stronger than I expect it to be, and I take a minute at the table to look through the rest.

As far as I've come over the past two months, there are still moments like these that stop me in my tracks. I still can't believe we came to an end like we did, and sometimes it feels like only yesterday. Then others, it seems like Bron and I were another lifetime ago because of how different things are for me now.

I wonder what would've happened if he had talked to me about how he was feeling and we had worked things out.

Don't dwell on that now.

I get up to add the cards to the other things I've found belonging to him—the odd shirt or gift from his parents, which I've put into a box already. I'm not exactly sure how he's going to get them though. I had thought of giving them to Dad so he could pass them on but had second thoughts due to Dad possibly using it as a reason to talk me around to getting back with him.

I'm hoping he still isn't hanging on to that idea, but deep down inside of me somewhere, I think he might be.

"Hello?" I hear Alicia shout after the front door opens.

"In here!" I jump off the stool to greet them, shaking my head when I see their arms full of liquor. "You know you're here to pack, not drink, right?"

"We can multitask," Rhian says, giving me a quick hug. "Glasses first, then we'll get to it."

I grab us all a glass, deciding to have one with them. Rhian pours me a glass of wine and then we all sit at the island. "It feels like forever since we did this."

Alicia nods. "It really does. I bet you need it. Moving is stressful enough without your job being a pain in the ass."

I groan. "For real." They've been so supportive in the group this week when I've constantly moaned in there. Rhian's even offered to help me set up a side-hustle selling things on Amazon so I can work fewer hours for the same money.

I said I'd think about it.

"You need dick," Chay says. "That would make you feel ten times better."

"Dick isn't the be all and end all," Rhian says, rolling her eyes. "You've got some toys now anyway, don't you?"

I nod, not so embarrassed about having this conversation this time. "That Rose is amazing."

Chay leans back so far on her chair, I worry she's gonna fall off. "I told you."

"I do miss physical touch though." I remember how nice it was when Mike held my hand at Overton. It was the littlest thing, but it still felt good.

Rhian's smile is sympathetic. "Nothing wrong with that. It's natural. How's the online dating going?"

I shrug. "It fills the boredom, but I can't see it going anywhere."

"What about Mike?" Alicia asks. "How you getting on with him?"

My mood lifts immediately. "Good."

"Damn, look at that smile," Chay says. "Maybe you should ask *him* for some D."

"Chay, really?" I shake my head, but if I'm honest, I have thought about it. What it would be like. "He's a little older, so I dunno..." I don't want to admit how inexperienced I am, but it's something I do worry about.

"Babe?" Chay says, grabbing my attention. "I wanted to ask you something."

Uh... That doesn't sound good. "Go on..."

"You can tell me to mind my own business, but how was the sex really between you and Bron?"

My stomach drops. "What makes you ask?"

"Well, I'm not calling you a prude, but some of the comments you've made when sex has come up have been... I dunno. Just something feels off."

"Right," Rhian agrees.

I sigh. I really need to come to terms with the fact that my girls know me too damned well.

"You can tell us now," Alicia says. "You're not together anymore."

Do I tell them the truth? Alicia's right, we're not together anymore, and it's not as if he'll know if I tell them...

"It was okay," I confess.

That grabs all of their attention, especially Chay's. "Just okay?"

"Yeah, I mean, I came a lot, and he did have a big dick..." The size and what he did with it was never the problem—it was everything he didn't do that was.

"But?" Rhian pushes, resting her glass down.

I mentally prepare myself for us to get into it. I'm also a little embarrassed, not only because I've hidden the truth for so long, but because it's just another thing in my life that I simply accepted and didn't stand up for myself about.

"You know he has Jamaican roots, right?"

They nod.

"Well, a lot of men from there don't go down."

I cringe from their chorus of "what?".

I knew they'd be shocked, but I wasn't expecting the blatant looks of disgust I'm seeing. Alicia appears pissed, Rhian is wide-eyed, and Chay is gaping at me.

"Yeah. Bron didn't do it."

"Hold the fuck on," Chay says, almost breaking my glass, "you're telling me you haven't been eaten out in three bloody years?"

I shake my head. "Or given it."

"Sis," Rhian says in disbelief, "you didn't go through a breakup, God *saved* your ass."

I chuckle. "Maybe."

"What kind of grown-ass man these days doesn't pray?" Chay says. "I don't get it. Can someone make it make sense to me please, 'cause I'm seriously struggling here, girls."

Alicia scoffs. "No man. That's a boy right there. Period."

"I dunno, but I think maybe that's what led to us breaking up. I suggested trying new things and I don't think it went down well. It wasn't anything too crazy; it was me suggesting things to try on him. I missed giving, y'know? And I was worried about things getting stale and him straying. Not that he ever gave me a reason to believe he would, I just... Maybe I hurt his feelings."

"Girl, fuck his feelings," Rhian spits. "Wow, I really thought Bron was doing his thing."

"So did I," Alicia says, sounding disappointed for me. "I really thought he was the whole package. Clearly not."

"Right," Chay agrees. "You need to get excited for what's coming, 'cause best believe that much better is. And it will be a real man of God that takes the knee because he likes to. As far as I'm concerned, no woman should ever settle when it comes to sex, because what one man won't do, a million more will. And better."

"She's right," Alicia says. "I would never put up with that shit. I'd become a lesbian before I let a man tell me he wasn't going down."

Rhian laughs. "And we'd have you with open arms, boo." She reaches over to hold my hand. "Don't you ever let a man take something away from you that you enjoy doing ever again. If someone doesn't give you what you need, they aren't for you."

"Everything she said," Chay says. "Never again."

Alicia agrees. "The right man will give you all you want in the bedroom and out, and you'll be able to live out all of your fantasies too, without the fear of being shut down, dismissed, or shamed for it either."

I smile. I hope they're right.

"Wow," Chay gushes. "That's blown my mind. I'm even happier that you're moving now. You can leave all those shitty-ass memories behind and really start living your life."

I take a deep breath as I look around. "This place has been

good to me, but I am excited for the next chapter. Whatever that may be."

"It's gonna be amazing," Alicia says. "Really. And you best believe you deserve it."

That makes me smile. "I'm definitely starting to see my worth, and it feels nice."

"And so it should."

"Yeah..." I drink the last of my wine before getting up. "Right, are we gonna get started? I have yoga in the morning, so the more I can get done, the better."

They all down their drinks, and as I find things for them all to do, I say a silent thanks up to the heavens for them. I really don't know where I'd be without my girls sometimes. I guess it's true what they say—that friends are the family we get to choose.

I chose good.

Chapter Twenty-Two

I get to Jenny's class a little early, as usual, and my eyes wander straight to Mike. He's started giving me this new look when he sees me now, and it makes my insides flutter in a whole new way.

I'm pretty sure he checks me out during these sessions, but I only know that because I do the same. His ass isn't the only great thing about his body, or his killer thighs. He's firm everywhere; broad shoulders, and the way his brow glistens from sweat and his arms flex during poses has my entire insides heating. Any time I face his direction, my eyes have a mind of their own.

He really does have a great body.

I say hello to everyone before rolling my mat out in the usual space between Emma and Mari. Today must be a good day for everyone, because Jenny comments on our timekeeping before grabbing her singing bowl to start the session.

"Close your eyes," she says softly as the bowl plays its tune, and then my favorite part of the week begins.

Total peace.

. . .

"You're definitely getting better."

I smile up at Mike as he holds the door for me. "Yeah, I feel as if I am. I've upped my practice at home. I never knew I'd love it so much."

"It's addictive."

"It really is. I can't wait to see how much better I am in another few months."

"You'll be running your own class."

That makes me laugh. "Let's not get carried away now."

He smiles, but it soon slips. "So, what are your plans for the rest of the day?"

That tells me he has something in mind, but I don't ask. "Packing, unfortunately. I seem to have a lot more to do than I thought." The girls and I made good progress last night, but when they left, I realized just how much stuff that house is holding.

He looks disappointed. "How much more do you have to do?"

"Most of upstairs. There are some things I'll need to wait to pack until the last minute, but with work being how it is, I don't want to run out of time." I think about whether I could spare a few hours if he wants to do something, because I do want to spend time with him.

"Want some help?"

That question lights me up inside. "You wanna help me pack?"

He shrugs. "Why not? The sooner you're done with that, the sooner we can do something fun."

My heart lights up at the term "we". "Ah, fun would be *so* nice. This week has been a nightmare."

"Okay. So packing, then fun?"

I'm intrigued to know what he's planned, because he clearly came ready for something different after the look he's sending my way. "What would be the fun this time?"

"Well… I wondered if you'd consider a little road trip."

It's been years since I've been on one of those, and the excitement is real. "Where?"

"Dauphin Island. Have you been?"

"No, I haven't. Isn't it like six hours' drive away though?"

"It is." He rests his arm on the top of my car, paying close attention to my reaction. "I'll drive."

Six hours? "Two hours of packing, six hours to get there… But we won't get there till six…" I wonder if he's intending for us to stay overnight. Should I ask or not? *Oh, screw it.* "We'll have to stay over if we want to make the most of the time."

Now his face lights up, and I'm glad I suggested it. "We can get a hotel. Separate rooms."

I smirk. Well, I appreciate the respect, but I wouldn't have minded sharing… *Ugh. Get a grip, girl. We're just friends, remember?* I check the time on my phone, but I don't know why. I knew my answer as soon as he asked. I'll just have to deal with a few more late nights of packing next week. "Let's pack."

"Really?" There's no doubt he's surprised I've said yes, but so am I that he thought I'd say no.

"Yes, reall—oh shit." My excitement is dashed when I remember that I have plans with Mom and Dad tomorrow. "I'm supposed to be having lunch with my parents tomorrow. I've been putting it off for a while."

He frowns. "So? Rearrange. The beach will be better."

Without a doubt, but… "Yeah, but as I've said, my dad is… I'll need a good excuse. He's kinda strict on the cancelling thing too."

Mike steps closer and rests a brief hand on my shoulder, and a rush of support floods through me. "Just tell him you're sick. You're twenty-six, Nikki. You're allowed to cancel shit. I thought you were trying to stand up to him more?"

"I am," I say, watching his hand fall to his side. "I'm not good at lying though."

He nods in knowing, and if I'm not mistaken, I think he likes that confession. "We'll think of something when we're packing. I'll follow you."

"Don't you need to go home and pack yourself?"

"I always have spare clothes in my car. Anything else I need, I'll get when we get there. I go with the flow, remember?"

I roll my eyes playfully. "How could I forget? You can shower at mine, if you want?"

"That would be great."

My excitement reaches new heights. "Then let's go."

Once we've both showered and changed, we listen to the radio while we pack. We both sing along, which is a nice surprise for me. Not only does it make me smile, but Bron never sang with me.

Mike packs fast, and I mean *superfast*. He grabs, wraps with newspaper if needed, then slots whatever it is into the box in a perfect fluid motion. It's like watching a magician with how quick he is with his hands, and after only an hour, we've done half the bedroom already.

"Right. That's the dresser. I've left your fragrance, a deodorant, and your makeup out. Want me to hit the wardrobe next?"

I turn from my current box on the floor. "Yes please. Did you want another water?"

He shakes his head. "I'm good. I don't wanna have to stop a million times on the way."

"Good idea." I should probably make this my last coffee.

He fixes another box and then heads to the wardrobe while I make my way over to the other side table. I've found a few more of Bron's things, but not many. He did a good job of taking most of his stuff when he picked it up.

I open the drawer and stifle a gasp when I'm met with my three new toys. *Shit.* I discreetly scoop them from the drawer into the box and quickly cover them with a few books.

"Thank God," I say under my breath. *I'd completely forgotten about those.*

"So do you have any brothers or sisters?" I ask. Mike's spoken about his mother and father but hasn't mentioned whether he's an only child or not.

"Yeah. Two brothers, but they live out in New York."

"That's far."

"My mom's family owns a real estate company. They work with them."

"Flipping houses not your thing?"

He laughs behind me. "Hell no. My brothers are a perfect fit for it though."

"Hmmm. Must be some juicy stories there."

"Plenty. I might tell you a few on the way."

"I'll look forward to that. Do you miss them?"

"Yes and no. They fly in regularly to see dad and Keosha, so I still see them quite often."

"Keosha?"

"Yeah, my dad's wife."

I turn to face him. "Is that the woman in the picture with you on your Facebook?"

"It is." He glances my way. "Yes, my dad is married to a black woman. She's amazing too."

"Too?"

"Yes, too." He smirks. "Did you like that?"

"Maybe." *Hell yes I did.*

"I know you did. I think I know you pretty well now."

He does, and that's so crazy to me. I've told him so much about my life and it's seemed natural to as well. I'd really like to know more about him though and feel as if this trip to Dauphin Island will be the perfect opportunity.

I really wanna know why he's been single for so long.

"Do you mind me asking how long ago your accident was?" I ask, hoping to get more of a timeline on his journey to where he is now.

"Four years…" His words drift off and I regret asking. Maybe he doesn't want to talk about it.

I turn around ready to apologize, but instead, I gasp.

Oh no. Please no. Please don't let what I'm seeing be real…

He's holding up my long-lost vibrator with two fingers, head cocked while he dangles it in front of him. "Is this what I think it is?"

The pink has faded, and I think there might be a cobweb hanging off the end.

"I…" I jump up to grab it from him, but he holds it higher and laughs.

"Your reaction must mean it is. How *old* is this thing?"

I cover my mouth with my hands. "Please don't… It's from college… I lost it ages ago…"

His eyes lower to mine, twinkling with mischief, but my face is on fire and I'm dying with shame.

"Please give it back."

"Here…" He finally concedes. "Better throw it away. I don't think it's safe."

I snort but can't bring myself to allow the laugh that wants to come out to break free. Instead, I snatch it from him and immediately throw it in the trash bag.

He's still laughing.

"Please stop…" I kneel back beside my side table to bask in my horror. *How the hell did it get in there? Did Bron hide it?*

"You really don't need to worry, Nikki. I've seen BOBs before."

Oh God. "Can we not talk about it?"

He's quiet, but then he's sitting on the bed next to me. "Nikki?"

I keep my focus on the drawer. "Uh-huh?"

"Look at me."

I take a steadying breath before lifting my head. "Yes?"

He's still smiling. "Why are you embarrassed?"

I scoff. *Is he for real?* "Wouldn't you be?"

He frowns. "No. It is what it is. We're both grown, and needs are needs."

My defenses rise. "As I said, I lost that years ago. I haven't used it since college."

"I hope not. You wouldn't want to electrocute yourself down there—or maybe you might."

I scoff again, but then I laugh when I remember how decrepit it looked.

And that cobweb on the end...

He watches me catch the giggles, the whole time shaking his head. "Exactly," he says, returning to the wardrobe. "Laugh it off."

As I look out at the view on the 45, I wonder again what Mike and I are actually doing.

Like, not once has he mentioned our days together being dates, or so much as hinted at this thing between us being romantic, but is it? Or are we really just friends?

I'm good with whatever, but if he does want something more, I wish he'd spit it out. I thought maybe he was stalling because he knows I've not long been through a breakup, but he knows I'm looking for a relationship because I told him I was talking to someone on a dating site.

Whatever we're doing though, I'm so glad we are. I used to look forward to Saturday mornings for the yoga, but now it's these trips and days out with Mike that I look forward to the most. Our conversations are always lit too, although they are becoming just a tad more personal recently.

And the touches are becoming a lot more frequent...

I finish booking two single rooms at the Holiday Inn before tucking my cell back in my purse. We had a little bicker about who was paying, but I point-blank refused to let him. I don't think he was too happy, but I argued that not only does he always pay when we go on trips, but that he's driving us and paying was my way of saying thank you.

I then turn my attention to how I'm going to cancel on my parents. "I could say I have food poisoning, but Mom would wanna come look after me."

Mike shakes his head at the road. "Just tell them the truth, Nikki. You've gone on a road trip with your friend and won't be back until late tomorrow afternoon."

"Yeah, but I made plans with them first."

"I don't get it." He sighs.

"Get what?"

"How a clearly independent, twenty-six-year-old woman is still living life under her parents' rules. Do they consult you on what they do?"

"No."

"Have they ever canceled on you before?"

I laugh. "Plenty of times..." My laughter ends abruptly, and then I frown.

"Exactly. You need to start putting yourself first. Text your mom and tell her you're not coming. I thought you read that book?"

"I did." He always calls me out on my shit. I think he might even be worse than the girls, but if I'm honest, I like that about him. "You're quite bossy when you want to be, aren't you?" *That's kinda hot too.* I didn't think he had any other sides in him besides understanding, encouraging, and fun.

He gives me a quick glance. "When needed."

My eyes hone in on his lips when he smirks at the road. *Definitely hot.*

I have no idea where all this attraction toward him is coming from, but no matter what I do, I can't seem to put a halt to it. The more time we spend together, the more I like him.

"I can feel your eyes burning a hole in my head."

"I'm looking out the window," I say, returning my attention outside. "You must be imagining things."

That makes him laugh. "Sure. Sent that text yet?"

I retrieve my phone from my purse to write it out.

Hey, Mom. My friend asked me to take a trip to Dauphin Island so I won't be back till tomorrow evening. Sorry to cancel last minute.

I leave it at that because I don't know what else to say. While I have my phone out though, I check my other messages and find some from the girls in our group chat.

Alicia: *Drinks today? Kids are with their dad.*

Rhian: *I'm good for drinks.*

Chay: *Me too.*

Rhian: *Nikki? Where are you? How was yoga? How's the packing going? You need help?*

Alicia: *She's probably off on one of her adventures with her hot nerdy boyfriend.*

Chay: *With the big dick she doesn't know about yet.*

There's that twinge again at the word "nerdy." I wish I never said that now.

Me: *Hey, girls. I've told you his name is MIKE and we're on the way to Dauphin Island. Packing is pretty much done now. He helped.*

Mom replies.

Mom: *Of course that's okay. Have fun. We can arrange for one evening in the week. Safe journey.*

I stare at my phone and the reply from Mom. Have I been imagining my parents' strictness all this time? I swear they'd usually protest at me canceling. Dad would be on a rampage about it being rude and disrespectful.

"Has she replied?"

I lift my head to see Mike turning away from me. *I hope he didn't see that shit.* "Yeah. She said that's fine."

"See. Nothing to fear, Nikki. I keep telling you you're stronger than you know."

"You might be right..." *I always say that around him.* "Thanks for the moral support." It means more to me than he realizes.

"It's nothing."

My attention diverts when the group chat starts going off.

Alicia: *I called it. Have fun, boo.*

Rhian: *Wow, I love that. He sounds like such a nice guy, Nik.*

Chay: *Oooh, Nikki's definitely got a boyfriend.*

Me: *He's just a friend, ladies. Calm your asses down.*

Chay: *Sure. Are you staying down there for the night? If so...*

I turn my phone on vibrate before shoving it back into my purse. They're doing the most, and I can't be bothered to deal with it.

"What's that sigh for?"

"My girls like to tease me, that's all."

He hums like he understands. "Well, now the stress is off your shoulders, how about playing some tunes?"

"Some tunes, yeah? What music do you like?"

"A bit of everything. You?"

"Same."

"Any guilty pleasures?"

"Hmm, if I told you…"

He laughs. "That's not putting me off. Spit them out."

My smile is instant. "I like Justin Bieber."

He laughs again.

"Hey, if you're gonna be judgy—"

"I'm not." He briefly holds his right hand up. "I'm really not. I like a few of his songs too."

"What's yours then? You can't ask me mine and not confess yours."

He glances my way and I see the slightest hint of a blush on his cheeks. "Adele."

I roll my eyes. "She's fire. That's not embarrassing."

"And Dolly."

"Better. I like her too, so how about we listen to all three? I thought you'd be into classical or something."

"Why? Because I'm white?"

That comment blindsides me completely. "Not at all. It's because—"

"It's okay, I grew up being ridiculed by my boys for liking anything by Nirvana and Green Day, so I'm used to the stereotypes."

My defenses rise. "I honestly thought classical because of how much you love yoga and the peaceful life *actually*."

He laughs. "Calm down, Nikki. I'm just teasing." He switches on the stereo and disconnects his phone. "Hook yours up."

I play Adele's first album, *19*, as I think about what he said.

Have I been stereotyping him?

I have no idea, but as I remember how Chay reacted to my meat comment in Sedona, I make a conscious decision not to from now on. The last thing I want to do is offend him, and I know for a fact I'd be hurt if he did that to me.

Chapter Twenty-Three

We reach Dauphin Island just before six, thanks to Mike's superhuman packing skills and slick driving. The raised buildings are few and far between on the part of the island we're on, but there's plenty of parking, and we can see the ocean from the left and right from where we are.

"Can we go to the beach?" I ask as Mike parks the car. The place is bustling with people, so it takes him a few minutes. "I'd love to put my feet in the water."

His grin when he looks my way tells me he's just as excited as I am. "We can do whatever we want."

There's that "we" again...

We make our way across the warm white sand to the water. The sound of the waves is soothing, and after I kick off my slides, I hurry to submerge my feet.

"This is everything," I say, watching him do the same.

"Agreed."

He's wearing shorts, so he walks deeper into the turquoise water until it's up to his knees. I have to pull up my maxi dress to follow. We must spend at least an hour like that, not saying anything much, just a few comments here and there about how beautiful it is.

It's absolutely stunning.

My happiness level is off the charts, and as corny as this may sound, I feel as if Mike is exactly what I've needed in my life. The spontaneous fun, the excitement of not knowing what he's gonna suggest for us to do next, the conversations. He doesn't push his views onto me either; he simply expresses them, and he forever makes me feel at ease.

Even with the dildo. *God, I still can't believe that happened.*

He's so carefree, and I love how it's rubbing off on me.

"Wanna eat?" he asks when we finally leave the beach.

"Yeah."

He brushes the sand off the back of my dress when we reach the car, and something about the way he does it has me smiling from the inside out.

He notices, but anyone would. "What's that smile for?"

"That was sweet."

He smirks. "Sand is a nightmare to get out of cars."

I roll my eyes. "Oh, thanks."

His smile gives me that special feeling that can only mean one thing. Back in the car and on the way to the hotel, I finally admit to myself how much I'm hoping this chemistry between us is leading somewhere deeper. I'm just not sure how to approach it, because if I have to choose between keeping him as a friend over something more, I'd keep the friendship no question, just for the fact he makes me feel so *free.*

After we check in to the hotel and find our rooms, we freshen up before meeting back in the lobby. Mike's wearing dark jeans and a semi-dressy cream shirt, and I've gone for comfort with one of the summer dresses I bought for my trip to Sedona.

"Looking good," I comment as we head out. *He looks cute,*

and he has that just-showered scent that he did after he washed at mine.

"You look beautiful."

I tame my smile on the outside but let it flourish inside me like a field of daisies. That comment though... "Thank you."

"What do you wanna eat?"

"Maybe seafood? A lot of it. I'm starving."

"Me too. They do great food at Pirate's Bar & Grill. We can sit outside and watch the water. You'll like it."

"Sounds amazing to me."

Mike was right, the view from the courtyard is spectacular. This bar is right on the beach, so close you can hear the waves, and although it's dark, the sky is crystal clear, so you can see the surrounding palm trees and the reflection of the waning moon in the water.

It's quite busy out here, but I'm not surprised by that because the food is great and so is the vibe. There are fire pits dotted around that are kicking out heat too, so although it's a little windy, it's comfortable.

"Who do you usually do these things with?" I ask him. He's currently devouring a piece of key lime pie. I picked the cheesecake.

"One of my friends, or sometimes my dad, but mostly alone. Everyone's usually too busy with work or their families to take time out like this."

"Are you not looking to settle down at some point?"

"I am settled down, but if you're asking why I'm not actively dating, it's because I don't feel the need to."

Interesting. "So it's not because women are too much work for you, or that they disrupt your life?" I'm deadly serious when I ask that question. He's clearly laid-back and said he takes each day as it comes, so I wonder if he enjoys that too much to give it up.

His brow lifts. "Not at all. It's more that I see relationships differently to most people."

"In what way?"

He wipes his mouth and hands on a napkin. "I don't rush into anything. I don't need to know every single detail of what's to come. If we like each other, that's cool. I like to live in the moment."

"Yeah, I can see how that's different..." I'm such a planner. I like stability, so to me, planning and structure in my romantic life gives me that.

He rests his fork down when he finishes his pie. "I don't pretend to be something I'm not. I stopped changing who I was to keep others in my life a long time ago. A lot of people can't handle that. It triggers them."

It's already triggering me a little, and we're just friends. "So you don't make *any* plans for the future?"

"After my accident, I realized you can't stick to any kind of plan you make for your life. So my only plan now is to be happy."

That part I do resonate with. Happiness. I'm starting to see how personal that is to everyone too. "How did your accident happen?"

"I was shunted into the back of a truck when I was switching lanes, and someone went into the back of me."

That makes me feel sick. "I can't imagine."

"I don't remember it; I found out from the police report. I just know I was running late."

"To a job you hated, right?"

"Exactly." He orders another round of drinks, while I sit in my feelings. I send a little thank you up to the sky too. I wonder what I'd be doing now if he hadn't survived.

"What about kids? Do you want them?" I ask when the drinks arrive. The alcohol is starting to kick in now.

He nods. "Without a doubt."

Well, at least that's something. "How many?"

He shrugs. "I don't know."

"Is that because you don't plan?"

"Nope, it's because I'm not the one actually having them."

I smile. "True."

My thoughts deepen as I finish off my cheesecake. I can understand why he is the way he is, especially when you have a life-changing moment like he's had, but still...

"See what happens when you start overthinking? It robs you of your happiness."

I smile as I look up. "You're very observant."

"I try to be. I think I know you pretty well."

"I think I know you quite well too."

His lip twitches as he sits forward. "You should, after all the time we've spent together."

My pulse races. "We do see each other a lot, don't we?"

"We get on." He looks down at my hand, but just when I think he might hold it, he sits up. "There's nothing wrong with that."

"At all," I muse, trying not to overthink again. However, it's hard not to notice that we're kinda in a relationship without the label, and without the sex.

Or maybe this really is just a friendship thing.

Waaaay too many drinks later, we're walking—or stumbling—through the cool white sand on the beach, each carrying a half-full bottle of wine.

You can hear the music from several beachside restaurants and bars, their lights keeping the area illuminated enough to see where you're going, and the beach itself is lightly scattered with visitors sitting by fires, listening to their own music, or in the water searching for crabs with flashlights.

It's a whole vibe, and it makes me want to start visiting more places further from home.

Swigging another mouthful of Pinot Grigio, I pick up the beat of "Lovelife" by Benny Benassi and Jeremih, and haphazardly dance while hanging on to Mike's arm.

"Can you dance?" I ask when he laughs.

He scoffs. "I think they came up with the saying 'white men can't dance' looking at me."

"Oh, please."

"It's true. I'm awful."

I roll my eyes and almost fall again. "I'll teach you."

He gives me a horrified glance while stumbling a few steps away. "Now? I'll fall over."

"No, you won't." I snatch his bottle of wine from him and wedge it into the sand along with mine. "I'm the best trainer at my job."

"I thought you were a project manager?"

"I started from the bottom—now I'm here."

He chuckles. "Okay..."

"Ready?" I ask, steadying myself in the sand.

"This *really* isn't a good idea."

I smile as I walk toward him. "It will be fine. It's not true what they say about white guys not being able to dance, y'know. Look at Magic Mike. He rolled the hell out of those hips."

He laughs. "He's an actor and probably had the best in the industry teach him."

"He still learnt though," I reply nonchalantly. "What happened to positive Mike?"

"I'm still here, I just don't need to gas up my dancing skills, no matter how intoxicated I am."

"Oh, come on. We'll start slow. Now, I'd ask you to close your eyes, but then you really would fall over, so just *feel* the music, okay?" I start clapping to the beat as I rock my hips a little. "Copy me."

He starts to move, but it's a little stiff.

"Not so jerky. Where's that grace you have in yoga?"

His eyes alight. "So you've been watching me?"

Now it's my turn to laugh, and I blush a little. "I just know you have it."

"I'm sure."

I ignore him and focus on his dancing, which he's right about: it's appalling. I'm about to say something, but then he suddenly takes my hand and swirls me around.

Don't fall...

I laugh when he swoops me down and back, but unfortunately, when he pulls me up to his chest, the whoosh results in a wave of sickness that I barely manage to keep down.

"I feel sick," I attempt to whisper, but it comes out much louder.

"Me too," he groans. "Let's lie down."

I practically drop to the sand and then concentrate on my breathing as I lie back, aware that Mike's done the same beside me. "Maybe dancing wasn't such a good idea."

"I told you it wasn't."

I take a deep breath, focusing on the clear sky. "The stars are pretty though."

"They are. That's the Pisces constellation." He points to a V of stars. "See how it kinda looks like a dog leash?"

I cock my head. "Oh yeah... That's cool."

"It is. Do you know yours?"

"Nope. I'm an Aries though, if you know it."

"Sorry, I don't. I'm sure my app could tell me."

"It's not important." I chuckle as I close my eyes but quickly snap them open again when the ground beneath me begins to spin. "Don't close your eyes."

"I did and regretted it immediately."

I smile. "As messed up as I feel, this is nice."

"You're good company, Nik."

He's been calling me Nik all night, and I *really* like it. "Same."

"Shame we have to leave early tomorrow."

My stomach drops when he says that. "Yeah, it is."

"Wanna stay the whole day?"

I sigh. "As much as it pains me to say no, I have to head home. I have work at eight on Monday morning."

He's quiet for a moment. "How about I drive us back through the night? You can sleep on the way, and I'll get you home in time for work."

I turn my head to find him already looking at me. "Won't you be tired though?"

His gaze travels the length of me. "No."

I consider saying no, but deep down I don't want to, so I say what I've been saying to everything recently. "Yes. I'd love to."

He nods before turning his head back toward the sky, so I do the same. "Would you ever date a white guy, Nik?"

My heart smiles, actually smiles. "A month ago, my answer would've been no..."

"Why?"

"For the reasons I already told you."

"About the having things in common and stuff?"

"Yeah."

"I understand that," he says softly, "but we're all human."

"True."

"People are only scared of what they don't know, but they fail to realize that deep down, everyone, no matter who they are, wants the same things. To be happy, and to be loved."

"I really do believe that." The way I feel about him is proof. "You said you've dated black women before, right? Has anyone ever said anything to you about it?"

"There have been a few comments."

"Like what?"

He sighs. "The usual. Some of their parents hated me because I wasn't black, some of their friends thought they had daddy issues—y'know, bad relationships with their absent or abusive fathers, and then there was the usual hate about interracial dating and how it's not natural."

What the hell? "Did you break up because of it?"

"It has led to a few breakups, but it wasn't because I cared—it was because they did."

I briefly turn my head, seeing him still focused on the stars. "Has it put you off dating black women again?"

"I wouldn't be here with you if it had."

That makes me smile. "So these trips *have* been dates."

I hear him turn onto his side, but I don't. "They might've been. Tell me, if you knew these were dates, and I'm not your usual shade, why did you agree to spend time with me?"

"Shade?" I shake my head. "When I spent that week in Sedona, my friends had just convinced me to be open to every kind of guy."

"Oh, so I'm an experiment?"

"What?" I turn my head. "Not at—"

He takes my hand, and I feel an electric bolt shoot through my body with his touch. "I'm just playing. I told you, it takes a lot to hurt my feelings, believe me. It means a lot, really, that you've given me a chance to get to know you."

"I'm glad I did. You've had a very positive influence on my life. From your book recommendations to all the new things you've invited me to try. I really like you, Mike."

His grip on my hand tightens. "I feel the same. I haven't made an effort to get to know anyone for such a long time, but with you, it's as if I haven't had a choice. There have been so many times over the past few weeks when I thought you might've friend-zoned me."

I laugh. "Friend-zoned? Why would you think that?"

"Well, when I first spoke to you, the story about my first time in Jenny's class slipped out."

"I thought you told me that to make me feel better."

"Believe me, I had no intention to make that your first impression of me. Same as what happened the first time we went to Greenway."

"When you fell off your bike to impress me?"

He rolls his eyes, but a smirk soon appears. "I didn't."

"Well, even if you didn't, all those things made me feel comfortable around you, so I'm glad they happened."

He smiles. "So I'm not in the friend zone?"

I shake my head, suddenly nervous of the way he's gazing at me.

"So... If I asked to date you, officially, what would you say?"

My stomach flutters wildly. I can't believe he's actually asked me, or that there's no doubt in my mind what my answer is. I must be crazy because we're complete opposites in some things, but... "I would say..."

"We can take it slow. As slow as you want."

I laugh at how the usual calm and collected Mike seems to be rattled. "Thank you, but my answer is still yes."

He recoils. "Are you for real? Should I ask you again when you're sober?"

I laugh harder. "My answer will still be the same."

"Shit... Then hopefully I won't screw this up."

Hell, I hope I don't either. I'd hate to lose what we currently have.

He perches on his elbow to lean closer. "So, as we're dating now, I can kiss you, right?"

A whirl of new emotions spirals inside me. "Yeah, but you better hurry. I can feel the water at my ankles now." The anticipation has been killing me too. I've been waiting for him to make a move on me since we left the hotel and he called me beautiful.

"We have plenty of time."

No more words are said by either of us, but the kiss we share speaks a million. It's as if the invisible elastic band between us has finally snapped, and the rush of emotion that follows is like nothing I have ever experienced.

Chapter Twenty-Four

I head out to find breakfast for us as soon as I'm up and ready. Mike and I stayed in our own rooms last night, and while I drifted off to sleep in my surprisingly comfy bed, thinking of Mike, I wondered if he was thinking of me too.

"Hey," I say when he opens his door. He's wearing dark shorts with a white tank top, and I can see where he caught the sun around his neck yesterday. I did too. "I got us breakfast."

The smile he gives me confirms my earlier thoughts, and so does the kiss he greets me with. "I thought I dreamt last night," he says as he lets me in and closes the door. "You didn't slap me just now when I kissed you, so I guess I didn't."

I laugh. "You didn't. How long have you been up?"

"About an hour. I went for a run along the beach. I would've knocked for you, but I thought you might still be asleep."

"I'm an early riser. I don't get hangovers either, no matter how much I drink."

He motions me over to sit on his bed. "Good. I know you have work early tomorrow and don't want you to be tired."

"I'm fresh as a daisy." I pass him the food before sitting

opposite him. "I got us some pastries, yogurt and berries. I hope that's good with you?"

"Anything would've been fine."

We eat mostly in silence, and to my relief, the vibe between us hasn't changed. I still feel comfortable in the lulls between conversations, and it seems he's not feeling any different either.

"I know I just kissed you at the door," he says as he lifts his head, "but we are dating now, right?"

That makes me chuckle. "Is this you asking me again while I'm sober?"

"Exactly that."

"My answer is still yes."

He's undoubtedly happy about that. "I thought we could explore the island. I grabbed a brochure while I was out this morning."

"I'd love to."

After breakfast, we check out of the hotel before beginning the day's adventures. I was so worried that things would be different now that our relationship is taking a more romantic route, but I needn't have been. Things are just the same. The only differences now are that he holds my hand and kisses me at random, which I absolutely love.

We visit the Sea Lab Estuarium, the incredible Indian Shell Mound Park—which is eerily peaceful and is home to some of the most magnificent trees I've ever seen—and then, after enjoying some ice cream on the beach, we head up to the bird sanctuary.

Mike holds my hand tight as we make our way through the trail, making sure to protect me from any flying branches released by the walkers in front of us. Unfortunately, though, one ends up smacking him on the cheek, leaving him with a red mark.

I pull him to the side to rub it for him while he glares at the people in front, merrily walking on. "Those things are a hazard."

I agree. "But at least you're not bleeding."

He turns to smile at me as I continue to stroke over the raised line, but then he pulls me into a hug. "Look at you, Miss Positivity."

That makes me laugh. "What can I say? You have a way of making me see the bright side of things."

"Good to know."

I step away when he suddenly does the same, but his smile is long gone and he's running a hand through his hair.

"What's... Oh God, is that..."

"Bird shit?" he asks, raising his hand. "Yeah."

"Mike..." I have to bite my lip to stop the laugh that wants to slip out from breaking free, but I end up snorting instead. "Shit..." I busy myself unscrewing the bottle of water in my hand to distract myself instead.

He grabs my wrist as I look up, and I see his eyes alight with humor. "You can laugh, Nikki. I'm not gonna cry."

"I never said..." I snort again before I catch the giggles. "I'm sorry, I don't mean to, I just can't believe your luck today."

"Me either." He's smiling though, but I think it's more at me. "I heard it's lucky."

"Me too..." Not that I see how. "Let me wash it out."

He bends to let me, and I quickly begin rinsing his hair. There's not too much, and I'm glad because although this doesn't stink, it reminds me of vomit.

"That's why you wear one of these," a passing man wearing cut-off shorts says, tapping his cap. "Happens all the time."

"Thanks," Mike mutters as he straightens. "I'll remember that for next time."

We shake our heads at each other as he passes me some

hand sanitizer, but I soon smile at him. His hair at the front has fallen over his forehead and he looks hotter than ever.

"I think I like your hair like this," I say, reaching up to run a wave through my fingers. "It suits you."

"I'll keep that in mind." I'm in his arms again after that, but this time he's kissing me softly. "Thanks for getting me right. *Again*."

"You're welcome." My voice is a little breathy, but that kiss was everything. I even have goosebumps. When I turn to step back onto the trail though, my smile wavers when I see a disapproving glance from a passerby at our hands.

I look up at Mike, but he doesn't seem to notice, so I let it go. *Maybe I imagined it?*

We stop for an early dinner around four, then spend the evening on the beach until the sun sets, mostly in silence. It is the perfect end to a pretty much perfect day, and although the thought of having to go home is hanging over me, I manage to block it out and enjoy every moment as much as I can.

Unfortunately, though, I do spot a few more looks, but Dauphin is far from diverse, not like where we're from, so I put that down as the reason why. I'm not imagining the looks, because whenever Mike notices anyone staring at our hands, he squeezes mine tighter.

He's used to this though, and although I'd heard from my cousin what interracial dating could be like, what Mike told me last night, combined with today's experiences, has been eye opening. I suppose we'll have to talk about certain things at some point and how we'll handle them, but for right now, I'm taking a leaf out of the latest book Mike recommended to me: *The Life-Changing Magic of Not Giving a F**k*, by Sarah Knight.

I wonder if that was part of his plan to date me.

. . .

We're back on the 45, on our way home now, and I've just asked Mike what happened with his last relationship. He's never gone into details about it before, but after I found out he'd been single since around the same time as his accident, I've wondered if the two things were linked somehow.

"I found out my girl was screwing one of my closest friends while I was recovering from my accident." He glances my way, but I can only shake my head.

"That is disgusting." *What the hell is wrong with people?*

"Tell me about it. It was for the best though. My life was going through all kinds of changes back then and I needed to be alone so I could focus on my recovery."

"What injuries did you have?"

"A few broken ribs, both wrists fractured, and a pretty bad head injury."

I sigh deeply. "Thank God you were okay."

"I wasn't for a while, but my family helped me out, and it gave me a chance to reevaluate everything. It was something that made me realize nothing bad really happens in life. At the time, yeah, it might seem like your world's falling apart, but give it time and I guarantee it won't feel like that for long."

"I really do understand that. It's like everything leads to something better."

He smiles. "Yeah?"

"Yeah." *Like him.*

He releases the steering wheel to tuck my hair behind my ear. "You should get some sleep, Nik. It's late."

"I know." I pull the blanket he took from his trunk over me and get comfortable with my head against the window. "Goodnight."

"Night, beautiful."

. . .

"Nikki?"

"Hmmm?"

"We're home."

I sit up to see my house out of the window. It barely feels as if I've slept an hour. "Thank you." I turn to face him as I attempt to fold his blanket in the small space, but he prizes it off me before throwing it in the back.

"I'll deal with that. Are you tired?"

"Not really." Groggy, yes. "Thank you for such an amazing weekend. I had the best time."

"Me too. Let me know when you're free in the week? I wanna see you. Maybe we could have dinner at my place?"

I hold his hand when he yawns, and I notice his eyes look tired. "That would be nice."

"When are you moving?"

"Sunday.

"And who's helping you?"

"The girls, and maybe, if I'm lucky, the guy I'm seeing."

He laughs. "I'm sure he will."

"Great. Well, I better go." I want to experience one of those amazing kisses he gives out, but my mouth tastes horrible post-nap. Almost like he senses my thoughts, he does one better by leaning forward to rest a soft kiss on my forehead.

My heart can barely take it. I've always loved when a man kisses me on the head, and the best thing about him doing it is that I haven't ever told him that—he just knows.

My smile must give away how much I love it though.

"Noted," he says, smiling. "Have a good day."

"You too."

I make it to work early, and it's a good job I do: two projects are starting today, and I need to pay close attention to one of them because it's the first time we're working on anything to do with organic food deliveries.

"Morning, Nikki. Here's your coffee," Kelly says, resting my mug down. "Good weekend?"

"The best." *Actually, saying that...* I grab my phone so I can delete the dating accounts. I've never ghosted anyone before, but I guess there's a first time for everything.

"Oh yeah? I know that look. Did you have a dick appointment?"

I laugh. "No, but I am seeing someone." I say that causally, but inside, there's a rush of excited and nervous emotions doing all kinds of things.

"Oooh. Do I get details?"

"Nope, but if someone called Mike calls, you can put him through."

She salutes. "Got it. Did you meet him online? 'Cause if so, I should get some credit. Maybe in the form of a pay rise."

I shake my head. "Sorry, but nope. I met him at yoga, of all places." I rest my phone back down and laugh when she gets up and pouts.

"Dammit—there goes my bonus!"

This woman.

"All right well, as you know, the accounts for OriginalK and 3DColor are starting this morning, so I've set up the interview room for you to listen in. Marcus will also be having a listen at some point, but he's quietly confident that there won't be any problems."

"Good."

That means a happy Marcus, which means a happy building.

Once Kelly leaves, I take a deep breath and check the group with the girls. I had to mute the chat yesterday because they were all up in there talking shit after I told them I wasn't coming home until this morning.

Chay: *Did you get the D then?*

Chay: *Nikki????*

Rhian: *LOL, Chay, leave her. Can't you see she's ghosting us?*

Alicia: *I wonder why.*

I don't even read the rest because I already know what they'll say.

Me: *You're all crazy. I'm at work now and have new projects to deal with but I can do lunch. Let me know.*

Alicia is the first to reply.

Dinner! Lunch won't be long enough. Should we do Memphis Soul?

Rhian: *Good with me.*

Chay: *Yassss! I could kill for some sweet potato pie.*

Me: *Okay. See you later.*

I almost put my phone down, but then I decide to send Mike a text instead. He'll most likely be sleeping, but he can get it when he wakes up.

Hey, if you're free after yoga on Saturday, I wondered if I could pick what we do. Let me know. Hope you sleep well.

Right, now to get to work...

.   .   .

I smile the entire way through telling the girls about my weekend with Mike. The mere memory of it makes me happy. Or maybe that's just Mike.

He called me at lunch, asking where I was planning to take him Saturday, but I said it was a secret and that he'd have to wait and see. We also planned dinner at his tomorrow.

"Well damn," Alicia gushes. "I know you've been spending a lot of time with him, but I never realized it was that deep. You've been holding out on us."

I roll my eyes. "I have *not*. It kinda just happened, and it seemed natural to say yes when he asked. It has shocked me, if I'm honest, because we're complete opposites in so many ways. He goes with the flow, is carefree, uber laid-back and isn't really bothered by anything, and as you know, I'm all about my job, easily stressed out, and I like to plan ahead by miles."

"Sometimes that's a good thing though," Rhian says. "Joi and I are completely different, but it keeps it interesting."

"It really does. There are some things I worry about, but I'm trying to take a leaf out of his book and take things day by day."

Chay's eyes immediately narrow. "Things like what?"

"The obvious. Us being from two completely different cultures. He was born and raised in Blackhaven, so he's been around black people all his life, and he's dated black women before, but some of the things he's said about interracial dating have me a little nervous."

Chay and Alicia both nod in knowing.

"And I noticed a few glances yesterday when we were holding hands, and I know he did too."

"Maybe you and I should talk," Chay says. "The world of interracial dating can be a minefield when you first get into it, and some people are hella judgmental."

"Ignorant too," Alicia adds.

Rhian scoffs. "And stuck in the past."

"Hmm, so I've heard..." I tell them what Mike told me about

his experiences of dating black women in the past, such as the daddy issues and their parents not approving, but they don't seem surprised.

"That's the least of it," Chay says. "Don't worry though, all right? As long as you remember that you're dating each other and not the whole world, you'll be fine. Leave those idiots to think whatever they want."

"Right," Alicia agrees. "We've made progress when it comes to race, but we still have a long way to go before everyone realizes that there's really only one and that we're all the same."

"Exactly," Rhian agrees. "This really *is* the time for you to start sticking up for yourself and not caring what other people think, because you won't be with Mike long if you let the naysayers in."

Chay and Alicia nod in agreement, but I try to keep calm. "I will. Thanks."

"What do you think your parents will say?" Alicia asks cautiously.

"I have no idea, but if they don't like him, it won't be because he's white—it'll be because he isn't Bron."

"I reckon your mom will be okay, but your dad... Is he still trying to get you back into church?"

"Since I told him not to tell Bron my business he's been a little better."

Alicia sighs. "If you like Mike as much as you say you do, I'd prepare yourself for a fallout, boo, and I say that in the nicest way possible. Boundaries need to become your best friends right now."

"I've actually read a book recently about how important they are. I'll make sure I'm ready."

"Good. We're always here for you, and you and I will talk."

"And so will we," Chay says. "I can give you the other side of the coin. Girl, I can tell you some shit, believe me."

I don't even know if I want to know. "I appreciate you all..."

My mood has undoubtedly taken a hit, so I decide to lift it by telling them about Mike finding my pink plastic "college boyfriend."

Rhian spits wine all over the table. "Oh my God!"

They're all hollering now, and the other diners are staring at us.

I ignore them. "And there was a *cobweb* hanging off the tip."

Chay screams as she holds her chest. "Babe... Stop... Please."

"I know. I can laugh about it now, but trust me, I wanted to die. You should've seen the state of it. All faded and..." I shudder. "It was doing the most."

"The most," Rhian hollers, and then they all get the giggles again.

I shake my head, but after the conversation we've just had, I'm glad of the laugh.

Chapter Twenty-Five

Mike's on the phone when he answers the door, but he holds my waist to guide me inside before kissing me on the head. He releases me and mouths "work," then gestures for me to take a look around.

"Have you checked the numbers?" he says to someone, but I tune him out as I make my way through his house.

I can't lie, I was blown away before I even got inside. The front of his house is stunning, old brick with cream pillars, and the entire house is surrounded by trees, apart from the open drive and lawned area at the front.

The inside is also filled with plants, and it's honestly like being in a tropical island in here, especially in the living room. The other rooms aren't quite as earthy, but they're just as peaceful and calming.

"You okay?" he asks, making me jump. I was just looking at the view of his street from one of his four spare rooms.

"Yeah, you?"

He hums but soon pulls me into his arms to greet me properly. "What do you think of my place?"

"It's beautiful. Very peaceful, but I expected nothing less."

He sweeps a few stands of hair away from my face. "Of course you didn't. Hungry?"

"Very."

He takes my hand to lead me back down to the kitchen. "Chicken okay?"

"Sure. Is it ready?"

"It is. Why?"

"No reason."

He turns from the stove. "Spit it out, Nik. I know there's something."

Ugh. I wanna let it go, but I can't. It may seem petty to some people, but when it comes to my food, I've always been a little cautious. I think it stems from watching my cousin's husband putting wings straight onto the BBQ from the packet when I was a little girl, and when I went to eat one, there were feathers still attached.

"Did you wash the chicken?"

He shakes his head. "I knew it."

My stomach twists. "Was it that obvious?"

"Yes, and yes, I always clean my meat. Does that surprise you?"

"A little. Not everyone does."

"You mean not every *white* person does." He turns back around but I see him still shaking his head. "Nikki, Nikki, Nikki. How about we get these conversations over and done with tonight?"

"What conversations?"

"You know what." He brings two plates over to the table of grilled seasoned chicken thighs, steamed potatoes, and greens. "Go on, as this is your first time, you can ask me everything you wanna know."

"This looks good. Thank you."

"I hope you like it," he says when he sits down, then he smiles when he picks up his fork. "So go on."

"You wash your meat, so that's good." I eat some of my chicken with the greens. It's really good, and I moan a little. "And seasoning's your friend."

He laughs as he pours us both a glass of water. "This is going to be interesting."

I smile across at him. "Hmm, maybe you should ask me some first."

"Oh no. You're not deflecting now. Next."

Dammit. "Okay... Do you like indie music?"

"Some."

I hide my smile, but that's because I do too. "So do I."

"Funny that, isn't it?"

That comment stings a little. "Hey, I didn't even know about most of these assumptions until my girls mentioned them."

He stabs a piece of his chicken. "Stereotypes are dumb, from both sides. Believe me."

I eat some of my greens while I think about that statement. He couldn't be more right about that. Those books he's put me on have really opened my mind to how the views of other people can affect your life. "You tell me some of the ones you've heard."

"Do you put Dettol in your bath?"

I laugh in surprise. "Sometimes."

"Yeah, well, so do I and so do about a handful of other white people I know. And bleach in with your dishwasher cycle?"

I nod.

"See. It's like white people like yoga and the outdoors, but you like those things, and you saw how diverse the people were at Shelby when we went."

"Right." I did.

"And hair is another big one."

"Hair?"

He nods. "Yeah. If you asked me if I dyed my hair, it

wouldn't bother me, but if I asked you about yours or touched it without asking, I'd be classed as racist."

That makes me frown because it's *so* true.

He rests his fork down before regarding me closely. "Don't get me wrong, I'm not oblivious to all the different types of racism there are out there. I've seen it from a young age, I've read about it, I've been told about it from family and friends, but I honestly believe that it has a lot to do with the way we've all been raised."

That hits hard, and it's something I've believed for a long time. "I agree, and I think that's why it gets better with each generation."

"Right. I also think some people ask 'just because.' There are a lot of things people ask because they simply don't know. It doesn't mean they have an agenda, unless they make it obvious they do. I asked an ex about her hair once, and the way she reacted..." He sighs. "I get it though, I do. Us humans haven't been the kindest to each other."

He's speaking all the facts now. "Y'know, I really love that you see these things, because a lot of people don't."

"I think more people do than we realize."

"Maybe..." I think about what he's said, especially the hair comment. I've seen him looking at mine countless times and always wondered if he was too scared to compliment it in fear of how I'd react. "I think hair is a sensitive topic because of how black people have been made to feel about it, but I wouldn't be offended if you asked about mine."

He smiles as he gives it another look. "Good to know, because when we do take it to the next level, I fully intend to touch you everywhere, and that includes your hair. I love it."

Whoa, I wasn't expecting the conversation to take that turn. My heart races a little with that comment too.

"I like when you blush," he says, eyes darkening. "And in

case I've not made myself clear so far, I like you for who you are, not the color of your skin. You make me feel good."

Another feel-good whiplash of emotion. "So do you."

He smirks. "Not to let the ego out, but that's obvious."

I laugh. "I didn't say anything."

"Yet. So, are there any more stereotypes you feel the need to find out the truth to?"

I blush again but for a completely different reason. "Um, like what exactly?"

He rolls his eyes. "We've talked about all kinds of things, Nik. We don't need to beat around the bush."

"Um, okay... Are you cut?"

He appears far from surprised by my question; expected it even. "Always the first one. Believe it or not, yes, I am. And...?"

Thank God. I don't know how to use the other type. "And what?"

"That question usually leads to the more obvious one."

Surely it can only be one thing... "Size of the goods?"

He shakes his head. "Seriously... Don't worry about my goods, all right? All you need to know is that it's bigger than that antique you had held captive in your wardrobe."

The remembered shame hits me, then I snort, but it ends in laughter. "That's forever going to haunt me, isn't it?"

He smiles, but he's soon serious. "Look, I know I'm not from the same background as you and I'll never pretend to know what it's like to live in your shoes, but I hope you can talk to me and be open about how you feel. I care about you, Nikki. I want to know everything about you, and I want you to know that I'm open to supporting you in whatever. And if you have questions, ask me. Some people will always have opinions of you and me, but all that matters is us and how we feel about each other. This won't work if we let bullshit stereotypes or opinions of others come between us."

I sigh. It's pretty much what the girls have said. "I know."

He drinks some of his water, eyeing me when he rests it back down. "Your parents, how do you think they'll react to us?"

"They won't care that you're white, if that's what you're asking; they'll be more concerned about you not being a man of God and that you're not my ex. Dad wanted me to fix things with Bron when we first broke up. I think he's still hanging on to hope that we'll work it out."

"All right, well, just so you know, I don't care what they think. Yes, I'd love to have a relationship with them and those you consider important in your life, but I'm with you, not them."

Those words mean more to me than he knows, but I still can't help but sigh. "I hope they don't make things difficult. As I said, Mom's not so bad anymore, but things are still a little icy with Dad. I really need to see them soon. I can't put it off any longer."

"Well, as I've said, I go with the flow, so don't think you have to tell them anything about us. I know where your mind is at, so I'm good."

I reach across the table for his hand. I don't know if it's who he is or his age, but his outlook on everything is refreshing. "I really appreciate how understanding you are, but trust me, I won't take that for granted. I'm not like that."

"I know. I keep telling you, I know you better than you think."

After dinner, Mike and I spend God knows how long in his living room, making out on his couch. He doesn't push me to go to bed with him though, and I don't initiate anything further than kissing and feeling a few places above the waist.

His body is really hard under that shirt.

"I better go," I say for the umpteenth time. We're by the

front door now. "By the time I get home it will be eleven, and I have a long day tomorrow."

He steps back a little but keeps his hand on my waist. "You gonna tell me what we're doing Saturday?"

I smile. "Nope."

He pouts but I stand my ground. "Did you wanna do something Thursday?"

"Like what?"

"Dinner?"

"A normal date night, yeah?"

"Yeah."

"Good with me."

"I'll text you tomorrow with details. Will you be finishing late?"

I shake my head. "Not as far as I can see."

"Good." He kisses me one last time before I leave, and I think I float home.

Chapter Twenty-Six

"Do you like to travel?"

Mike and I have been playing twenty questions over dinner at River Oaks. He's wearing a suit, of all things, and my eyes almost escaped my face when I saw him in it. He figured as I was meeting him straight from work, he would dress smart too. I more than approved.

He licks cream off his spoon and smiles. "I love it. You?"

"I haven't traveled too much, but I plan to more. Where did you go last?"

"Lake Como in Italy. Ever been?"

"To Italy, yes. Lake Como, no."

His nod is thoughtful. "Where did you visit last?"

"Antigua, two summers ago. The only place I haven't been to in the Caribbean is Barbados."

He smirks. "I've been. You'd love it for the walks alone."

"I've heard." I wonder if there's anywhere he hasn't been, and to think there isn't is a little disappointing.

"Are you ready for moving day?"

That question distracts me from my thoughts. "Yep, but I'm

looking forward to yoga first. I'll be able to relax before the stress of all the unpacking I need to do."

"I bet. You still want me to help?"

That makes me smile. "If you want to, yes. Why?"

His eyes narrow. "It means I'll meet your friends."

"And?" I shrug. "They know about you."

"Yeah? What have you told them?"

I finish my water. *Ugh*...

He leans back in his chair with a look of knowing. "Go on, Nikki. That look is screaming something that needs to be confessed."

"Well, I kinda said something to Alicia after the first yoga class and it sort of might've stuck."

That piques his interest. "What did you say?"

I bury my head in my hands. "I may have said something along the lines of you being 'hot but a bit nerdy' when we first met."

He laughs, so I lift my head and see him shaking his head. "Nikki, Nikki, Nikki. I don't know whether to be offended or flattered, but I suppose I should take you mentioning me to your friend from our first meet as a compliment."

"You should. I didn't mean it in a bad way."

He leans forward to tuck my hair behind my ear and then in one fluid motion holds my chin. "Gates or Kent?

Gates or Kent? Oh, Bill Gates or Clark Kent. "Definitely Kent."

He drops his hand to finish his drink. "I hope to be."

"I'll be glad when you've moved," Mike says as he kisses me goodbye in the parking lot. "It will mean I get an extra hour with you."

"Me too." I smile up at him. "See you at yoga?"

"You will."

I'm in my feelings the entire drive home. I really, *really* like him, but I am scared. I only broke up with Bron two months ago, and I'm worried I'm rebounding with Mike. I don't think I am, but after all the relationship advice I've read and listened to, I know a lot of people end up doing that.

And then there are our differences...

The girls, and especially Rhian, said I was never broken from my relationship with Bron, so I should take advice from relationship gurus with a pinch of salt. And no, I might not think about Bron anymore, but is that because Mike has been distracting me?

Am I just enjoying the attention and newness more than him?

I don't know, but the last thing I wanna do is hurt him.

"Your form gets better each week."

I smile as I hold Mike's hand on the way to my car. He had his dad drop him off because I'm driving us for our Saturday outing today. "Any particular pose?"

"All of them."

I smirk. The sexual tension has definitely escalated between us now that kissing and groping has become a regular part of our relationship.

He is such a passionate kisser too.

"I appreciate the observation, especially coming from a pro."

"You're welcome. Are you not going to tell me where we're going yet?"

"Nope."

"I always tell you," he complains.

"I'm not you," I say as we jump in the car, then once he's buckled up, I begin the three-hour drive, hoping I've chosen well.

He's more than likely been there before, but in all honesty, I don't think there would be anywhere he hasn't been when it comes to places like this. Shame the drive is so long, but going by the pictures, I know it will be worth it.

"We have a bit of a drive, but we can stop for something to eat on the way."

"Good with me."

"How about you pick the music this time? I'm in the mood for a bit of Mariah," I say as I indicate.

He laughs, but he plays it.

After driving around like a crazy person in Maury County, I find somewhere to park a mile away from Rattlesnake Falls. We're going to have to walk the rest of the way because the only parking I saw close by was marked as private land.

Never mind though, I'm up for a hike.

I watch Mike's reaction as I grab my pre-packed rucksack from the trunk of my car. I brought us water, fruit, and some protein bars this morning because I thought maybe we could spend the afternoon here by the water.

"Have you been to Rattlesnake Falls before?"

He shakes his head. "Nope." He looks up at the sky. "You picked a good day for something like this. Not too hot."

"Good. I'm excited." I close the trunk and throw the rucksack onto my back, but Mike takes it from me as quickly as I get it on.

"I'll carry that."

"Forever the gentleman. Thank you."

He takes my hand. "I try. Ready?"

"My head says yes, but my thighs are already calling me a bitch."

He laughs. "Prepared to be sore tomorrow. You're moving too. You sure about this?"

"Yep, we're here now."

He shrugs. "All right."

I use the GPS on my phone for directions and we get moving. *I hope we don't get lost.*

"What made you choose this place?"

"I googled 'waterfalls near Memphis'. I liked the pictures and thought you'd like it too."

"I'm sure I will. I'm with you."

That makes me smile. "Exactly."

We don't get lost, and we make it to the falls after half an hour's walk.

"This is a bit steep," I say as I grab onto Mike's hand tighter. "I'm gonna fall."

"You won't. Hold my back instead."

I do as he suggests and follow him down the hill step by step. It's a little tricky and we both almost fall on our asses, but we make it in one piece.

"Wow. Now this was definitely worth the near-death experience."

"Without a doubt," he replies. "Wanna get in? It's not too busy."

"Are we allowed?"

He shrugs. "I don't see any police here. Why, are you scared of getting into trouble?"

"It would be a first if I did."

His eyes light up. "Then we're definitely getting in."

We put the bag and our shoes in a shaded area beneath the trees before making our way over to the falls, still in our clothes from yoga. We both brought spares though. I told Mike to make sure he did when I text him goodnight last night.

I gasp when I step into the water. "It's cold as hell."

"It is." Mike releases my hand as he wades a bit deeper.

"Really cold." He suddenly splashes water at me, and I squeal.

"What the—" I gape when he laughs, then he splashes me again. "Is that how it is?"

"Get him back, girl," an older woman says on her way past. "Get him good."

I kick the water toward Mike, but I miss because he leaps like a cricket. He doesn't dodge the next spray I send his way though.

His laugh stutters as he arches his back. The entire right side of his tank top is soaked through now. He gapes at me. "I splashed you, not soaked."

I cross my arms. "Too bad."

He kicks the water back my way, but I'm not the only one who shrieks when it hits its target. Turning around, I see a couple glaring over at Mike.

"Apologies," he says, holding his hand up. "She started it."

I almost choke from how shocked I am. "I did not!"

"Not the most mature thing to do when other people are here," the woman says. "Who raised you?"

"I..." I bite my lip so I don't laugh. If only she knew. "You're right. We'll stop."

After she turns away and continues walking with the guy she's with, my laughter unleashes as I playfully narrow my eyes at Mike.

"I started it, yeah?"

He laughs. "I'm sorry."

"'Who raised you,'" I say, mimicking the woman. "Miserable ass."

Mike laughs harder as he comes over to hug me. "If only she knew what your parents were like."

"That's what I thought." I link my arms around his neck to get closer. "Can we dry off now? This water really is freezing."

He nods above my head, shivering the same as me. "Let's find some sun."

. . .

I untie my hair so that can dry too. God knows what I look like because I didn't bring a mirror. I only know that Donna, as Tabitha would say, is no longer presentable.

"The sun feels so good," I say as I lie down on my back and close my eyes.

Mike's sitting cross-legged beside me. "It does. How's the meditation going?"

"I'm still doing it every morning, but although it's getting better, my thoughts refuse to shut off. The only time I ever accomplish it fully is when Jenny guides us through her ten minutes."

"There are lots of guided meditations online. Maybe you should try some of those."

"Yeah, I might have to do that. The books I've read make the benefits sound amazing, so I would like to be able to do it properly."

"How do you feel now?"

I take a deep breath and smile. "Happy." The heat on my skin is soothing and so is the sound of the water cascading over the rocks. I can hear Mike breathing softly beside me too, the light chatter of the other visitors close by, the birds chirping, and the rustle of the trees around us...

It's pure bliss.

I'm not sure how long I stay like that. I might even have fallen asleep, but when I open my eyes, Mike's smiling down at me.

"Did I fall asleep?"

"I don't know, but you looked like an angel."

My smile is instant. "Are you a magician like Jenny?"

He laughs. "No, I just know that happiness brings peace."

He's not wrong. "Have I told you how happy I am that I met you?"

"A few times."

"I'm saying it again." We always do the most spontaneous things, but I've never had as much fun in my life as I've had since I met him. He's really made me see the beauty and joy in the little things in life. Where I was always go, go, go before, now I long for the quiet moments.

The simple things.

"Should we make our way back?" he asks.

I nod. "Yeah, we should."

"I had such a good time today, Nik." He lowers to rest a soft kiss on my lips. "I don't want it to be over."

"Neither do I."

"Do you want to stay with me tonight?"

I sit up to start packing up my rucksack. "I'd love to... but I'm not ready," I confess, hiding my face and the blush covering it. "I'm not prepared." I haven't shaved since Dauphin Island, and I'm due a wax.

My legs are not only like cactuses, but I have an entire weave growing between them. I could probably braid it if I tried...

He grabs my hand to stop me picking up the water bottle. "I don't mean to stay overnight for that, Nikki—and even if I did, I wouldn't care about whether or not you'd prepped for the occasion."

I believe that.

"I..." I'm a little torn, but the desire to spend more time with him wins out, so I say yes. "The removal people are coming at eight in the morning though."

"So? I'm helping anyway, aren't I?"

"You are." I can't wait for the girls to meet him. Hopefully they'll stop calling him the hot nerd in the chat after they see him in the flesh.

"Well, then. We can leave at the same time."

He helps me up and the excitement takes hold. "All right."

Chapter Twenty-Seven

I used Mike's razor to shave my underarms and legs but that's as far as it went. I didn't have time to do anything else, but I gathered as long as my legs are okay, that would be enough, especially because the T-shirt of his that I'm wearing only covers down to the middle of my thighs.

I'm nervous, because although Mike has been single for years, he's older than me and likely has a lot more experience. I'm rusty as hell too. I haven't even given head for three years.

I'm not even sure I remember how.

As long as I don't choke. Or bite it...

Ugh.

Stop.

It will be fine...

I find him in the kitchen dishing out the takeout we picked up on the way home. He's showered too and looks good enough to eat in those cream pajama bottoms and matching tee. The attraction I have for him has certainly increased the more I've gotten to know him. The girls were right; being friends with someone first is definitely the way to go.

"It's been years since I had Thai food." I'm looking forward to it. Those snacks I bought were nowhere near enough.

Mike looks up from the plates and makes me shudder with his gaze. "I could get used to seeing you in here like that."

I don't hide my blush this time. "Is that so?"

"Without a doubt. Did you want wine with this, or water or juice?"

"Wine would be nice. I can get it."

"It's in the fridge."

"Do you have underfloor heating in here?"

"I do. I love the stone, but not the cold."

"Same." I find a bottle of white wine and then go in search of glasses and a corkscrew. "How long have you lived here?"

"Four years. I rented a few blocks up before I found this place."

"I don't blame you. If I'd found a house like this, I'd have bought it too."

"You might be able to buy yours eventually though, you said?"

"Yeah, and I probably will if I get the chance. I'm looking forward to everyone seeing it. It's so nice. You'll love the backyard."

I show him some pictures of the house over dinner, but not any of the garden. I want everyone to see it in the flesh when they see it for the first time.

"I love it just for how close you're gonna be. I can slip out and sneak through your bedroom window at night."

"A bit creepy. And another first for me."

He smirks. "Noted."

Silence falls between us after that. I'm dying to know what he's thinking about and if it's along the same lines as me. I wonder if he's nervous about us sleeping in the same bed too, because I get the feeling something might happen other than us getting some sleep.

"I have a spare toothbrush here," he says when we finish clearing up the kitchen.

"Thanks. I kinda already used your razor on my legs, so you might wanna change the blade before you use it again."

He laughs behind me as we head upstairs. "Kinda, or did?"

"I did. I didn't want to slice you to shreds in your sleep."

He runs his hand up my calf a little before humming to himself. "Looks like I'm safe."

My skin warms. *He won't be if he keeps touching me like that.*

As promised, he finds me a toothbrush, and after having a mini panic attack in the bathroom and psyching myself up, I join him in bed.

I need to calm down. He hasn't even hinted that he wants to take things further than this.

He rests his hand on my hip and gently tightens his grip before loosening it again.

Who am I trying to kid here? We're definitely going a few bases.

"Are you nervous?" I ask quietly, my nerves getting the better of me.

"A little." He looks up from my neck. "I don't want to disappoint you."

I practically scoff at that. "*I* don't want to disappoint *you*."

He gently shakes his head. "You won't."

"How do you know that?"

"I just know."

I take a steadying breath to calm my racing heart. "I've had one serious relationship in my life. Before that, I barely dated. I wasn't allowed."

He frowns. "They restricted that too?"

I nod. "Really. My experience is... let's just say, limited. My ex didn't believe in certain acts either, so I'm kinda out of practice with anything other than maybe three positions."

"Are you saying he never..." He glances to where his hand is beneath the covers.

"Nope. So while you're worrying because you've been single for years, I'm worrying because I barely have any experience whatsoever."

He curses under his breath, but then his hand lowers to my bare thigh before slipping it beneath the tee I'm wearing. "I can though, right?"

"Yeah, but not now. It's not—"

"I don't care."

Panic rises in my throat as I try to find a way to distract him, so I touch him instead, but I'm not ready for what I find.

I blink. "Is that...?"

His nerves seem to dissipate with the laugh that follows my question. "Told you I was better than your college boyfriend."

I snort, but then he's disappearing under the covers. "Mike, please. I haven't—" I gasp. "Oh God!"

Far from ready.

Stayed at Mike's last night. Will be at mine by 7:45-ish. See you all soon, and thank you so much!

After I send the text to the girls, I close my messages before the ambush begins. I wouldn't know what to say if they asked me the inevitable anyway.

I've barely been able to look Mike in the face over breakfast. We need to leave soon but between each mouthful of the porridge he made me, I keep zoning back out to the memories of last night.

I've been seriously missing out.

Thank God I decided to go natural with my hair too, because with the way he was pulling it when it was my turn to get beneath those covers, even the most heavy-duty lace front would've been ripped off my head.

I shudder. *Really missed that.*

"Beautiful?"

I turn my head to him beside me. "Yeah?"

"We need to leave in a minute. Are you not hungry?"

"I am..." To be honest, I wish we didn't have to leave this house. I feel as if I need to go back to bed with him to make sure last night was real. "We did have sex last night, didn't we?"

He smiles. "Y'know, if I wasn't so sure of how much you enjoyed yourself, I'd be upset by that question."

"Shit. I'm sorry, I didn't mean—"

"I know." He shakes his head as he gets up to clear his bowl. "Nikki, Nikki, Nikki... I never knew you were hiding such a wild side to you."

I blush all over again. He kept asking me questions, so I answered, or moaned my response. I may have even screamed a few times. Either way, I somehow managed to get out the answers he wanted to hear. He was a completely different man. He said he was nervous, but I saw not a glimpse of it.

'*I wanna know all the things you like. Don't hold a thing back from me, babe...*'

Those words had me heated, and the memory of him saying them has me feeling exactly the same way now. I've always loved how free he makes me feel, but to experience the kind of sexual freedom I did last night took that statement to an entirely new level.

He kisses my cheek when he returns. "The sooner we get you moved, the sooner we can be alone again."

My heart leaps, and so does another part of me. "I'm almost done."

. . .

The girls are standing at my door when we arrive at the house, so I point them all out for Mike so he's not going into this completely blind.

"Alicia is the mother of the group and the most serious, Rhian is carefree and is a lot like you—goes with the flow. And Chay, well, she has no filter, so just be prepared for anything with her."

Hopefully she'll behave.

"Got it."

The girls don't pay me one bit of attention as we make our way over to them: it's all on Mike. They seem impressed.

"Hey girls. Mike, this is Alicia, Chay, and Rhian. Girls, this is Mike."

"Hey," they all say innocently, all smiles too.

"Nice to meet you," Alicia says. "Nik's told us all about you."

He gives them all one of his cute smiles, and I feel it too. "So I've heard. It's a pleasure to meet you ladies."

The girls eye me, Alicia especially. She gives me a look as if to say, "Okayyyy, sis. I see you."

I shake my head as I open the door. "The movers will be here any minute, so we can start taking the boxes outside."

I know they're desperate to get me alone, but they're gonna have to wait.

Chay slams her hand over the box I've just opened. "Spill. *Now.*"

Mike's just left with the movers to collect the last of the boxes at the old house and leave my key, so we have about two hours before he gets back.

"Can you calm down?"

"Calm down?" she practically screams. "*Calm down?* Babe... This is big."

"Humongous!" Alicia says, appearing with Rhian. "You were glowing like a lighthouse when you arrived with him this morning. You slept with him, didn't you?"

I laugh. "Sorry, am I not allowed to have sex with the guy I'm seeing now?"

They all scream, deafening me in my left ear.

"What was it like?" Chay asks, and although I feel like holding back, I don't.

"Amazing. Girls, the way he spoke to me was everything. No one has ever said such sweet things to me before, and when I gave... The sounds he made took me right back to that karaoke night."

I was as high as a kite.

"Lawd," Alicia gushes. "I can't deal."

I laugh. "What do you think of him?"

"He's lovely," Chay says. "I like him for you. We kept clocking how he looked at you too. It was so sweet, babe."

Rhian and Alicia agree, and it's a relief.

"He makes me feel so good, girls. Like, *so* good. I feel so free when I'm with him and we always have fun." I tell them about our trip to the waterfall yesterday. "I never would have done that before."

"It's the little things," Alicia says. "I feel like a lot of people don't get that."

"Right." I'm only just beginning to.

"So just to clarify, the sex was good, right?"

I roll my eyes at Chay. "I just told you..." More memories surface and I smile, but then I giggle. *Actually giggle.* "It was unbelievable. Dare I say I'm actually a little sore, in several places, and it's not from yoga or that hike yesterday. I may have even invented some new yoga poses last night."

The girls literally scream my new house down with that information.

"Is he big?"

"Screw the size," Rhian says to Chay. "What was his stamina like?"

That makes me blush. "I have no complaints with either."

"And," Alicia starts, "did he pray?"

I laugh again. "Several times. I tried to stop him because I hadn't waxed, but he didn't care." All the guys I've been with before have preferred me practically bare down there. Bron was the exception, but I always made sure to keep on top of it when I was with him.

"That's a grown-ass man for you. They see past all that superficial crap."

"And women," Rhian adds, shooting her a look. "Us grown Queens like a little natural beauty too."

"Right. Craig takes me any way he can get me. Whew..." *These girls.*

"Have you told your parents yet?" Alicia asks.

"No, but I'm going to soon."

"How do you feel about that? Are you nervous?"

"A little, but like you and Mike keep telling me, it's my life."

"About time, boo," Rhian says, suddenly hugging me. "About bloody time."

"Yeah, well, I have to see how it goes first, but I don't want to think about that right now. What do you all think of my new place? You should see the yard."

"We love it. It's so you."

I take a look around the living area filled with boxes. "It really is. Mike lives in Collierville too, so I'm closer to all of you."

"You should have a housewarming party," Chay suggests.

"I was thinking about it."

"Let us know if you do. We can help you with the food."

"I will. Thanks girls, for today and for Sedona. If we had never had those conversations about me being more open and saying yes to all those things, I might not be here now."

"No thanks needed," Alicia says. "You've been there for all of us just the same. We love this new you. You deserve all good things."

Those words touch me deeply, and I pull them all in for a group hug. "Don't make me emotional, all right? God, I love you all so much."

"We love you too," they reply.

"Come," I say, releasing them to wipe my teary eyes, "let's start unpacking this stuff so I can make us all a drink at least."

I need to find the box with my toys in too, before it gets into the wrong hands.

Once Mike gets back, I give him and the girls a proper tour of the house. This place has two beds, two baths, and although smaller than my last home, it's more open-plan which makes it feel much bigger.

They seem to love all the rooms I show them, but I save the best till last. The one part of this house I wanted everyone to see in person.

"And this is the backyard," I say, leading them through the sliding glass doors off the living area. "My little paradise."

I watch their eyes light up as they come out onto the little decked area, and then I step down to the lawn to show them all my favorite areas. Starting to the right.

"These two trees here, I'm going to hang a hammock on. I thought it would be the ideal place to read, so you can send me book recommendations, Chay."

"Great idea. Who's gonna have your spare key?" She smiles sweetly. "This garden would be perfect to write in."

"You're more than welcome to, sis." I'd love for her to write out here. "I'll hook you up."

"I love this part," Alicia says, over by the raised flower bed to the left. "The people before you really took care of these." She runs her fingers over the yellow roses. "So pretty."

"I know. I'm hoping I don't kill them off. I might get a gardener." Really, I'd like to ask Mom to help out here, but with everything so up in the air with Dad, I don't know how that will work.

"Are you gonna put some lights up out here?" Rhian asks.

"I hope to. Especially over there." I point to the end of the yard where there are dozens more trees. "I can imagine lying under there on a soft, fluffy blanket." *Maybe making love...*

"Sounds like heaven."

"Doesn't it? I might put some kind of water feature in somewhere too."

"I love the sound of water," Chay says. "You should see if you can."

"Well, the landlord is pretty laid-back, so I'm sure he wouldn't mind."

I return to Mike and hold his arm. "What do you think?"

He rests a kiss on my forehead. "I think it's beautiful, just like you said. I can imagine you falling asleep out here after getting some yoga and meditation in."

"So do I," Alicia agrees. "You picked good, boo."

That makes me smile no end. "I did, didn't I?"

Almost everything is in its rightful place not long after midnight, with only a couple of boxes left to unpack downstairs. The girls were a godsend, and Mike overdid himself helping me get all my furniture rebuilt.

It's just him and me here now, and we're both exhausted.

"Thank you so much for today," I say, collapsing onto the couch beside him.

"You're welcome." He kisses my head when he pulls me

into his arms. "It was nice to meet your friends. It's clear to see how close you all are."

"We really are, and they liked you too."

"Good to know." His chest rises and falls, but I'm not sure if it's with contentment or relief. "You should sleep, Nik. It's late."

"I know."

"You've not got much left to do in here now. This place is nice."

That makes me smile. "It so is. I'm thinking of having a party to celebrate."

"You should."

I sigh. "I have dinner with my parents, my brother James and his wife after work tomorrow. Mom and Dad are visiting Spain the week after so they want a family dinner before they leave."

He holds me tighter. "It will be okay. I already told you, there's no rush for you to tell them about us."

"I know, but I want to. You're not a dirty secret, Mike."

"Hey, you've never made me feel like one." He yawns. "I know how you feel about me and that's what matters."

I turn in his arms and feel bad when I see his tired eyes. "I'm glad you know. Wanna stay over?"

"Yeah." He gets to his feet, and after helping me up and throwing me over his shoulder, he takes me up to my new bedroom, making me laugh the entire time.

I've always loved a man that could pick me up.

I let him shower first and find him a toothbrush, but when I finish showering, I throw on a nightdress, knowing that if I'm naked too, there'll be no way we'll be sleeping.

He pulls me closer when I get into bed. "As much as I really want to take advantage of you, I think it's best if we actually sleep."

I bury my head in his chest, closing my eyes and inhaling

the freshly showered scent of him. "I think you're right... You smell so good."

"You always smell good."

I pull away a little to kiss him, hoping he'll feel my happiness in it. "Goodnight."

He gently kisses my forehead before pulling me back into his arms. "Goodnight, beautiful."

Chapter Twenty-Eight

Something feels off when I wake up without hearing Alexa, and after grabbing my phone to check the time, I realize why.

"Shit!" I have an hour to get to work.

"Nik, what's wrong?" Mike asks as he wakes.

I've already jumped out of bed to look for clothes. "I'm sorry for waking you. I forgot to plug in Alexa, so I'm late."

He laughs. "You don't like to be late, do you?"

"Not if I can help it. It throws me off." I run to the shower and return in record time to find Mike drinking a coffee on the edge of my bed. Naked.

"You look good," I tell him, throwing him a glance. "No clothes really suits you."

"Oh, Nik... If only you hadn't neglected Alexa."

I want to roll my eyes but end up laughing, which calms me down. "You really balance me out."

"Glad to hear it. I made your coffee in your travel mug so you can take it with you."

"Thank you. Do you want me to drop you home on the way? I don't mind being late for you."

"As much as I appreciate that, no. I'll get a ride. You go." His eyes drop to my breasts when I button my shirt. "I'll plug Alexa in too. I might set her a little earlier though."

"Good idea. There's a spare key in the kitchen. Use that to lock up." I run over to kiss him quickly, before hopping out of the room with one heel on. "I'll call you at lunch," I shout, but I don't hear his reply.

I hope he doesn't try to unpack any more of those boxes before he leaves. My toys are in one of them...

But at least they're new.

Kelly keeps me plied with coffee all morning while I make my way through another two projects, and after the busy weekend I had, I'm glad. I can't stop thinking about that night with Mike either, which slows down my work pace. Still, by lunchtime, I've made good progress.

"I'm out for lunch today," Kelly says, popping her head in the door. "Need anything while I'm out?"

"A protein shake would be good." I need all the energy I can get.

"I'll grab one. See you in an hour."

She closes the door, and I call Mike. I'm fretting over the box my toys are in.

"Hey, babe," he answers.

"Hey. You okay?"

"Yeah, you? How's work?"

"The usual. Busy. What are you doing with your day?"

"I have a webinar in half an hour, and I need to pick up some groceries. I might go for a run. That's about it."

I wonder again how he doesn't get bored with working so little, but with how busy work is at the moment, I kinda envy him. "When did you leave mine?"

"Not long after you left. I forgot to post the key through the door so I'll give it to you tonight. Why?"

"No reason. I wanted to ask you something."

"Yeah? What's that?"

"I don't know if you saw it, but there's a box at the house with Bron's name on. I was gonna arrange to drop it to him this week."

"And?"

"Well, as we're seeing each other, I thought I'd ask how you felt about it."

"Fine with me, Nik. It's just a box."

I'm relieved. I know we're only dating, but I still don't want to hide anything from him. "Okay cool, 'cause I didn't wanna give it to my dad. He's already feeling a way about me not getting back with Bron so I'm trying not to encourage him to spend any more time with him than he currently does at church."

"Ah, so that's why he's so eager for you to go back."

"I think that might be part of it, but believe me, it's more about him thinking that's where I should be. If he asks about me going back tonight, I'm gonna tell him straight that I'm not."

"Whatever is best for you, babe."

"Yeah..." *Whatever's best for me.* "All right, I'll talk to you later. I'm gonna work through lunch so I'm not late tonight. I'll text you later. Good luck for your webinar."

"Thanks, beautiful."

I hang up and decide to text Bron now so I can get it over and done with. The sooner that box is out of my house, the sooner I can close out that chapter all together.

Hey, hope you're well. I have a box of your things if you want them? I thought I could meet you somewhere downtown this week. Let me know.

He replies almost immediately.

Bron: *I would like them thanks. I can swing by tonight if you're free?*

Me: *Meeting downtown would be easier.*

The last thing I want is for him to come over to my new house. Definitely not.

Bron: *Okay, that's fine. Can I get back to you? I'm out of town right now.*

Me: *No problem.*

At least that's over and done with. Just dinner with my parents to get through now.
It will be fine.

I find my brother and Vanessa already out in my parents' back yard, standing by the apple trees to the left of the patio table that's set for dinner. I smelt beef casserole as I came through the house and I'm almost certain Mom will have made her herby potatoes to go with it.
"How are you, sis?"
"Good," I reply, hugging Vanessa. "You?"
She steps away, back to my brother. "Tired, but I'm well. How are things?"
"I'm honestly good. You really don't have to worry."
She shakes her head as if she can't quite believe I'm telling the truth. "I can't say I've taken any breakup as well as you have."
My brother playfully punches my arm. "Runs in the family, huh, sis? We don't mope over spilt milk for long. Not allowed to anyway."

He's got that right.

Vanessa turns to glare at him. "Oh, so if I left you then you'd be back out dating tomorrow? You wouldn't be heartbroken, no?"

I watch the argument brewing between them, quickly thinking how to put an end to it. "Um, I was a mess at first, believe me," I say loudly, drawing their attention back to me. "Luckily though, I have some pretty amazing people in my life that made me see how great I am, which helped." I smile at my brother when he winks at me. "Thank you, both."

"You know we've got you, sis."

"I do, and I appreciate it."

"Dinner is ready," Dad announces, appearing with a casserole dish. Mom's following him out to the table with a crock pot too, so we all take our seats.

"Are you excited about your trip, Mr. and Mrs. Mack?" Vanessa asks my parents once we all have our plates.

"Very," Dad answers. "We had an incredible time when we visited last."

Mom smiles wistfully. "We did. Byron took me dancing and I ended up with sore feet, so he carried me all the way back to our suite."

That makes me smile. If there is one thing about Dad, he's forever the gentleman when it comes to Mom. Shame he can't seem to transfer that care to his kids.

Dad pats her hand. "I'd do it again too." He turns his attention to James. "Are you still okay to keep an eye on the house?"

"Of course."

We usually take turns to look after the house for Mom and Dad, and as I did the England trip, it's James's turn this time.

"And how's your new house?" Dad asks as he plates up the food. "I really wish you had let us help. Did you manage to get it all done?"

"I forgot you moved yesterday. How'd it go?"

"It was fine," I say to my brother, "and thanks, Dad, but I had plenty of help, and I'm pretty much all unpacked." I think about the box with my toys in again, but Mike didn't mention anything earlier when I called him, so I let it go. "The house itself is everything I could wish for and more. You'll all have to come over to see it. I'm thinking of having a housewarming."

"Be careful who you invite. You don't want people getting overexcited and trashing the place."

"I won't, Dad." I swear he thinks I'm still a teenager with the things he comes out with sometimes.

I'm relieved when he turns his attention to my brother. "And how are things with you, James?"

"Good. Business is doing well. We landed a high-profile wedding last week, so things are improving steadily."

"Well done, son. That's brilliant news."

"Yeah, well," Vanessa says, clearing her throat, "hopefully he can hire some other photographers soon, because he's going to be needed at home a little more than he currently is."

I frown, but then I widen my eyes at her. "Are you...?" I'm scared to say the word because they've wanted it for so long.

Her entire face lights up. "Yep, three months tomorrow."

Mom is already saying her prayers of thanks, and Dad is up shaking James's hand.

"I'm so happy for you both!" I gush. "So, so happy."

"Thanks, sis. Appreciate you."

"I'm gonna be an aunt." My happiness is overwhelming, and I experience a sudden rush of emotion. I really do have so much to be grateful for in my life at the moment.

Vanessa smiles. "It will be you one day."

I brush off her comment. "Oh, there's plenty of time for that. I'll let you keep the baby limelight for a while before I steal it from you."

"If you get back with Bron, you could have one now. Babies always bring people together."

I gape at my dad, barely holding my shit together. Why the hell would he bring that up now? "Can we not talk about that?" I say as calmly as I can manage. "This is James and Vanessa's moment."

"Thanks, Nik," James says. "Dad, Bron broke up with Nikki. It's not her responsibility to run after him."

I love my brother. He forever has my back.

"Nonsense. In my day—"

"Byron," Mom says shortly, resting a hand on his arm. "Please. We spoke about this."

"I'm seeing someone new," I blurt out. "He makes me happy."

James's smile is a smug one. "Nice. I told you you would."

"Excuse me?"

I turn back to face Dad. "I'm seeing someone."

He scoffs. "You only just broke up with Bron, Nicola. Don't be stupid."

"It's been ages, Dad."

"Byron, please," Mom insists. "Don't do this."

He shrugs his arm away from her hold. "No, I'm sorry, Annie, but I don't understand why she's being so difficult. She's only doing this to make Bron jealous, and it's wrong."

I see red. "I'm not doing anything because of Bron. I don't even think about him anymore."

"Of course you do. Bron feels the same too; he told me this morning at service—where you should have been, may I add—how much he misses you. Toya and Calvin said the same. He's been doing nothing but moping around, talking about how he should never have let you go. I told him to call you."

Anger explodes inside me, and I almost send the entire table crashing over when I stand up.

Calm down, Nikki. Vanessa's pregnant.

"I'm leaving."

Mom stands. "Nicola, please... Byron, why did you

encourage Bron that way when Nicola has told us loud and clear that she wouldn't be taking him back?"

"Nicola doesn't know what she wants."

Mom looks lost now, and I'm disgusted. "Nicola—"

"I'm sorry, Mom, but I'm not sitting here listening to this. I told you I'm not getting back with Bron, Dad. I've moved on. I'm the happiest I've ever been. I do fun stuff. I'm living life for the first time ever and I'm not going to let you ruin it."

He stands now. "Who do you think you're talking to?"

I ignore the fear rising inside me and turn to my brother and Vanessa instead. "I'm sorry to ruin your evening. I'll call you tomorrow, okay?"

James shakes his head. "Don't worry. We're good."

I grab my purse from beside my chair before storming toward the house. "Have a good trip, both of you."

"Nicola!" Mom shouts.

"Let her go, Annie. She's clearly lost her manners."

"Dad," I hear James begin, "why would you do that—"

I barely control the urge to slam the back door before making my way out of the house. I'm so angry I could smash up my car. How dare he tell Bron to call me! He's always had my number, and not once has he said anything about missing me in any of the messages he sent, and even if he did...

Maybe that's why he said he could've been better?

I push away those thoughts and scream when I get inside my car. Dad just doesn't know when to stop. It's like he has no respect for my boundaries whatsoever.

He's gone too far this time.

My mood has barely changed when I reach home. *How could he!* How could my own father continue to completely and utterly disrespect me like this? And to tell Bron to call me, even though I have repeatedly told Dad that I wasn't getting back with him, has quite honestly stunned me.

I slump down on the couch and message the girls, filling them in on everything Dad said.

Alicia is the first to reply.

What the fuck? You really need to put him in his place, Nikki. This has gone on long enough!

Chay: *I agree with her. This really needs to stop.*

Rhian: *You have to tell him how you feel, Nik. It's all good your mom talking to him, but I really don't think he'll get it until you tell him yourself.*

Me: *I know. I'm so angry! And they're going away for two weeks on Monday so I'm here feeling guilty that we've argued before they go.*

Alicia: *It's probably a good thing. It will give you a chance to calm down before you speak to him, and to think about what you're going to say.*

Me: *I don't know if I'll ever calm down. I feel disrespected by my own father!*

Chay: *I would too. He should have your back. It's awful, babe. I'm so sorry you have to deal with this. Are you gonna tell Mike?*

Me: *Probably. He's supposed to be coming over later.*

Alicia: *Talk to him. Don't hold any secrets back.*

Me: *I won't.*

I sigh as I rest my head back on the couch. I've been so happy, so chilled out, and now I feel as if my whole peaceful attitude has been smashed to pieces. How dare he?
How could he?

I try to relax in the bath before Mike gets here but it barely works. I try meditating too, but I'm way too riled up. I feel like texting my dad a ten-page message telling him exactly what I think of him, but the thought of hurting his feelings the same way he's hurt mine makes me feel even worse.

Maybe the girls are right. Maybe I need to take some time to calm down. Think logically about how to get my point across to him in a respectful way, even though he has no respect for me whatsoever.

There's a text waiting from Mom when I get back downstairs.

I'm so sorry, Nicola. I had no idea, I promise. I saw them talking but I didn't know what about. I'll talk to him. Please don't be upset. We love you so much.

I don't blame Mom, so I text her back, telling her I love her too, but I ignore the rest. I don't want to hurt her feelings or upset her any further before she goes away. When they get back though, I will be having words with Dad. I can't keep living like this.

My feelings matter.

I hear the door, so I get up from the kitchen table to answer and find Mike holding up my spare key.

"I didn't want to use it. Here."

"Keep it," I say, hating how snappy I sound.

"What's wrong?"

I usher him inside before locking the door. "Dinner didn't go well." I'm hungry, so I make my way to the fridge to find something to cook. My meal preps from Vegan Sistas came last night so I put one of those in the microwave.

"You haven't eaten?"

I scoff as I turn around. "Didn't get a chance. What my dad said made me sick." I sigh. "I'm sorry. I don't mean to be a bitch."

"You're not."

He comes to hold me, and I almost cry. "I don't think my dad respects me."

"What did he say?"

"He spoke to Bron's parents at church. Apparently, they were saying how unhappy he is, and then he told Bron to call me."

"Shit, your dad really is something else."

"I know." I pull out of his arms. "I told him I was with someone, that I was the happiest I've ever been, but he completely dismissed me and accused me of doing it to hurt Bron."

His jaw clenches. "No wonder you're upset."

"I feel so angry. I almost lost it."

He wipes my eyes. "No one can force you to do anything you don't want to do, Nik. You just have to be firm with him, and Bron, if needs be. Set him straight yourself when you give him his stuff."

"I will, and once Mom and Dad get back, I'll be telling Dad exactly how I feel too."

"And so you should." He pulls me back into his arms. "I know how hard this must be, beautiful, but it will all work out for the best."

I close my eyes. "I really hope so."

Chapter Twenty-Nine

Work the next day is tough.

I've barely been able to focus, and I'm finding it hard to get the torment out of my head.

My brother called me to let me know he isn't speaking to Dad either. They got into it after I left, and he and Vanessa ended up leaving too. I thanked him for the support but equally encouraged him to make it up with Dad. This problem is between Dad and me, not James, and I don't want it getting any messier than it already is.

My heart feels for Mom too. I don't want her being caught in the middle, and right now, she is. She tried talking to Dad after I told her how I feel, but everyone's right—it's not her responsibility to make him understand, it's mine.

But the worst and most worrying issue that seems to have come out of this is the fact I'm now suffering with being all up in my thoughts about my love life again. I keep replaying what Dad said over and over again, worrying whether there's any truth in it.

Bron replied to my message yesterday too, and I've ghosted it. Mike knows and still insists he isn't bothered by whether I meet up with him to give him his things, but with all the thoughts that are racing through my head, I'm worried about seeing him.

All my thoughts have become overwhelming, and I think I made the biggest mistake yet by googling "can interracial relationships really work?" for reasons unknown to me, and what I read has me not only confused but scared.

I text the girls.

Anyone free for lunch?

Chay: *Me!*

Alicia: *Me!*

Rhian: *I'm not. I have to get this blog post up by tonight before the sponsors withdraw. Will call you later though, Nik.*

Me: *Good luck, Rhi. Where do you girls wanna meet?*

Chay: *Gus's?*

Alicia: *Good with me.*

Me: *And me. See you two at 1.*

Hopefully they can help me see sense.

I relay my fears to Alicia and Chay, hoping they'll be able to reassure me in some way that all I'm currently feeling is merely a result of me letting people get into my head and stoke my anxiety, which I thought I'd seen the back of.

"Firstly," Alicia says, "just take a minute to calm down. We get that this is a lot for you, but it really is normal to be feeling this way."

I sip my wine. "Really? Because it doesn't feel like it. I mean, I don't regret saying yes to dating Mike, but I think I'm out of my depth."

"Okay, let's start with what your dad said. Do you feel as if you're using Mike to make Bron jealous?"

"Of course not. I'm with Mike because he makes me happy. I rarely think of Bron... But is that because Mike's distracting me?"

"Only you know that. Would you take Bron back if he contacted you and said he wanted to try again?"

"No."

"It's easy to say that though," Alicia says. "I know from experience how convincing exes can be."

Chay nudges her. "Don't say that to her."

"I'm not gonna sugar-coat shit for her. Sorry, Nik, but it's true. If what your dad said is true, you might be in for a comeback."

I sigh. "It's okay. I need the truth." No matter how much I don't want to hear it.

"And sorry to break it to you," she continues, "but looking up stupid shit about dating outside of your race isn't a good idea either, especially when you have two possible partners to choose from that are complete opposites."

Chay nods. "Now that part I do agree with. Your relationship with Mike is new so it's already sensitive, so looking for possible 'outs' at a time like this won't do you any favors."

I frown. "I'm not looking for an out."

"Maybe not consciously. Look, I've been where you are. You know I always dated black men before Craig, so I know how difficult that can be. Most of the people in my life didn't agree with it or encourage it, and their families were often the same. I couldn't tell you how many times we heard comments like 'you should stick to your own,' 'you're only dating him because you want mixed babies,' or even 'you're stealing black men' like they were some kind of "fashion accessory" to me. Trust me, I heard it all."

"What?"

She nods. "Yep. Sometimes, I think that until we all look the same, these problems with interracial dating won't ever go away."

Alicia agrees. "And it's not just black and white either. Dating Sean—"

I raise my hand. "Hold up, we have a name at last?"

"Oooh," Chay sings. "Alicia and Sean, that's cute."

She rolls her eyes. "He always had a name. *Anyway*, as I was saying, dating Sean's opening my eyes to a whole new side of interracial dating. His culture is different to any I've been involved with before. The key is not to care about the opinions of others. Sean's family isn't all mixed, yet they have been nothing but welcoming, for the most part."

"I forgot he was mixed."

"Yep. Stereotypes and other peoples' opinions are the devil, I'm telling you."

"The problem is," Chay says, "a lot of people only know what their parents, the media, and our societies have taught us about other cultures. People are naturally curious, so if and when people ask you something, nine times out of ten it's because they really are just asking. It's not always about color."

"Mike said that."

"You said Mike's dated black women before and already knows a lot of the territory, so the best advice I can give you is to learn not to give a shit about what other people think. You can't, otherwise you might as well just end things with him now."

I don't want to end things with him.

"Love is love," Chay says. "Anyone who genuinely wants you to be happy will support any relationship that does that. And if they don't, screw them."

"Says more about them than it does us anyway," Alicia says. "Let them be insecure in themselves. That's their problem, not yours. You think I'd be here now if my parents cared? My grandad tried to hide letters my dad used to send my mom when they first started dating. She only found them by accident."

I gape at her. "What the hell?"

"I know. Every generation gets better, but like Rhian said before, we still have a long way to go."

Ugh... I don't think this has helped at all, but I still thank them. "I appreciate you."

Chay rests her hand on mine. "Just do you. Leave everything else, all right? Block out the entire world and their opinions if you have to. Do not let other people ruin your happiness. You get one life. Live it."

"I'm trying to."

"Does Mike know you're planning to meet up with Bron?"

"Yeah. I asked how he felt about it before I even messaged him."

"If you do," Chay says, "you need to just hand that shit over and leave. If he tries bringing up anything personal, he'll reel you in."

"I already stopped him from coming by mine. I didn't tell him I moved, but he did offer."

"Good. He doesn't need to know where you live or what you're doing. He gave up that right when he left you."

"Exactly," Alicia agrees. "Meet, drop, leave. That's it."

"I will."

.   .   .

I answer the door to Mike when he arrives an hour after I get home from work.

"Hey."

He smiles as he comes inside and rests a kiss on my forehead. "Good day?"

"So far so good." I lead him into the kitchen. "I cooked us salmon with potatoes for dinner."

"Good with me."

"How was your webinar?"

He shrugs off his jacket to rest it on the back of a chair. "The turnout was good. Want some help?"

"No, I'm good. You sit down and I'll bring it over."

I feel his eyes on my back while I'm plating up the food, and I begin to wonder if he cares more than he's letting on about me meeting up with Bron.

Why is everything triggering me today?

"Here," I say, resting his plate down in front of him before sitting down with mine.

"Thanks, babe. Looks good."

"It's one of my favorites so I hope you like it."

He takes his first bite and says he does, but the usual silence that falls between us seems tense to me.

Am I becoming paranoid?

"You sure you're okay?"

He nods. "I'm good. Why?"

"No reason."

Maybe I am being paranoid. Mike usually says if something's bothering him. Besides, we're dating, not officially in a relationship, so technically it's not as if I'm crossing any boundaries.

Is it?

I wish I had more relationship experience.

I'm sure he would say something if he was bothered by it.

As much as he goes with the flow, he's always good at communicating. Maybe I'm projecting. How would I feel about him meeting his ex to give her things back to her?

If it was somewhere public, I wouldn't care. Going to her house, now that would be something else. I don't think I'd be upset though.

Or would I?

I give Mike a quick kiss on the cheek before I leave for work, careful not to wake him. He was up late working on his laptop when I finally fell asleep, at almost eleven, so God knows what time he eventually came to bed.

I'm trying not to overthink myself to death over him working around me all of a sudden, but it's hard not to. Since I mentioned that box and giving the contents of it back to its owner, things have been... weird.

The fallout with my parents isn't helping either. *Everything's such a mess.* I just need to put on my big girl panties and give Bron his shit back so I can tell him to stop talking to my parents. Then all of this can stop.

Just before I leave work, I decide to reply to Bron's message. I'm sick of the stress.

Hey, sorry it's taken a minute to get back to you. Work's been manic. When are you around next?

He calls me back before I've even left my office, so I go back inside and close the door.

"Hello?" I answer.

"Hey, Nik. I'm Downtown so I can grab those things, if you have them with you?"

Now? Uh...

Just do it!

"I do. I'm just finishing work, so I can meet you wherever."

"I can come to you if it's easier?"

"Uh, yeah, okay. I'll wait in the parking lot."

"All right. Give me ten."

"Okay."

I hang up and realize I'm shaking with nerves. I need to get a grip. It's just Bron.

"Nikki? You ready?"

"Yeah," I tell Kelly when I open the door. She's all ready to go with her jacket and purse. "I am."

"Cool. Any plans for tonight?"

I follow her out into the hall, toward the elevators. "I'm giving the ex the rest of his stuff. That's about it."

Her eyes widen as we step into the elevator. "Oooh. Meeting with the ex? You sure you're prepared for that?"

"Why wouldn't I be?"

"Have you seen him since you broke up?"

"No... Why?"

She stabs the first-floor button. "Be prepared for the feelings to rekindle. Those bitches ain't no joke."

"I'm seeing someone, Kelly. I have no intention of rekindling any feelings with my ex. The girls warned me already anyway."

"That's what we all say," she mutters. "Good luck."

We go our separate ways in the parking lot, and my heart beats a little faster as I walk to my car. I'm only giving him a box, so I honestly don't see what the big deal is here. Bron and his parents might've told my dad he misses me, but not once has Bron messaged or called to say that.

I get in the car and open up a message to Mike.

Bron finally called, about to give him his stuff back now. Am I seeing you tonight?

He said he'd let me know earlier on if he'd be coming over, but he never did.

Mike: *I have some online training to do tonight. Tomorrow?*

Online training? Since when does he do online training? He's definitely not telling me something, and the only thing that's changed is this situation I'm in now. If it bothered him, why not just say so?

Okay, cool. Good luck.

I startle when there's a knock on my window, and I look up to see Bron there. Remembering what Kelly said, I wait for the rush of emotion to come. I have to admit that I'm genuinely surprised when it does.

Meet, drop, leave, I hear Alicia say. *That's it.*

Maybe this wasn't such a good idea...

After I clear my throat, I reach for the door, and he steps back so I can get out.

"Hey," he says, smiling.

I look away as I head toward the back of the car. "Hey. It's in the trunk."

"Thanks. How have you been?"

I *was* fine... "Good, you?"

"So-so."

I open the trunk and Bron grabs the box while I barely resist asking him what's wrong, especially because his expression tells me he wants me to. He doesn't look any different, apart from the fact his beard isn't as neat as he usually keeps it. Apart from that though...

Just the same.

"Thanks for this. What are you doing now?"

"Going home." I close the trunk before walking back around the car, hoping that's the end of this conversation. I need to remember what the girls said and not complicate my life any more than it already is.

"I miss you."

I sigh. Why have those words hit me straight in the chest? "Please don't," I say, turning to face him. "It's been months."

His eyes soften. "I know. I still care though."

Is he serious? "Well don't waste your time. I know you've been talking to my parents at church, and I really wish you wouldn't."

He looks hurt by that. "You don't want me talking to your parents?"

"Not about me, no. I don't know why you're even interested after all this time." I'm a little taken aback by the sudden anger I feel, but I'm proud that I'm standing up for myself.

"I wanted to call, Nik, so many times, but I felt guilty over what happened. I didn't think you'd want anything to do with me."

"Could you blame me if I didn't? You walked out without talking to me about whatever was bothering you. I thought we were friends and that we could talk about anything. I thought we were a team, but you decided to make the decision to break up with me on your own, so whatever."

He holds the box tighter against his hip. "I was confused. You'd asked me for things I wasn't comfortable giving you."

So it was *about that.* "Well, there you go. It was for the best."

He steps closer. "I could try though. For you, I would. We could try new things, we could buy a house of our own, have kids. Whatever you want."

My heart aches a little when I think about the future I used to see for us. "It's too late now."

"Why is it? Are you seeing someone else?"

My defenses rise when I think of Mike, and then I remember how his ex did him. Maybe he thinks I'm going to do the same. "I'm not doing this."

He steps closer. "You are?"

"That's none of your business. The point is that I wouldn't trust you not to do it again, so it would never work."

"Look, I know what I did was wrong, but I still love you. I thought I was doing the right thing. I didn't want to put my shit onto you."

"So you do now?"

He shakes his head, frustrated. "That's not what I'm saying. I'm saying I was wrong. I'm saying... I fucked up."

The anger I feel is replaced with sadness. Those last words were so genuine, and I know he's telling the truth.

"Listen, I don't hate you for what you did. At first I was hurt, and I missed you. When I text you about the lease, I hoped you'd change your mind about us, but now... I honestly think it was for the best. You were right. We were more like friends."

"We weren't. Just give me a chance to show you."

"We are. I'm not the same. I've changed."

His eyes widen. "Changed how?"

"It doesn't matter. I just don't think it could work anymore."

"At least think about it. Please? I miss you in my life. No one has my back like you did. Whatever it takes, Nikki. I'll do it."

"There's nothing you can do; it's just too late. I'm sorry."

"Nik, please."

As quickly as the guilt comes for upsetting him, it leaves. He had me when all I saw was him, but I'm just not that woman anymore. "I've gotta go. Take care, Bron."

"You too," I barely hear.

I breathe a sigh of relief when I close the car door and he

walks toward his. I can't go back—it wouldn't be the same. I'm free now and it's true what I said, I'm different.

If he'd said these things sooner, then maybe it could have worked out with us, because we always saw the future the same. But he ruined it, and now I have to do what's best for me.

I have to put my feelings first.

Chapter Thirty

"That cheeky prick," Chay says on the three-way.

"Right," Rhian agrees. "Like you'd take him back after how he did you."

Chay laughs. "He thought he was talking to the old Nikki. I bet he got the shock of his life."

"Right," Alicia agrees. "The audacity."

I smile sadly as I pick at my food. "To be honest, I did feel kinda bad for him. He offered everything I ever wanted."

Everything I'd like from Mike.

What Bron said has me questioning what I truly want in life and where my happiness lies. Bron and I always saw the future the same way—our own house, kids, marriage, but Mike lives in the present, and he never so much as mentions anything to do with the future. And I know we're only seeing each other, but if I'm going to invest more in him emotionally, I need some reassurances...

"We told you not to let him get in your head," Chay says.

"He didn't," I lie, knowing full well he did, "and I'm not getting back with him. Not because of Mike, but because I'm just too different now. I mean, could you imagine what Bron would say if I suggested coming with me to yoga?"

That makes them laugh.

"Whatever the reason," Alicia says, "I'm proud of you. You've stuck up for yourself, which is something we've all been waiting to see more of."

That lifts my mood and distracts my thoughts. "I know. It feels pretty amazing."

"What did Mike say?"

"I haven't spoken to him. He's training tonight."

"Oh, well that's shit. Are you seeing him after?"

"I dunno yet. Work's tough right now, and with the mental stress of the fight with Dad on my shoulders, I could probably do with an early night anyway." I don't tell them about the weirdness between us. I didn't really want to tell them what happened with Bron before I told Mike, but I needed to talk it out.

It's how I deal with stuff.

"All right. We'll let you go," Rhian says, "but we're glad you're feeling a little better."

"So am I."

"Definitely gonna be a book," Chay says, and I roll my eyes.

"Any date for the housewarming yet?" Alicia asks.

"No, but I'll have one soon. I know you need it for the girls. I'll see if I can have it on a weekend you're free."

"That would be good but let me know either way."

"All right." I say goodbye to them all before going up to collapse onto my bed. I'm mentally drained. What a day.

Thank God it's almost Friday.

"Nikki?"

"Hmm?" I moan, opening my eyes. It's dark and I'm still fully dressed. Mike's sitting beside me too. "What time is it?"

"Just after eleven. I called you, but you didn't answer."

"My phone must still be on vibrate." I rub my eyes. "I'm tired."

"Clearly. You left your front door unlocked."

I smile. "You didn't climb through my window then?"

He chuckles. "That would've been my next move. Are you all right? I didn't hear from you after you saw Bron. Did it go okay?"

I nod. "Yeah. I need to talk to you, but it went fine."

"We can talk tomorrow. Go get changed. I'm tired too."

I leave him to wash up and can't help but feel good at the fact he's here. After the way the past couple of days have been, in all honesty, I'm surprised.

"Have you eaten?" he asks when I climb into bed.

"Yeah, earlier."

He pulls me closer and kisses my forehead. "All right. I missed you," I think I hear before I fall asleep.

I missed him too.

The next time I wake, it's to the sound of my alarm going off.

"Alexa, stop," I say. I don't even open my eyes.

"Call in sick," Mike says, sounding groggy.

"I've never done that." I turn to look at him. "I'm seriously considering it though."

"Text Kelly and say you're not coming in."

I feel a twinge of guilt, but before I can let it really kick in, I reach for my phone.

I'm taking a personal day. Let Marcus know please. Be back tomorrow.

Kelly: *No problem. Sending love.*

The last thing I remember is Mike putting my phone back on the side.

After I wake up in an empty bed, just after eleven, I take a quick shower and then find Mike downstairs in the kitchen. He's on his laptop but closes it when he sees me.

"Hey, beautiful. Feeling better?"

"Much, although I do feel a little bad for calling in."

"Don't be. You clearly needed it. I made breakfast. Come sit down. I'll get it for you."

He retrieves a covered plate from the oven and then reveals French toast and berries when he places it in front of me.

"This looks amazing, thank you."

"You're welcome. So how did yesterday go?"

I decide to ask him a question first. "Did you feel a way about it after I told you?"

He frowns. "What do you mean?"

"Things between us have been weird since I mentioned giving Bron his things back. You've even started working more."

He appears genuinely surprised. "Nikki, I swear, I didn't feel any sort of way about that. I have changed a few things with work recently, yes, but mostly I was trying to give you space. I know we've spoken a lot about your ex, but I didn't want to get involved with that."

"So you weren't upset that I decided to see him?"

"Of course not. I've told you, I know where your mind is at, so why do I need to be concerned?"

"But you becoming distant made me unsure about us, and it added to the stress I was already feeling after the argument with my dad."

He holds my hand across the table. "I'm sorry, Nik. That wasn't my intention."

I sigh. "I know that now." I suppose I need to get better used to his laid-back way of doing things. "Anyway, I spoke to Bron when I saw him…" I fill him in on what was said, but again, he doesn't give the reaction I was expecting.

He pretty much just shrugs it off, and it triggers the hell out of me.

"Hopefully your dad will get the message too."

"Yeah, I hope so."

I try to swallow down the wave of insecurities and emotion about Mike's seeming lack of empathy, but it's difficult as hell. *Does anything ever bother him?*

"I didn't get to ask you how lunch went with the girls on Tuesday?"

"Uh, it went okay."

He gives me the look he always does when he knows there's something bothering me. At least he's observant that way. "Spill."

"Well…" I hesitate telling him, but I'm still feeling annoyed, even if I don't really know why. "They were giving me the lowdown on relationships from their past experiences."

Now that seems to shift his mood. "Right…"

I look down at the last of my berries, bracing myself for his reaction to what I'm gonna say. "What Dad said had me stressing, and I somehow ended up googling interracial relationships."

"Nikki…"

I lift my head. "I know I shouldn't have—"

"Do you want to be with Bron?"

I recoil. "What? No, of course I don't. Did you not just hear what I told him yesterday? And I was talking to someone while we were spending time together as friends, remember, but I cut him off as soon as I got back from Dauphin Island."

"So is me not being black the problem? Is it going to be a problem? Because if it is—"

I reach across the table to hold his hand, hating how what

I've just said has made him feel. I wanted more of a reaction from him, but not this one. "It's not. You make me happy. That's why I'm with you. I'm an overthinker, you know that. I also research everything. It's what I do. I'm trying to get a handle on everything..." I'm rambling. "Does that make sense?"

He nods.

"The last thing I want to do is hurt you, Mike. You can't begin to understand how much I love being around you. How much joy you've brought into my life. I'm trying to be prepared for anything, that's all. Not only do I not want to ruin this, I don't want anyone else to be able to either because I wasn't ready."

He sighs deeply. "You're stressing me out, and I haven't been stressed out in years."

"I'm sorry. I'm not trying to."

"I know. For some reason, you seem to have a way of getting to me like no one ever has. I worry more now than I have in a long time."

"It's hard to believe that. You barely show emotion over anything."

"It might not look that way, but I still feel."

That's news to me. "Over what?"

"Mostly you. Like when we go out and I see people looking, I worry if you see them and what you think if you do. I worry someone will say something to hurt your feelings because this is so new for you. So, when you say you want to be prepared, I do understand. I just wish you didn't have to be."

"The girls said to block the whole world out if I have to, just don't let anyone come between us."

He tugs my hand to lead me around the table so he can pull me onto his lap. "I like your friends more every day."

"Me too." I rest my head on his shoulder and let my worries fade. "You've changed so many things in my life."

"So you said the other night." He slips his hand up my

nightdress. "That's really why you're with me, isn't it? For the sex."

I lift my head as I laugh, and it feels really good to. "I agreed to date you before we had sex, so not really."

"But you knew I'd be different. White guys are known for their 'freaky' shit."

I smile. "Is that stereotype true?"

"It is when it comes to me." He kisses me, and my heart races because of how passionate it is. "I like you so much, Nik," he says when he pulls away. "You're all I think about these days. Planning trips with you is the highlight of most of my days."

"I feel the same," I reply breathlessly. "I can barely remember what life was like before you came along. I think I was just existing."

"Do you believe in fate?" he asks.

"Sometimes. I believe I was meant to meet you."

"So do I." He lifts me off his lap and then takes my hand. "Come with me. I think I need to remind you exactly how good we are together."

"Yeah? And how are you going to do that?"

His eyes light up. "You'll have to wait and see."

"I'm gonna have my housewarming next weekend," I tell him over dinner. We ordered takeout because we spent most of the day in bed and are both tired again.

For better reasons this time though.

"So you decided then?"

"I did. I don't want to miss yoga, so I planned it for the Sunday afternoon."

"Good idea."

"And... I was thinking maybe you could invite a few of your friends and family too, if you wanted to?"

I hold my breath after I ask him that. If he says yes, I can take it as a sign he's thought of us long term, not just someone in his life for right now.

He smiles. "Sure. I can do that."

I'm relieved. "Great."

"Did you not want your parents there?"

"If they weren't away then I would've invited them, but it's probably a good thing that they won't be. Dad would ruin the fun."

"Ohhh, I see, so while the parents are away..."

"Exactly. My brother and his wife will come though, and Kelly from work. The girls obviously, and their partners. Most people will bring a plate too, so I won't have to cook a whole lot. It will be nice."

"I'll look forward to it."

"Me too."

"There's something I wanted to ask you, Nik," he says as he rests his fork down.

My nerves rise. "Okay..."

"How would you feel about being my girlfriend?"

I smile, but a part of me feels uneasy. "Are you asking me because of what we talked about earlier?"

"This has nothing to do with that. I've actually wanted to ask you for a while now."

I'm a little surprised by his answer. "Does that mean you're deciding not to always stay in the present? 'Cause if you're asking me to be your girlfriend, it must mean you see us somewhere in the future."

His expression turns thoughtful. "I like spending time with you, and I care about you a lot. I don't know what the future holds, but right now this between us is good, don't you think?"

I nod. "I do, but sometimes..."

"Go on."

"Well, I kinda wish you planned ahead a little bit."

He frowns. "In what way?"

"In life. Five-year plan maybe? Or even two? It's just, although I'm in your present and things are good, it would be nice to know we're headed toward the same future."

"I don't want to make promises that I might not be able to keep. I almost lost my life, Nik. It's why I live it like I do. Is anything wrong right now?"

"Not right now, no."

"Well then." He smiles. "So? Yes or no?"

"Yes or no?"

"Will you be my girlfriend?"

Do I want to be? Yes. Am I still a little worried about where we're headed, even though he wants to put a title on us? Yes. But I decide to take another leaf out of his book and live in the now. "I'd love to be your girlfriend."

"Good." He picks his fork back up to continue eating, and I watch him smile to himself. "Now I can stop adding 'the girl I'm seeing' after your name every time I mention you to someone."

I laugh, and it lightens my mood. "Such a romantic."

He pops a sweet chili chunk into his mouth and winks. "I know."

Chapter Thirty-One

Mike: *Can we rearrange tonight? I forgot I have a webinar at eight.*

The excitement I'd been feeling about trying the new vegan restaurant that's opened up near my house leaves me as I read Mike's message.

Really?

I stare at my work emails, looking for an outlet, like it's their fault.

Just let it go, it's only dinner...

Me: *No problem,* I reply. *I'll see if I can get into Jenny's class tonight instead.*

Mike: *Sorry, beautiful. We can go Monday evening, if you want?*

Me: *Sure. See you later and good luck.*

I swipe out of his messages to send one to the girls' chat instead.

Alicia, do you think Jenny could fit me into her class with you tonight?

Alicia text last week to let me know she'd started Jenny's new class over our sides. Jenny also mentioned how nice it was to have her back again on Saturday when I saw her.

Alicia: *Let me text her. It's new so I'm sure she could.*

Rhian: *Me too. I'm free tonight and could do with some destressing. This new blog is kicking my ass.*

Chay: *Not me. Tummy's playing up and I don't wanna shit myself. Have fun, girls.*

Alicia: *Haha, Chay. All right. Give me ten.*

Ten minutes later, she replies.

Alicia: *All good to go. Meet at 7?*

Me: *Yep.*

Rhian: *Hell yes. See you later girls.*

"Here's your coffee," Kelly says as I rest my cell down. "And I got you a cupcake too."

I smile at her. "Thank you."

"No worries." She sits opposite me with one of her own. "I made sure I got first dibs this time. Those new project managers don't play about their cupcakes."

"So I heard." Still, I don't mind missing out on cupcakes for less stress.

My phone vibrates again, but the smile that was gracing my face leaves with the name I see on the screen.

Mom: *Hope you're well, baby. Please let us know when you're free.*

I groan.

Kelly shakes her head. "That doesn't sound good."

"Because it's not."

"Wanna talk about it?"

I sigh. "I kinda fell out with my parents."

"Oh... Sounds tense."

"It was. My dad only sees life one way, and that's his."

"Just cut him off."

I scoff. "That's easier said than done."

"Why is it?" She takes a bite of her cake. "Regardless of it being blood or not, if someone isn't adding value to your life, what's their purpose for being in it?"

I peel the wrapper from my cake. "That sounds toxic as hell, Kelly."

She laughs, like I'm delusional. "No, what's toxic is keeping people around when they make you unhappy. For what? Self-harm?"

I silently eat a bite of my cake. *When she says it like that...*

"You *do* wanna be happy, right?"

I nod.

"Well then. If it makes you sad, give it up. Life's too short."

"He's my dad though."

"So? You still don't owe him anything. Besides, he's not loving you unconditionally if you can't do anything right. Trying to be something you're not is toxic."

"Maybe..."

She screws up her wrapper. "Stick with me, Nikki. I speak nothing but facts."

That makes me chuckle. "Thanks."

"That was well and truly needed," Alicia says after we leave class. "Sean loves my yoga poses."

Rhian and I laugh. It's so nice to hear how happy she is these days. Not so stressed out all the time. "I agree. It was."

"I thought you were having dinner at that new place you've been gushing about?"

"We were, but Mike's been working more and had a webinar."

I see the looks between her and Rhian while I hold the door to the parking lot open, but I keep quiet. I wonder if they know something's off, because I swear I feel it.

"Why don't we still go?" Rhian says. "Alicia, do you have to get back?"

She shakes her head. "I'm sure Mom wouldn't mind staying a little later. I'll text her."

The three of us end up at Maya's Kitchen twenty minutes later. It's really nice here, and much larger in size than I expected. They also have a wide range of imitation meat dishes, which goes down well with the girls.

Once we order, I send a message to Mike. He didn't say how long his webinar was running for, but I guess he'll get my message at some point. He's meant to be staying at mine tonight...

Hey, hope your webinar's going okay. Girls and I went to Maya's so I'll see you after

"Right, what's going on?" Rhian asks when I put my cell back in my purse.

I laugh uncomfortably. "Nothing."

"Don't start that shit again," Alicia hisses. "Yeah, I understand wanting to keep your relationship private, but we're still here for you."

I take a deep breath, uncertain of whether I should get into this conversation. I'm worried about what might come up. "Mike's working more, that's all."

"And?"

"We've not been seeing eye to eye on some things."

Their nods are knowing.

"It's my fault—"

"Hold up," Rhian says, lifting her hand. "Before you start internalizing everything, tell us what's been going on."

"He's canceled dates last minute, and I've kinda been nagging—"

"Nagging in what way?"

I sigh. "He's such a free spirit, y'know? And it's something that I do love about him, but..." *Ugh, how do I say this?*

"But?" Alicia pushes.

"It doesn't make me feel safe." I close my eyes briefly when I admit that. "I've tried so hard to let it go and stay in the moment, but the more time that passes without knowing where we're going, the more I realize how important it is to me."

Their faces fall. "Oh..."

"Yeah. He's always been that way too, so I feel bad for complaining about it now, and he is an amazing guy..." I stop there. I knew we were different when we were getting to know each other, so I don't really have any right to moan about it.

Rhian's smile is sympathetic. "Security is important to any woman, Nik. You shouldn't feel bad about it. Joi's asked me the same things, especially with me traveling so much, but I found a way to make her feel secure."

"But I don't know if I only feel this way because I'm used to having that with Bron, y'know? We always saw the future the same, so I guess I'm just used to that. I honestly don't know."

"What's he said when you've told him how you feel?"

I clear my throat. "He says things are good right now, and he's right."

"But they're clearly not though," Alicia says, leaning back when her food arrives. She thanks the waitress before returning her attention to me. "You should talk to him about it properly, Nikki. I don't think he's grasping just how important this is to you."

"Me either," Rhian agrees. "I know you really like him and he's fun, a great guy even, but your core values have to match, otherwise you're just wasting your time."

I hate that she's said that.

"You don't think..."

"What?"

"That I've got swept up in a fantasy, do you?"

The consensus is no, but I don't miss the concern in their eyes that mirrors mine.

"I think you just need to talk to him properly, and maybe do a little soul searching yourself. You've come a long way. You don't wanna go back to putting your own feelings aside again, no matter how amazing someone is."

"Agreed," Alicia says. "You have to be honest, to yourself and him."

"Yeah... Thanks." I smile as I watch them eat, but my appetite seems to have left me.

Be honest with myself.

Mike's already at mine when I get home. He's in the kitchen on his Mac but closes it when he sees me. "Hey."

"Hey." I rest my purse on the side. "You okay?"

He nods. "Tired, but good. You?"

"Same. How was your webinar?"

"Good." He leans over to kiss me when I sit beside him. "How was dinner?"

"Really nice, and the food is great. You'll like it."

He nods as he sits back down, but then I see something that looks a lot like hurt in his eyes. "You should've said you were still going and I would have come after I was done."

"It was a last-minute thing. The girls suggested it after we left yoga."

He's quiet for a moment. "I wanted to take you there."

"But you canceled." I surprise myself with how blunt I am, but the talk with the girls still has my feathers ruffled.

"Not on purpose." Now he *sounds* hurt. "I really did forget about that training."

"I know." I sigh. "I was disappointed when you canceled, but as I said, I didn't plan on still going."

He sighs deeply. "I'm sorry. I'm glad you had a good time."

"Thank you."

He holds my hand, stroking his thumb over mine like he always does. "No more canceling, all right? I'll get a planner."

I laugh. "A planner?"

"Yeah." He's smiling now. "Let's go to bed. I'll make it up to you."

I smile in knowing. "I thought you were tired?"

He shakes his head while pulling me up with him. "Never too tired for that."

Chapter Thirty-Two

Mike and I settle into a routine of spending alternate nights at each other's houses, and with Alexa waking us up a little early, we even get time for "adult meditation" before I have to leave for work.

I still haven't spoken to him about my continuing fears about us, which I know I should, but with things being up in the air with my parents, I haven't wanted the additional stress. I'm trying to go with the flow.

Still, I wonder what life holds for the both of us, and I can't lie and say that I'm not missing the security of knowing that my partner feels the same way I do about the future. With Mike being so carefree and changing what he does every second, it's hard not to wonder if he could wake up one day and decide to just up and move or something crazy.

I'm trying to respect the way he is, but I can't lie and say it's not hard sometimes.

Mom and Dad have been away for five days now. Mom's sent me pictures of various places they've visited and random dishes of paella—which I expected, but our messages to one another have been brief. I've asked how Dad is when I've checked in on them, but that's as far as it's gone because I'm still upset.

I don't want to hold on to the bitterness I'm feeling, but until they're back and I can tell Dad how I feel once and for all, I don't think I'll be able to forget about it.

Work has also been manageable—the new project managers have taken a massive weight off all of us—so all in all, life is good.

I've been spending the past few days shopping for decorations for my housewarming tomorrow evening. So far, I've hung lights in my garden, placed the banners, and right now I'm finishing up laying out the disposable tableware. Mike bought me a firepit too, and enough logs to last me a year, and we had dinner beside it last night, which was wonderful.

The garden really is the best part about this house, or at least it will be as long as I can keep those plants alive.

Mike's invited his friend Kevin, his dad, and Keosha to my party, but I'm not nervous about meeting them, I'm excited. Mike wanting me to meet some of the important people in his life tells me that I mean as much to him as he does to me. It even makes me wish I'd waited until my parents got back so he could meet them too, but then again I don't think it will be a good idea for him to see Dad until I've set my boundaries with him first.

The girls are all bringing their partners. Craig, I already know, but I'll finally be meeting Alicia's boyfriend Sean, and Rhian's girlfriend, Joi. Rhian and Joi have been spending almost every day together—they've even joined forces and have planned to set up a joint blog, combining food and travel, which launches next month. Rhian does nothing but gush about it and her. She was single for two years before Joi and has struggled with issues within her own family. She didn't tell them she was gay until she was halfway through college and her grandmother —God rest her soul—far from approved. It caused a lot of tension within her family and resulted in her father cutting his mom off over it. They only made up a few months before she passed away.

"Right, I think that's everything," I say, placing the last pile of paper plates on the kitchen table. All the food is prepped in the fridge, ready to be put into the oven tomorrow, and the girls are bringing the drinks, so I don't need to worry about that.

Mike checks his phone on the side. "Be prepared to receive a mountain of food tomorrow. Keosha's been cooking up a storm, so Dad said."

"That's so sweet of her. Tell her thank you." I did say not to worry about bringing anything when Mike asked if I wanted them to, but they wouldn't hear of it. I overheard his dad telling him to "be quiet" when he refused.

"Already did." He drops his phone and comes to wrap his arms around my waist. "Still excited to meet them?"

"Very."

"I told them all about you."

That makes me smile. "Did you now? Well, I can't wait to meet them. Especially Kevin. Are there any skeletons in your closet that you wanna confess to before he tells me?"

He smirks. "You'll have to wait and see."

"That's a yes. Tell me."

"Nope." He tickles me, and after screaming my lungs out and fighting for my life, I manage to break free from his hold.

I hold my chest. "It's been years since anyone tickled me."

"I didn't realize how ticklish you were."

He comes toward me, but I step back. "Please don't—ow!"

I turn around to the cactus he bought me as a house-warming present. "Your plant pricked me."

He laughs. "I told you to put it higher up."

"There is nowhere higher up for it to go. I need shelves. Better put that on the list."

"I can grab some," he says as he picks up his jacket.

"Where are you going? I don't need them now."

"I know. I have to pick Kevin up from the station, remember?"

"Oh yeah. Is that the time already?"

"Yep. You know what they say about time flying." He comes to kiss me goodbye. "I'll be here by ten, without Kevin. If you need anything, let me know."

I grope him. "I will."

"Careful, I may sneak over in the middle of the night to see if your window's open."

"You know where my bedroom is. You'd fit through it too."

He smiles as he steps around me. "Nikki, Nikki, Nikki. It's a good job I don't have a corporate job with how insatiable you are."

I mock gasp. "I am not. If anyone is, it's you."

"I don't know what you're talking about," I hear before he leaves.

I'm still smiling long after he's gone.

If I'd have known just how much Keosha was cooking, I wouldn't have bothered making any food myself. There's an entire buffet lining my kitchen sides, and only one tray so far is something I cooked.

"You really didn't have to. Thank you though. I'm sure it won't go to waste."

"It definitely won't with Kevin around," Mike mutters.

"Don't you worry, hun. It was my pleasure." Keosha introduces herself properly, followed by Mike's dad, Peter, and I like them immediately.

"It's so nice to meet you both, and thanks for coming."

"Thanks for having us," Keosha says. "Your new home is beautiful."

"Very nice indeed," Peter agrees. "Reminds me of my first place. I loved that house. Where are you originally from?"

"Raleigh growing up, Midtown more recently. Mike told me you're from Whitehaven?"

"That's right—"

"Blackhaven was the best, ain't that right, Mikey?"

We all turn to Kevin when he finally reappears from the bathroom.

I only caught a glimpse of him when he arrived with Peter and Keosha. He said he'd eaten something that didn't agree with him before he ran up the stairs, two at a time.

"It was," Mike replies, dapping his friend. "This is Nikki. Nik, this is Kevin."

He smiles as he shakes my hand. "Nice to meet you, Nikki."

"And you."

"Now I see why he's obsessed with you. You're all he ever talks about."

I laugh. "Nice to know."

Mike shakes his head. "Bro, can you not?"

"I'll give you the juice later," he says quietly, but Mike still hears. Kevin ignores the look Mike shoots him and compliments the house instead. "Real nice."

"Thank you. The garden is the best part. Please all make yourself at home while you're here. Drinks are in the fridge, and there's a cooler out the back too."

"Will your parents be coming?" Keosha asks.

"They're actually in Spain right now."

"Oh, how nice."

"They travel a lot. I'm sure you'll meet them soon though."

She smiles. "We'll look forward to it."

"Hey, hey, hey," Kelly says, walking straight through the open door. "Where's the party at?" She looks beautiful, as always, dressed in a light pink wrap dress, and is holding a bottle of Cîroc in her hand.

"You're early." I'm not used to people arriving at my parties on time.

"I thought I'd come see if you needed help." She takes a quick look around. "Wow, love the house."

"Thanks. Everyone, this is my friend, Kelly."

She says hello to everyone in here but smiles a lot harder when she shakes Mike's hand. "The 'if Mike calls let him through' Mike."

This girl. "That's the one."

Mike chuckles. "A pleasure to meet you, Kelly."

"And you. Nikki's all brand new since she started dating you."

I roll my eyes. "Thanks, Kelly, but he's actually my boyfriend now. Do you wanna put that bottle over on the side?"

"Sure."

She wanders off and Kevin follows close behind her.

"Should she be worried?" I whisper to Mike.

"Should *he*?"

"Knowing Kelly... I'd say yes."

It's half an hour before Alicia arrives. She's hand in hand with Sean, all giggles and smiles and... *different.* I've honestly never seen her like this before, and Sean is pretty much the same.

"Sis, who's glowing now?" I say quietly, cornering her in the kitchen.

She smiles as she looks over to him. "He does that to me. Do you like him? We look good together, right?"

"You really do. You have no idea how happy I am for you."

"I do. Trust me."

"Nik?"

I peek my head around the kitchen alcove to see Rhian and who must be her girlfriend, Joi, chatting to Sean and Mike. I wave her into the kitchen, where she introduces us, but we're soon interrupted by Chay arriving with Craig.

"I can't believe you're all in here introducing girl and boyfriends without me."

"Maybe your ass should've been on time then," Rhian snipes. "You knew we were bringing plus ones."

Chay rolls her eyes and introduces herself and Craig to Sean and Joi. "I'm the best friend and this is my boo."

"Girl, stop. Seriously. Craig, get your girl."

"You know I can't." He pulls her closer though and kisses her cheek. Those two are always loved up, always smitten, always all over each other.

"Hello?"

"That's my brother and Vanessa," I tell Mike when I hear James. I steal him away from the others. "My brother's cool. You'll get on."

Neither my brother nor Vanessa so much as bat an eyelid when I introduce them to Mike. They're all smiles, but I expected nothing less. They were never obsessed with Bron like Dad was.

James gives Mike a solid handshake. "Nice to meet you, Mike."

"Likewise."

"My sister said you're into stocks?"

Mike chuckles. "I am."

"Mind plugging me in?"

"Sure..."

Vanessa pulls me away to the kitchen. "Good for you, sis. He's cute."

I smile at him from the kitchen table. "I said the same."

Chapter Thirty-Three

Mike and I leave the group in the yard to get some food in the kitchen. Everyone seems to be getting on well and enjoying themselves, and I'm happier than I've ever been.

"Your dad and Keosha are so nice. No wonder you looked so close in that picture."

Mike smiles wistfully as he grabs a plate from the side and hands me one. "We are. Keosha appeared like an angel not long after Mom died, so she's helped raise us really."

"What happened to your mom?" I finally ask, having wanted to for a while now.

"She had an asthma attack when we were at school. Dad found her."

My heart hurts when he tells me that, and I almost drop my plate. "Oh, Mike..."

"She was the best mom, always put us first. She was everything to my dad, and I honestly can't remember one bad memory with her in it."

"She sounds amazing."

"She was."

I change the conversation to a lighter one while I heat our

plates in the microwave. There's no doubting how much I like him, and the last few days have shown me how much he cares for me. But even with all that, the nagging thoughts about our future remain.

"Why the long sigh?" he asks, suddenly holding me around the waist.

I don't want to ruin my own party, but... "Where do you see us going?"

He sighs himself. "What do you mean?"

I pull back to look at him. "Say, three years from now? Where do you see us?"

"Happy, together hopefully. Why? Don't you?"

"Yeah... I mean, I'd like to think we'd be more than just happy though. I guess I just like to know where things are going in my life."

He tucks my hair behind my ear. "I know you like to plan ahead and be in control, but things are good between us right now, aren't they?"

"They are..." Maybe he's right. Maybe I need to just let it go.

"We're good, Nik," he says as he pulls me back into his arms. "Stop worrying."

I close my eyes. "All right."

"She snitched on him cussing in the street, so he put dog shit in her mailbox."

I gasp at Kevin as he finishes telling us another story about his and Mike's childhood. "He did *what* to his neighbor?"

Mike shakes his head from beside his father while the girls and I continue to laugh. "Who's the snitch now?"

Kevin smirks. "My bad."

"But didn't that just get him into more trouble?" I ask, fully invested in the outcome of this story.

Kevin shakes his head. "Peter didn't believe her."

I bite my lip, but the laughter keeps coming.

"He didn't get away with much, believe it or not," Peter comments.

"We did," Kevin whispers. "Trust me."

"Can you shut up now?" Mike says. "I won't have a girlfriend for much longer if you don't rein it in."

"Nikki's cool, ain't you, Nikki?"

"I dunno," I tease. "Dog turd in mailboxes is kind of a deal-breaker for me."

"I could tell you something worse than that... But I won't," Kevin adds after Mike sends a coded look his way this time. "Some people are such killjoys."

"And some people are assholes."

"Language," Peter snaps at Mike.

"Sorry, Dad."

Kevin smirks before unleashing a full-blown smile on me. "Better keep an eye on him, especially when he starts traveling for those conferences."

My eyes immediately find Mike's after I see the girls' faces fall. "What conferences?"

Mike shrugs. "I've made some changes at work. Means I'll be traveling."

The relaxed atmosphere immediately shifts, and not only between the two of us. "Oh, right. How long for?"

"I'm not sure yet. It might be a long-term thing. The webinars have been going really well so the next logical step would be to take it face-to-face."

"That's great news, son," his dad says, shaking his hand.

"It is," I say, because it is, but I'm also hurt. Why the hell am I only hearing about this now? And where do I fit into that plan? I didn't sign up for a long-distance relationship.

"Girl," Rhian says, pulling me from my thoughts. "Are you okay?"

I nod, but my attention's on Mike, who has passed his beer to his dad and is coming my way.

He leans into my side when he reaches me. "I know that look. Come inside with me?"

I nod before following him into the house, and after checking no one's in the front room, he sits me on the couch.

"Tell me what's wrong," he says, sitting beside me.

I couldn't stop the shock I feel, even if I wanted to. "Are you serious?"

He frowns as he holds my hand. "Of course I am."

It takes everything in me to keep a level head, but I'd be lying if I said I wasn't borderline seething inside. "Why didn't you tell me about your new job?"

"I only decided on it a few days ago."

"Which means you called Kevin to tell him?"

"Yeah."

I scoff. "We've practically been living together, yet you didn't think to tell me?"

"I was going to. I've just been busy. Why are you so upset?"

That hurts my feelings, a hell of a lot more than they have been for a while. "I can't understand how you don't think I wouldn't be. You didn't tell me something that could have massive implications for our relationship."

"But things are good—"

"Right now," I spit out. "That's all you ever say, and that's why this never gets resolved. You say not to worry, but when you make plans for your future, like traveling for conferences, it's hard not to wonder why you can't give me any detail about where you see us going."

"It's not the same."

"How isn't it?"

"It just isn't. You really do need to stop worrying."

This again. "But don't you see how selfish it is to keep saying that, while not giving me any guarantees? I keep apologizing for wanting to know where we're going, but it's important to me."

He sighs, and my defenses rise.

"Have you ever considered that maybe you're too used to being single and that you're not taking my feelings into account? I'm trying to change my way of thinking, but you're not budging."

"I always think of you," he says quietly, but I feel a chill in his words.

"But you're not now. You never do when I bring this up. I can't feel safe when you won't plan beyond right now. You can swap and change what you're doing for work but won't tell me if I'm a permanent feature in your future? Make it make sense."

"You're my girlfriend, we're happy." He rubs his head in his hands. "I don't understand what you want."

I don't want to do this now, but I can't hold it in anymore. I've been swallowing down my feelings, trying to keep the peace, and I'm sick of it.

"Well, I know you want kids. Will you want them with me? What about marriage? Do you even want that?"

"Right now, no, but one day, yes."

"But do you want that with *me*?"

"Shit, Nik, I do right now, but I don't know what the future holds. I've told you this. You can make plans all you want. It doesn't mean you'll live to see them."

"I feel like your accident's tainted your view of relationships."

"Maybe it has."

I nod slowly. "Right."

He sighs, but so do I. This isn't how I wanted this to go, but I can't really blame him. He's always been this way. I told myself so many times we are different. Now I'm realizing just how different.

I can't keep doing this.

He suddenly tugs on my hand. "Why are you looking at me like that?"

"Because—" I turn to the door when there's a knock.

"Did you invite more people?"

I shake my head when I get up. "No, I didn't."

Answering the door, it takes me a second to grasp what I'm seeing.

"Nicola."

"Hey, Nikki."

I turn my attention from Bron to my dad. "What are you doing here?"

"Your mother decided to end our trip early so I could work this situation out with you." He steps inside with Bron, and I feel like I'm tripping as I slowly close the door. "You're having a party?"

"Yes." I eye everyone outside, praying to God they don't come in here.

"Nikki..."

I flinch when I hear Bron say my name. "You shouldn't be here."

"Don't be ridiculous, Nicola. He told me what you said to him."

My fury rises. "Why are you two still talking about me behind my back?"

"Because Bron is good for you."

Stay calm, you have guests.

"Nik, I know I messed up, but I swear I'll make it all up to you." Bron reaches into his pocket before getting on bended knee. "Please give me another chance?"

Horror and embarrassment for him rushes through me, and when I spot everyone outside looking through the glass doors, I close my eyes to make it all disappear. "Get up."

"Nik—"

"Stop saying my name like that," I snap, ignoring the ring in his hand to pull him to his feet. "I'm not Nik to you anymore."

Dad apologizes to him on my behalf, but that's not what triggers me most, it's the fact I spot Mike beside the sofa, just standing there. Emotionless.

So much for him being my boyfriend.

"Nicola!" Dad says angrily, "what is wrong with you? Bron is everything you could want in a husband."

I scoff. "Actually he's not. That's why we're not together. Bron might've been bored in our relationship, but so was I."

Bron gasps. "Nik, how could you say that?"

"Because it's true!" I shout, exasperated.

He pulls his jacket closed and shifts from foot to foot. "I swear I didn't know what I was saying, Mr. Mack..."

I feel the resentment rise further hearing Bron playing victim, then when Dad starts trying to reason with me, something inside me snaps.

"Mom said she spoke to you after we had lunch together. Did you listen to anything she said? Did she tell you how you've made me feel my entire life? Like such a constant disappointment that I've basically been walking on eggshells for twenty-six years?"

He clears his throat. "She did. I never meant to."

"Well, you did. I feel as though I've been starved of fun. Fun, of all things. I couldn't party, I couldn't date." I'm flapping my hands around like a crazy woman now. "I barely learnt any social or life skills because of the fear of doing something *you* didn't like. Even now, your opinions are suff-o-ca-ting me!"

He straightens. "I want the best for you, Nicola. I'll never apologize for that."

"But what's best for you is not what's best for *me*. I'm allowed to make my own mistakes. Even with him."

I see the admiration in Bron's eyes when I look at him, almost making me not want to say my next words, but I know right here and now, I have to start being truly honest with not only myself but everyone else.

"He left *me*, Dad, and yet you had no sympathy for how I felt, only disapproval that I was single at my age. I should've been able to come to you for support, yet I felt worse after I told you. Do you have any idea how that made me feel? And it's not the first time. You do it all the time. The things I'm learning now are things I should have learnt years ago."

Dad scoffs then. "Don't be so dramatic."

My heart breaks with his comment, and as the sickness settles in my gut, I finally realize that my dad is never going to take me seriously. He's never going to see things from my point of view, never going to respect my decisions, and I'm forever going to have to consider his feelings before mine.

And I can't do it.

I catch sight of Bron, smirking now. He thinks he's being discreet, but I know that look—he's proud of me for standing up to my dad. "I know you care about me, and I'll always care for you, but you need to accept that *we are over*."

Bron nods, and I sense he finally, *finally* gets it. "I'm sorry."

"I know, and I'm sorry for how my dad's led you on, but I'm not gonna change my mind."

He sighs. "I see that now."

I offer him a sympathetic smile before turning my attention to Dad and dropping it. "Leave."

That stuns him. "Excuse me?"

"I said, please leave my house."

"How dare you be so ungrateful—"

My fury reaches a completely new level. "No, you're ungrateful!" I yell. "You don't even appreciate your own children's decisions. You're a bully!"

Mom gasps as she walks inside the front door, followed by my brother and the girls from the back. "Nicola, calm down!"

"No!" I practically scream. "I've been calm for long enough.

I'm sick of always having to put my feelings aside for people, especially you, Dad. All you ever do is make me feel not good enough!"

"How dare you speak to us like that?" Dad shouts, stepping toward me, but before I know what's happening, my brother blocks my view of him.

"Dad, you need to leave."

"Not until we've sorted this out."

"Fine," I say, storming into the kitchen to grab my keys. "I'll leave."

"Sis," Alicia says, rushing to my side. "You want us to come?"

"No." I snatch my keys off the side. "I'll text you later."

Her nod is knowing. "Okay. I'll see everyone out for you."

"Thank you."

She squeezes my arm before I head for the door, ignoring all the looks, but as bad as I feel for abandoning my own party, I still leave.

I don't even turn back when I hear Mom crying.

Chapter Thirty-Four

I ended up at Shelby Farms car park. I've been staring at the bridge for so long, it's dark now, and only a few cars are left parked around me. I should probably move from here and go home because I have work tomorrow, but I can't be bothered to drive.

My cell rings again on the passenger seat, but I ignore it. I know my house is safe and I'm not going back to a mess to clean up, so everything else can wait. Besides, anyone I spoke to now wouldn't like me very much. I'm still reeling from the nightmare of earlier.

It's almost laughable how quickly my life has gone from almost perfect to messy as shit, but after sitting with my feelings, I've realized I've only got myself to blame. I tried to go back to people-pleasing Nikki, and God well and truly told me that I can't.

On the positive side, at least I don't have to worry about Bron trying to get me back anymore, and at least we're not on bad terms. I meant what I said: I'll always care for him, but we can't go back.

Shame too, 'cause that ring was a stunner.

And Dad... I don't know if we'll ever talk again, but if we don't, I'm just gonna have to be okay with it. I'm done worrying about what he thinks of me, and if that makes me selfish, so be it.

The guilt of making Mom cry makes me tear up again though, and when she calls again, I send her a quick text telling her I'm fine. But the other calls and messages, I ignore.

Including the ones from Mike.

I can't believe he just stood there while all that craziness was going on. What happened to having your partner's back? To supporting them? What happened to a man standing up for his woman as her protector?

Yes, we'd not long had a disagreement, but regardless of that, he still didn't seem to care one bit. I deserve a man who's absolutely certain about me. Who doesn't make me feel bad for wanting to know his future plans. I deserve a man who includes me in his life and tells me when he's making life-changing decisions, and the fact Mike didn't see a problem with what he did is a massive red flag that I just can't ignore.

But it's not all his fault.

He's been nothing but himself. It's me that got swept up in the exciting new life I was creating, and somewhere along the way, I thought he would change. I thought he would change into what I wanted him to be, but all I got was my feelings hurt.

The funniest thing about all this though is how much credit I've given him for the changes in my life. Yes, he's suggested his fair share of things to do, but now I realize that I'm the one who did the work. I'm the one who turned my life around by trying new things.

It turns out that I don't need him, Bron, or any other man to live my life. The happiest people I know are those that put themselves first. So maybe I should stop focusing so much on other people, so I can do the same for a while.

What do I want though?

To disappear for a while, away from everyone and everything.

Maybe I will.

"Are you sure you're okay?"

I nod as Kelly rests my mug on my desk. "I'm fine." I've barely said more than a sentence to her since she got here. I wish I'd called in sick. I'm tired because I barely slept, and my tank of peopling is depleted.

"All right, well, Marcus closed a big account Friday evening at a business dinner and is overly cheerful, so watch out for that."

Good. I like Marcus, but I'm not dealing with his assholery either.

I'll quit.

"Nikki?"

I look up. "Yeah?"

"You zoned out there."

"I'm fine."

She sits down opposite me, and I watch as her expression turns thoughtful. "Have you spoken to the girls yet?"

I frown. "No. Why?"

"Well, after you left yesterday, your brother and your dad got into it."

I groan. "Great."

"Your brother really stood up for you, Nikki. Told your dad point-blank he was going to lose you if he didn't sort his shit out. What shocked most of us though is what your mom said."

"What did she say?"

"She said she'd leave him if he didn't make it right with you. He seemed heartbroken after that."

That makes me sigh. "I want him to understand where I'm

coming from on his own, not be forced to because he's been threatened."

She nods. "Yeah... I get that."

My mood plummets as I pick up my mug, so I change the subject. "I saw you getting on well with Kevin." *That should distract her.*

Her eyes immediately widen. "Girl..."

I knew it.

"He spent most of the night at mine. He's crazy. Into spanking and all sorts."

I almost spit out my coffee. "Excuse me?"

"And he ate my boot—"

"Please stop. I just had a visual, and I feel sick enough as it is."

"Sorry. He is crazy though. Different."

"So you like him?" I can't tell when it comes to her sometimes.

"At the moment I do. I'm seeing him tonight. He's staying in Memphis for a few weeks."

"At yours?"

She grins. "Probably."

Good for her. "Well, whatever happens, I'm happy for you."

"Yeah. He's a lot like me, y'know? We have a lot in common."

"Oh... Do you eat the groceries too then?"

She frowns, as if I don't know. "I do everything. I used to be on a sugar daddy website in college. Whew..." She stops when she clocks my expression. "Anyway. It opened my eyes to a lot."

I shudder. "I'm definitely more adventurous now, but that's a step too far for me."

She laughs as she gets up. "Don't knock it till you try it."

I glance at my phone as it vibrates, seeing my brother's name. "Nah. I'll let you keep that."

She laughs when she leaves, and I shake my head.

That girl is cray-cray.

My phone stops vibrating but starts right back up again. I suppose I can't put him off forever, so I answer. "Hey."

"Thanks for finally answering the phone. You're lucky I didn't call your damned office."

"Sorry. I needed a minute."

He sighs deeply. "I get it. How you feeling today?"

"Not as bad as yesterday. I heard what you said to Dad, and I do appreciate it, but as I said before, I don't want you getting involved."

"You're my little sister, Nik. I'm not gonna let anyone come at you like that, regardless."

I smile. "I know. Thank you. Do you know how Mom is?"

"She's okay. Livid with Dad though."

"So I heard."

"His loss, sis. Honestly, unless he's gonna respect that it's your life, you're better off without him anyway."

"I think you might be right."

He sighs. "I get how you feel though. I've been there, remember? But at least you did it. I'm proud of you. You stood up to Bron too. That's massive."

"Thanks, Jay. That means a lot."

"And you never know, maybe he'll see the error of his ways now."

I chuckle. "That would be nice. Anyway, how is Nessa and my baby? I didn't stress her out yesterday, did I?"

"Not at all. If anything, she's stressing me. I swear she's been running me ragged with her cravings. Who the hell eats dills with Skippy, dipped in Cool Whip?"

I laugh. "Women growing the next generation."

"True."

"It's all worth it, Jay. Remember how long you've wanted this."

"Right. I'm not complaining. She knows I'd do anything for her."

That makes me smile. "You're a really great guy, y'know? I dunno if Dad's ever told you, but I'm proud of you."

He's quiet for a moment. "Respect, Nik."

"It's all true." I hear my email alert, so I turn back to my desk to take a look. "I better go, but I'll check in with you soon, all right?"

"All right. We're here if you need us."

"I know."

He says goodbye before I hang up, and I scan through the email from Marcus. He's approved the time off I asked for this morning.

I call Kelly.

"Hey."

"Could you please only bother me this week if it's urgent? I don't want to take any personal days, but I could do with some peace."

"No problem."

I glance down at my phone. "I might give you my cell too. If that's okay?"

"Sure. I can be a Rottweiler when needs be. I've got you."

"Thanks." I hang up.

Now I can book my flights.

My front room lights are on when I get home from work. Either Mike's here or he was.

"Hello?" I say, dropping my keys on the small side table beside the door. "Mike?"

"In the kitchen."

I find him sitting at the table, a backpack by his feet, and although the sight of it makes my heart twinge, I more feel relieved. "Hey."

He smiles as I make my way over to him, but he doesn't move to get up. He pulls out the chair next to him so I can sit down. "How was work?"

"Good thanks. You?"

"I didn't work today."

"Oh."

He rests his elbows on his knees and then sighs deeply when he looks up at me. "I'm sorry. I fucked up."

I nod slowly. "What makes you say that?"

"Hindsight. Have you spoken to your parents?" he asks cautiously, and by the look on his face, I get the impression he was worried about asking me that. I also sense he's longing out the conversation he knows is coming.

"No. I figure time heals and he needs time to process what I said. I think I finally realized too that I can't control what Dad does, only me."

He appears impressed. "And that's what they call 'facts.'"

I chuckle. "It is."

"You were right, Nik..." Mike pulls back a little to hold my hands in his. "I should have told you about the conferences first. I was being selfish. I've been alone for so long, I've forgotten what compromise is. I wasn't considering your feelings or your needs, and I failed to see the effect that was having on you..."

My heart flutters with those words. He finally understands.

"It's more than reasonable for you to expect to know where you stand in my life, and I never wanted you to second-guess that." He takes a deep breath before exhaling slowly. "I know how independent you are; it's one of the many things I admire about you, but I want you to know that I'm here for you in all things. I want you to feel secure, safe enough for you to talk to me when you need to—about anything. We were friends before we took things further, and I truly only want for you to be happy."

Tears well in my eyes when he finishes. "Thank you." *It's everything I wanted to hear.*

But now I have to tell him how I feel.

"I wanna say that I love what a free spirit you are. You go with the flow and don't let much bother you, and it's been really inspiring to me. I always used to notice how different we were, but I pushed it down. However... now I have to be honest about how I truly feel, because I haven't been."

I see the confusion on his face, but I stick to what I need to say, knowing I have to do this.

"You've taught me so much... How to slow down, to have fun, to be more present... And I love how you've taught me that I don't have to be strong all the time, that I can rely on someone else other than myself... that I can speak my mind..."

He holds my hand tighter. "Nik—"

"See, you've brought emotions out of me that no one ever has. I care about you so much, and I'm so grateful to have met you... But I've also realized how different we are, and as hard as I want us to work, we don't fit."

He frowns. "What do you mean?"

I take a deep breath, hating how tight my chest feels. "I have to let you go."

He sits back and blinks, as if he can't grasp what I'm saying.

"You're amazing, without a doubt. You have so much going for you, but I'm not the woman for you. I need time to focus on me. I've spent my entire life thinking about other people, and as much as I know you'd try to make me happy, you couldn't, because I don't even know what that looks like, and I know that might sound selfish—"

He sits up straighter. "No, it's not selfish, I'm just... I wasn't expecting this."

"I'm sorry. I never wanted to hurt you, but I have to be honest."

He slowly nods. "I respect that," he says, rubbing his head. "But it hurts."

I almost apologize again, but I stop myself and give him a moment.

"Well, I think this is the most speechless I've ever been, but I understand."

"You do?"

"Yeah... I've been there, remember? It's like you've just mirrored me four years ago, so I get it."

He falls silent, and I eye the bag by his feet again. I thought he'd come here to get his things, that after yesterday he'd come to the same conclusion as I had, but I was clearly wrong.

I leave him staring at his hands to make myself a drink. "Would you like a coffee?" I'm not going to force him to leave.

"No, thanks. I'm gonna head out, but before I do..." He grabs the bag beside him. "I have a confession."

My stomach twists as I turn around. "What...?" I gasp when I see what's in his hand, but when he smirks, I laugh. "You thief!"

He had my Rose!

"I heard how good they were and got jealous."

I shake my head as I run over to take it from him. "You stole my Rose because you didn't want me using it?"

This is the first time I've seen him truly blush, and it makes me sad to think it's also the last. "Kinda, sorta, maybe..."

"How could you?" I tease.

His eyes narrow. "Have you missed it?"

Do I make him suffer a little longer? "I had the others to fall back on, so not really."

He gapes at me. "You were using them while we were together?"

"Not much. You took my favorite one."

He gasps, and I barely contain my laughter.

"If you knew how good that Rose really was, you'd miss it too."

"Did I not—"

I burst out laughing. "I didn't even realize you had it."

He's relieved. "I didn't think you could wound me any more than you have already."

Guilt threatens, but I don't let it take hold. "I'm sorry. I really do wish things could be different. You're an incredible guy, Mike, and I know without a shadow of a doubt you'll make someone extremely happy."

His smile is a sad one. "Y'know, as hard as it is to accept us breaking up, I don't regret a thing. You've changed my life too."

"I'm really happy to hear that."

He stands to pull me into a hug. "I'm gonna miss you."

I close my eyes. "I'm gonna miss you too."

He's smiling when he releases me, and so am I, because as much as I really am gonna miss him, there's no doubt in my mind that letting him go was the right thing to do.

Chapter Thirty-Five

I send a voice note to my brother while I wait for the girls to arrive at Gus's. My flight to Bali is later today, but between work, shopping, beauty treatments and packing, we haven't had the chance to meet in person until now.

There was no way in hell I was leaving the country without seeing my sisters first though.

Hey, Jay-Jay, just want to say thank you to you and Vanessa for all the support over the past few months. I dunno if I would have found the courage to stand up for myself if it wasn't for you. Love you so much. Dinner when I get back? I'll show you my vacation snaps.

"Hey, hey, hey," Chay says as she leads the girls to the table. "How sexy do you look?"

I laugh as I stand to hug them. "This dress is everything, right?"

"Very."

I picked it up online a few days ago and was so damn happy

it arrived in time. It's a lilac wrap dress that's just above the knee, and it makes my tits and shape straight "pop."

"You're glowing too, sis."

"Right," Chay agrees with Rhian. "Anyone would think you just spent the night getting dicked down."

"I did. By my toys." I made sure to pack all three of them too. There's no way in hell I'm going on a two-week trip empty-handed.

Rhian and Alicia snort as they take a seat opposite me and Chay, but Chay seems a little speechless.

"You didn't tell me off."

I frown at her. "Huh?"

"You always hate when I say things like that."

"I guess I've changed. What did you say before? Everyone masturbates?"

She smirks. "They really do."

"Well then." I call the waiter over to order some drinks, then I show them all where I'll be staying in Bali. I went all out and booked myself into a five-star resort. I'm so excited I could burst.

"You're gonna be in heaven," Alicia gushes.

"Sis, I hope so."

While we wait for our food, I tell them what happened with Mike. I told them in the group I'd ended things, but they didn't know exactly why.

"I think you've done the right thing," Chay says, taking her hot wings and fries from the server. "You seem a hell of a lot less stressed."

"Believe me, I am."

"Are you really gonna stay single for a while?"

I nod. "That's the plan. This chapter of my life is all about me."

"Good for you," Alicia says, getting us all to toast. "It's been a long time coming."

I agree. "It has."

"Have you heard from him?" Rhian asks cautiously.

"You can talk about him, y'know. I'm good. And yes, he recommended some beauty spots to check out while I was away. He was at yoga on Saturday too."

"Aww," Chay gushes. "He really is such a nice guy."

"He is. He'll make someone very happy one day." Mike deserves to be happy after what he's been through. With the right person though.

"And no news from your dad?"

I shake my head. "I'm not stressing over it either."

Alicia's the most surprised. "Wow. I didn't think I'd ever see the day. Nikki is officially Miss 'I don't give a fuck.'"

"I love it," Rhian says. "Look at you now. Boss bitch."

That makes me laugh. "Thanks, girls." I rest my fork down. "Thank you all so much, for all the talks, late-night messages, the advice. A girl really feels like she can take on the world right about now."

"That's what we're here for," Alicia says. "But we will have to kick you out of the group now you're single."

I hold my chest and gasp. "How could you?"

"Bitch, shut up," Rhian says. "Nikki ain't going nowhere."

I glare at Alicia before blowing Rhian a kiss. "Thanks, sis."

Alicia rolls her eyes. Dramatically.

"So," I say as I pick my fork back up, "now I'm settled and have no drama going on, can we focus on someone else please? I'm done with being the drama queen of the group."

"Yasss," Chay says. "Let's focus on our next girls' trip. What about Vegas?"

"No," we all tell her, and she sulks.

"Boring arses..."

"Nicola! *Nicola?*"

Mom?

I turn around from the check-in queue to look for Mom, who's shouting my name from somewhere in Departures. She sounds distressed, so I rush through the crowds to find her, leaving a mass of smacked ankles from my suitcase in my wake.

Dad must be going mental at her drawing attention to herself, and sure enough when I spot them, he's following behind her, complaining.

"We've probably missed her."

"Mom," I yell, holding my hand in the air. "Over here!"

There's no doubt she's relieved to see me, and when I reach her, she hugs me tight. "I thought we were too late. James only just told us."

"You almost were."

She's teary-eyed when she steps back. "You weren't going to tell us?"

I shoot Dad a quick glance. "I didn't want any drama before I left."

Mom nods knowingly before dragging Dad to her side by his shirt. "Your father has something he needs to say to you before you go."

"If he's going—"

"Please listen to him," she says in earnest. "I know he doesn't deserve it, but please?"

I sigh, but instead of letting my nerves get to me, I remember that I'm not the frightened little girl I was, and that if things don't work out, it's okay.

I'll be okay.

"All right."

Dad shifts uncomfortably and fiddles with the car keys in his hand, but just as I think Mom's gonna have to push him again, he looks me in the eyes. "I'm sorry, Nicola."

My entire body relaxes when he says that.

"You're my baby girl. I just want what's best for you—" He sighs when Mom elbows him. "But I now see the mistakes I've made. You were right. I've been trying to control how you live your life, and I was wrong."

Wow. Never have I heard him sound so remorseful before, and it makes me emotional. "Thank you."

"And...?" Mom pushes.

"I'm sorry for what I said, and my actions regarding Bron. For not being more sympathetic to your feelings... I didn't realize how stubborn I was until your mother... Well, your mother here has given me a taste of my own medicine recently, and I've seen the error of my ways."

I smile at Mom. Seems as though she's found her backbone too.

She reaches forward to squeeze my hand. "Your father cares for you deeply, but like you, he hides it behind a mask. It's not easy for him to say how he feels, but I hope now he'll be able to express himself better and consider things from other people's points of view, not only his."

"Well, I appreciate that, Dad, and I accept your apology. I never meant to upset either of you—I love you both more than anything. I just want to be free. I've been so happy. I've done so many things I've never done before... The past three months have been life-changing."

Mom wipes her eyes. "We can see that. We're sorry for making you feel as though you weren't good enough, Nicola. That has never once been our intention. We're both so very proud of you."

"We are," Dad says, backing Mom. "Very proud."

I smile. "Thank you. That means the world to me."

Dad looks around, and I immediately know where his thoughts have gone. "You're alone?"

"I am. Mike and I broke up. I'm going by myself."

His eyes widen. "Alone to Bali?"

I hold in my laughter. "Yes. The resort I'm staying in is completely safe. Please don't worry."

"Nicola—"

The glare from Mom halts his next words, and we both smile at each other, harder when Dad asks why I broke up with Mike.

"It's none of your business, Byron," Mom berates him, shaking her head. "He can't help himself," she says to me.

Dad shakes his head, but I laugh before reaching forward to rest a reassuring hand on his arm. "I know you think I shouldn't be single at my age, but it won't be forever. I still want to get married and have grandchildren for you one day, just not now."

He's instantly relieved. "Thank goodness. You know, you could meet a lovely man at church..."

Mom scorns him, but I just shake my head. I don't think he'll ever give up trying to get me to go back to church, but for the first time, I don't take it personally. That's just how he is.

"I should go," I say, turning to look at the empty line. I stayed longer than I should've with the girls, so I was cutting it close as it was. "I'll see you both when I get back."

They both hug me tightly, and I feel lighter than ever afterwards. I wasn't expecting to resolve our argument before I left, but I'm so thankful we did.

It's lifted a massive weight from my shoulders.

"Have an amazing time," Mom shouts as I leave them. "Take lots of pictures!"

I smile. "I will."

Excitement takes hold as I check my case in, and after a quick wave to my parents, I head toward my gate. I can't really believe I'm doing this, but I'm so glad I am.

For the first time in my life, *I'm* the priority, and I don't have to answer to anyone.

And it feels fucking amazing.

Epilogue
Three days later in Bali...

I scrape the sand off my legs with my French-manicured toes before settling back on my luxury sun lounger. This resort is right on the beach, next to the turquoise water, and the view is absolutely breathtaking.

There was a wedding party out here earlier this morning, but the beach is practically dead now. It hasn't been busy like the other resorts I've been to while traveling, but that may have something to do with how much staying here dents your credit card.

It's been worth it, though.

So far, I've made good use of the spa facilities, yoga classes, and the unlimited food, and they knew me by name at the beach bar within the first few hours of me arriving. I didn't unpack until the second day I was here. The excitement of being left to my own devices may have gotten to me a little too much, but it's exactly why I went all inclusive.

I wave down a server while adjusting my bikini, not wishing to do a Rhian out here. This two-piece is a little small, but it's purple and I couldn't not wear it.

"Could I get another Red Rainbow, please?" I ask, holding up my empty glass.

The guy smiles as he takes it. "Of course."

I slip my sunglasses back down when he leaves, then I close my eyes and listen to the calming waves. I've never felt such peace. Yeah, things may not be perfect in my life, but at least I've made a start.

This is heaven after the week of crazy I've just seen the back of. Arguing with my dad, turning down a marriage proposal, another breakup...

I still can't believe I'm here now, but I'm so glad I did this. It's allowing me to process everything that happened.

Really process it.

Dad finally saw how his actions were affecting me and apologized, which is massive for him. James was right; I had to confront him myself, and I wish I had done it sooner. Him acknowledging how his ways had affected me is all I ever wanted, and now that I finally feel seen by him, I have no doubt our relationship will be different.

He knows I won't tolerate him running my life anymore, and I've learned that although he's set in his ways, deep down, it really is just because he cares.

I've been lucky in my life with all the people who have cared about me. Like Bron. Looking back, I can see that about him now. Even when he broke up with me, he did it in a way that considered my feelings. Still, I was right to turn down his proposal, regardless of the fact that at one time that was all I ever dreamed of. He has his closure now and it sits well on my heart to know he can start moving on with his life.

Don't get me wrong, before we broke up, I would've loved for us to have worked. I shared a lot of my firsts with him, such as renting my first home and taking my first trip outside the States. I'll never forget our Christmas in the Bahamas and the bikinis he bought me, and I'll forever remember him every time someone leaves crumbs on my kitchen counter.

But as much as I wish I could've had all my lasts with him too, if I'd have gone back to him, I always would've wondered if everything he offered—including that marriage proposal—was because he wanted that himself, or because he felt he should.

We were together three years and he never proposed. And yeah, he always said he wanted marriage, kids, and to buy a house of our own, but did he do anything to make it happen? No.

"Here you are," the server says as he sets down my cocktail on the table beside me. "Enjoy."

"Thanks, I will." These vibrantly colored cocktails not only look amazing with their mix of orange juice, vodka, grenadine, and curaçao, but they taste incredible too.

The server smiles before tending to a woman further down the shore while I sip my ice-cold drink through an already flimsy straw. This reminds me of when Mike and I went to Dauphin Island and got wasted. We drank a ton of cocktails that night.

I sigh deeply when I think of him. There's still no doubt he was brought into my life for a reason, but a part of me wishes we'd never taken things further than our friendship.

As friends, we fit perfectly, and there were never any expectations, but as soon as we moved into dating territory, that's when things seem to have gone downhill. We tried to change each other into people we weren't. Him with getting me to live in the moment and go with the flow, and me wanting more of a future plan from him.

Things got messy at the end, no doubt, but I know I'm lucky to have met Mike. He taught me how to have fun and not take myself so seriously. The memory of our bike race especially always makes me laugh... up until the part where he ended up on the ground. So does the thought of our water fight at the falls where we both got told off like we were kids. His hugs were everything too, and our first kiss under the stars was the best I've ever had.

Maybe I rushed us, considering we hadn't been together long, but I'd spent my entire life going along with what everyone else wanted, and I'm not sorry for not wanting to do that anymore.

Besides, I don't want to settle, whether that's at the beginning of a relationship or after years in one. If it isn't working from the get-go, what says it will work later on? Mike may not have wanted more serious commitment without me pushing for it, but I know out of all the billons of men in the world, one of them will.

Which has me thinking, what do I actually want in a man?

Mike and Bron were completely different, but both had amazing qualities. Bron was career driven, was stable, and led in our relationship—which I've learned are absolute dealbreakers for me. I don't just want those qualities in a man. I need them. I liked knowing that Bron saw his future the same as I did.

But on the flip side, Mike opened up a new world for me. He proved that love is love and neither looks nor color mattered when it came to that. He was adventurous too; held deep, meaningful conversations; and was always fun to be around. A lot of the things he taught me will stay with me for the rest of my life.

Now I just need to find one person with all those traits... *when* I start dating again.

I smile to myself when I remember the conversation I had with Alicia when I was trying the dating apps. "Look, at least you're finding out what you don't want. This is a good thing really. It means you're fine-tuning what you *do* want. Besides, there's no harm being single for a while. That's where the growth is. And you don't want to settle again, do you?"

She was so right.

My phone buzzes, and my mood lifts when I see Chay's name on the screen.

You hook up with anyone yet? xx

I smirk.

Me: *Nope. That's not what I came for.*

Chay: *Even better. It means you'll be surprised when it happens. We're just heading to Gus's. We miss you!*

Me: *Only a week left to go.*

Chay: *That's ages without my Nikki fix. What are you doing?*

I send her some pics. One of my cocktail, my toes hanging off the lounger, the clear blue sky, and then a ten-second video of the tide coming in.

Chay: *Bitch. Xx*

I chuckle.

Me: *We have Jamaica soon, remember?*

We decided our next girls' trip would be there when I saw them at lunch before I left. Rhian's already looking into flights and hotels.

Chay: *True. Alright, have fun. Love you.*

Me: *Love you all too.*

"Mind if I take this?" I hear a voice beside me ask when I tuck my cell back into my purse.

Even with my sunglasses on, I have to shield my eyes when I turn to my left *and* hide the smile that wants to escape when I catch sight of the guy the voice belongs to.

"Not at all."

He drags his towel off his broad shoulder before laying it perfectly on his lounger, and I don't miss how his bare back muscles flex.

Saying that, *all* of him does, and his dewy skin literally looks like he's been kissed by the sun.

That's hot.

My thoughts have wandered so far, I don't notice he's laid down until he turns my way and smiles.

"Joe," he says, reaching across to offer me his hand.

I reach over to shake it, remembering my promise to stay away from men for the foreseeable.

"Nice to meet you, Joe. I'm Nikki."

A Letter from LeeSha

Thank you so much for reading *White Boyfriend*. What did you think? If you have a moment, I'd love it if you could drop your thoughts in a review. I read them all to improve future books, so please don't be shy having your say.

Also, if you'd like to keep up with my future releases and news in general, please click the link below. It's the best way to stay in the know about all things me. Your email address will never be shared and you can unsubscribe at any time.

www.bookouture.com/leesha-mccoy

White Boyfriend was such a personal book for me to write. I always like to weave my life experiences into my books, and if I don't have any experience in what I'm writing, I use my very vivid imagination to live what my characters do. However, with this book, the universe decided to really make me understand how Nikki felt, by throwing a divorce at me.

Although when I began Nikki's story, I was heartbroken and hated love for how it was making me feel, with her I found it again. She was therapy for me in a way, and now I'm out the other side, I can honestly say that it was one of the best things that ever happened to me. Because of how much I grew.

I've discovered who I *really* am, my likes and dislikes, what I want from life, and what I will and won't tolerate from others anymore. Pretty much all Nikki learnt, I did too. She taught me that life is just a series of present moments, and as bad as we may believe one is, when you look back, it may have actually been exactly what you needed.

So, as always, I hope you took something away from this book, even if it was merely the importance of putting you first and making yourself happy. Because as Nikki learnt, when you do, life gets really exciting.

Lots of love,

LeeSha xx

www.leeshamccoyauthor.com

 facebook.com/leesha.mccoy.7
 instagram.com/leeshamccoyauthor

Thank Yous

To my mother, Lynda, and my sister, Leanne, thank you for all your support since forever. You were the first to read my work, and always gave honest feedback to me. Even during times I thought about giving up because my life was falling apart, you encouraged me to keep going through it all. I love you both.

To my Queens, Jen, Kayleigh, Nikki, Chay, Chinita, Joyalynn & Grace, you have all been such a massive support to me, with my books and private life. You are my sisters in my heart, and I appreciate everything you've done and continue to do.

I want to say a huge thank you to Kathryn, Jessie, and everyone at Bookouture. Kathryn, the belief you showed in me at a time I needed it most in my life is something I will never forget. Thank you so much for giving me this opportunity. You will never know how much it has meant to me.

Jessie, you have made this entire experience so easy, from the moment you took the reins until the moment you handed them back. Your words of encouragement, support, and hard work has led to a book I'm more than proud of. Thank you.

And finally, but probably the most important thank you of them all, goes to my forever amazing readers. God knows how much I love each and every one of you. From reposting my links, sharing your struggles and life experiences, to harassing my inboxes for my next release (LOL) you are always reminding me why I do this.

Without all of you, I wouldn't be sitting here writing this.

So please, believe in yourself, and go make your own dreams come true.

www.ingramcontent.com/pod-product-compliance
Lightning Source LLC
Chambersburg PA
CBHW061556190726
48288CB00007B/2054